For
Emily

Katherine Slee studied Modern History at Oxford University and formerly worked in investment banking. She is a graduate of the Faber Academy and now lives in Kent with her husband, two kids and a crazy puppy.

For Emily is Katherine's debut novel.

For Emily

Katherine Slee

ORION

An Orion Paperback

First published in Great Britain in 2019 by Orion Fiction
This paperback edition published in 2020 by Orion Fiction,
an imprint of the Orion Publishing Group Ltd.,
Carmelite House, 50 Victoria Embankment,
London EC4Y 0DZ

An Hachette UK Company

1 3 5 7 9 10 8 6 4 2

A CIP catalogue record for this book
is available from the British Library.

ISBN (Mass Market Paperback) 978 1 4091 8734 9

Typeset by Deltatype Ltd, Birkenhead, Merseyside

Printed in Great Britain by Clays Ltd, Elcograf S.p.A.

www.gollancz.co.uk

For Dylan & Scarlett

The fishermen know that the sea is dangerous and the storm terrible,
But they have never found sufficient reason for remaining ashore.

Vincent van Gogh

CATRIONA ROBINSON'S SWANSONG

Or does Britain's favourite children's author still have one last adventure to share?

Interview by Suzie Johnstone

Catriona Robinson was one of this generation's most beloved and best-known authors. Her series of children's books, about a girl in a wheelchair who discovers a magical atlas that transports her all over the globe, have been read and adored by millions. She has also written several works of adult fiction, most recently *Enchantment*, which was shortlisted for a number of literary prizes last year.

A notoriously private person, Catriona spent the majority of her time at her home on the Norfolk coast, but in recent years was also a guest lecturer at the University of Cambridge for their Creative Writing course. It was at Cambridge that I was fortunate enough to meet her. She was giving a lecture to the upcoming Finalists and, from what I have heard, it was both inspiring and humble, with a sprinkle of humour thrown into the mix.

The hotel in which we met was perhaps not what you would have expected from a woman who, by her own admission, was most comfortable in dungarees and wellington boots. The establishment in question had a double-height reception hall, an industrial spiral staircase and contemporary lighting. There was also a mezzanine library with recessed shelving and plush velvet furniture, which is where I chatted to Catriona over a pot of tea and a slice of her favourite lemon cake. She was wearing a pleated black skirt with turquoise silk blouse and her hair was styled in a loose chignon. She was animated, relaxed and even asked our waiter if she could buy the tea set, which was decorated around the rim with paintings of turtle doves, from the hotel. If I hadn't known otherwise, I would never have guessed the woman sat across from me had only months left to live.

You're about to give a lecture to the next generation of writers. What is it you've enjoyed most about teaching here?
I never had the opportunity to go to university myself, not least because it wasn't as commonplace for women back then as it is now. But also because I never believed I was good enough, certainly never thought I would end up here. I am a strong advocate of the fact that all children, irrespective of their gender, race, socio-economic background, should be encouraged to reach for the stars, to be the very best version of themselves they can possibly be.

But Cambridge is an elite institution.
It is, but part of the association with places such as Oxbridge, and large corporations, is that unless you fit a certain mould, you may as well never bother applying. I have no degree, no formal literary training, and yet am now teaching at one of the most renowned universities in the world. There is no one pathway to success any more, indeed what does the word even mean?

What does it mean to you?

When I first began to write, it was out of a simple curiosity for the world. A way to put down onto paper all the crazy ideas and characters I kept thinking about. But I never considered it to be anything more than a hobby and certainly never dreamt it would take me on the incredible journey I've been fortunate enough to enjoy. Success should never be measured by the amount of money, or things, you have, but more the sense of achievement it gives you.

How much of your own success do you put down to happenstance?

One could argue that life is nothing but a series of serendipitous events, both good and bad. I try to adhere to the rule that there's a balance to this universe, this life, and no matter how much pain and hardship we face, there is always something, or someone, to give you hope.

There's a famous quote from Leonard Cohen that I have pinned up on my refrigerator at home, which pretty much says it all: *Ring the bells that still can ring, Forget your perfect offering, There is a crack in everything, that's how the light gets in.*

What gives you hope?

My granddaughter, Emily.

You've spoken before about how the idea for Ophelia came from her.

Yes. As I'm sure everyone is aware, she was severely injured in a car accident fifteen years ago. I used to tell her stories whilst she was recovering and she liked to draw pictures of

3

the characters. My publisher saw something we had been working on, just for fun, and the rest, as you say, is history.

It seems to be a real collaborative effort between you and Emily. Does that come with its own challenges?
(Laughs.) Of course, we're family, which means we're always going to have disagreements. But Emily's real talent is knowing exactly what it is I am trying to describe to the readers and, somehow, she manages to reproduce it in her pictures.

Did Emily's own disability influence the stories you wrote?
Emily doesn't have a disability, but people will believe what they want to believe. My books are there to entertain, but also to educate, to inspire. So many people stay in one place for too long, become stagnated by society, by money. But there are all sorts of wonders out there, just waiting for us to find them.

What made you change direction in your writing, move away from children's books?
As a writer I'm always looking to explore new ideas, find new challenges. Ophelia and the world we created became such a huge part of our lives for such a long time that it seemed necessary for me, for both of us, to draw a line under it all. Try something different.

Enchantment **has had mixed reviews from readers, despite its literary success. How much of this do you think is due to the fact it's aimed at an adult, rather than a younger, audience?**
It doesn't surprise me, because people come to expect a

certain style, a certain subject, from well-known authors. And yet if I'd written another children's book, it would have been criticised for not being about Ophelia. Life is about experimentation, about exploring the magic hidden within the world. I wanted to look at the links between science and philosophy, about how it affects the human spirit. About the finite amount of time any one of us has on this planet and how, when forced to confront that, we would each change our behaviour, our outlook.

In reference to the main theme of *Enchantment*, if you knew this was your last day on Earth, how would you want to spend it?
You do know I'm dying? Oh goodness, your face, I'm sorry. Death seems to have this effect on me. I forget how hard it is for other people to deal with.

What was the question again? Oh yes, last day on Earth. Crikey (more laughter), wherever did I come up with that idea?

There is a place, on the coast of France, that holds a special place in my heart, not least because it's where I wrote my first book. There's something about the light there that is so peaceful. I would wake early, have warm croissants and strong, black coffee for breakfast, followed by a long walk along the beach, with the sea between my toes. Then I would dive beneath the waves and feel the strength of the tide, a reminder of all the power in this world we have no control over. Fresh langoustines roasted on an open fire and champagne drunk at sunset. All with Emily by my side.

Nothing spectacular, nothing fancy. Because when you wipe away all the layers of spit and polish, all anyone ever has are the relationships, the memories, they forge along the way.

Do you have any advice for aspiring authors out there, no matter how young or old?

Say yes to everything. Take the risks, regret only the things you don't do, because mistakes are more important than success. You can't write, you can't connect with people if you haven't any memories to draw on, no matter how painful they might be. You see, the things I remember most clearly from my life are those I wasn't supposed to do, but I did them anyway.

Did any of those things involve men?

Aren't all the best mistakes about love?

Have you been working on anything new?

There's always something new. Another idea, another character, another story.

Is that the reason for this interview?

I haven't always been so elusive, so reclusive, as it were, but rather my lifestyle has simply been a result of unfortunate circumstances. This interview is most likely to be my last and, to be completely honest, I no longer feel the need to hide behind the veil of my stories. I only hope that something good can come out of what Emily and I have created, that the end of one journey could perhaps mean the beginning of another.

Does this mean there's some truth to the rumours about a new series, featuring a grown-up Ophelia?
There's always an element of truth to every rumour. Let's just say there is something, but I'm not yet certain it will ever be shared with the world.

You're famous for leaving clues in all of your books. Is this another treasure trail, another puzzle, you want your readers to solve?
Well, that would be telling.

Catriona Robinson died peacefully at home last month, after a long battle with cancer. She is survived by her only granddaughter, Emily, who has remained unavailable for comment.

COCKATOO

Cacatuidae

Emily was sat by the back door, sketchbook open on the kitchen table, waiting for something to happen.

The shadows on the lawn were slowly disappearing as the sun rose in the summer sky, and next door the church bell-ringers were warming up for their weekly practice. Everything was as it should be on a Monday morning in August, but Emily felt that there was a gap in the day, one which she was trying to figure out how to fill.

She was stuck, waiting for inspiration to strike, but even a second cup of tea and slice of lemon cake had done nothing to shift her focus back to the task in hand. A selection of inkpots was stood next to the sink, ready for when Emily decided which colours to add to the picture of a cockatoo she had drawn over breakfast.

The problem was, the brief she had been given by her publisher was for a lifelike depiction of the bird, with no whimsy or magical elements, but whenever Emily looked at him (for he was most definitely a him, with such a proud crest on his head), she was struck by a desire to paint his feathers with all the colours of the rainbow. Her mind was misbehaving and kept going off on tangents, imagining the cockatoo being able to transform, much like a chameleon, whenever he needed to hide from whomever or whatever he was flying from.

There was another picture in her head too, of a little girl sat in a wheelchair with the cockatoo perched on her shoulder. She was whispering to him, gently stroking his breast and watching as ripples of colour passed from the bird and onto her skin. For no matter the pictures that Emily was asked to draw, her imagination always seemed to bring her back to Ophelia, the iconic character her grandmother had created all those years ago.

'Cacatuidae,' Emily sounded out the Latin term for the bird as she wrote it underneath the branch he was perched on. She spoke slowly, feeling her way through each syllable, and realised it was the first time she had said anything out loud for days.

The whole point of agreeing to the illustrations was that it was supposed to be distracting her from the fact she was all by herself. Naively, she had thought a new project would be all it took to fill the hours of the day, when she otherwise had nothing in particular to do and nowhere to go.

The song on the radio changed, the velvet notes of a clarinet playing *Peter and the Wolf*, which filled Emily's mind with a picture of a boy running through the snow, longing to get back home where his mother was waiting with a turkey on the table and presents under the tree.

I'm sorry, she thought, looking at the cockatoo as she turned the radio off, before closing the sketchbook and tidying away the pots of ink. *It would seem you're destined to be decidedly ordinary after all.*

Emily had spent years creating illustrations that were anything but ordinary. Her pictures were filled with fantasy and make-believe, designed to bring to life the incredible stories her grandmother had written. But ever since her death, Emily had found herself unable to concentrate on anything new.

She looked across to the room that led off the kitchen, her grandmother's study. One wall was taken over by shelves filled with dozens of her grandmother's red notebooks, which contained all the ideas for every book she had written about Ophelia and her pet duck. Ten books in all, no more, no less. But now the whole world seemed to think there was another, one that Emily knew there had never been time to write.

How could she do this? Emily thought to herself. The doctors had said there was still time. Time to finish her work. Time to seek out another possible treatment.

Time to fight.

Her grandmother was the one person in the world who understood. Who had shared in the misery of losing both parents in a car crash so many seasons ago and the pain of Emily's subsequent recovery. She was the only person who had been there throughout the years of cruel taunts, from children who were supposed to be her friends.

She had promised to love Emily, to take care of her always. But now her grandmother, the famous Catriona Robinson, couldn't protect anyone.

Outside came the sound of footsteps on the garden path, a pause, then a tumble of post that appeared through the letter box and landed in a heap on the doormat. No doubt more notes of comfort, of sorrow, from people Emily had never met. Handwritten notes from grieving fans – all of them detailing how amazing and talented her grandmother had been. Every one packed with personal stories of how her books had helped excite their early imaginations.

Emily went into the hall and bent down to retrieve the post, began to sort them into piles of letters and junk, catalogues and bills, when the shrill sound of a telephone disturbed the quiet. The answerphone clicked on to record.

'Emily, darling, it's Charlie.' A woman's voice crossed the distance from London to Norfolk and Emily could picture the person on the other end of the line, sat in a large, bright office on the twenty-second floor of a skyscraper overlooking the River Thames. 'Look, I'm sorry to keep asking you the same question, but I'm being pressured by the board to put out a press release about this damn manuscript.' There was a long sigh and Emily closed her eyes, waited for what she sensed was coming. 'Are you there? I know you don't want to talk about this, but at some point you're going to have to answer all these questions about Catriona, about her life. It doesn't have to be in person, but you owe it the fans—'

The room fell silent as Emily pulled the plug from its socket, then threw it to the floor, where it landed on the carpet with a soft thud. She looked down at the letters clasped tightly in her hand, before walking into the living room and over to the fireplace, where she tossed them all into the grate. Next, she went back out to the hall to retrieve a large cardboard box by the front door, taking it back to the fireplace and opening the lid. Inside were hundreds of fan letters, most of them unopened.

I don't want your pity, Emily thought as she began to take them out and stack them in four neat piles by the fire.

Emily had never before wanted to run away, had in fact done everything she possibly could to stay within the safe confines of Wells-next-the-Sea, a happy little town on the Norfolk coast where life moved at a suitably slow pace and the wider world largely left her alone. That was, until her grandmother had given that interview, telling the world and everyone in it that there was, quite possibly, another manuscript ready and waiting for all to discover. There had been such an incredible frenzy after it was published, with phone calls and emails and strangers turning up at the door, thrusting phones in Emily's face and asking her if it was true. The kind of chaos Emily had been sheltered from when her grandmother was alive. But she didn't have any answers, neither then nor now, because she hadn't asked her grandmother about the unfinished story. It was beginning to feel as if she had never asked her anything of importance, and now it was too late.

On the opposite wall to all those notebooks hung a small, square picture of two bluebirds. It was so very different in style to all the other paintings in the house, but Emily had never asked where it came from, or why it was right next to the space where her grandmother always worked. It was just one example of how Emily had simply assumed, in that slightly arrogant way of a child, that adults had no real past before their children were born. Now, more than anything, she wanted to be able to talk to her grandmother, to discover everything that had happened before.

Emily went over to the mantelpiece, looking at each of the photographs stood on top. She wished she could go back, find at least one answer to all her questions.

For years, Emily had allowed her life to be decided for her, first by a long series of doctors and then her grandmother. It was always Catriona to whom she had turned whenever she was in need, relied on her to make all the decisions, allowed her to take responsibility for pretty much every aspect of her life. It wasn't until Catriona had decided to forgo further treatment that Emily was forced to acknowledge how isolated, how dependent on her grandmother, she had become.

Emily looked across at the piles of letters she had created, thought of what would happen to all those words if she were to set them alight. Imagined them dancing up the chimney and into the sky, where they would mix together and perhaps create something new, or get caught in the beak of a passing cockatoo who would fly across the ocean and deliver them to a boy who dreamt of one day growing up to be a famous author.

'What am I supposed to do?' Emily sighed as she sank to her knees and looked across at her grandmother's desk, where an ancient typewriter had sat, untouched for months. Twenty-eight years old with nothing to show for her life other than a shelf full of books. What was she, who was she, without the late, great Catriona Robinson?

2

ROBIN

Erithacus rubecula

Mr Thomas could see someone moving around inside the house as he approached. The outline of a person who dipped and turned beyond the window. The house itself was tucked away at the end of a long, gravel path next to the church. A blink-and-you'll-miss-it sign for *Meadows Cottage* written in the same hand as that on the envelope he'd been instructed to deliver by the woman whose absence he felt each morning when he woke.

It was his dog Max who'd first brought them together, just shy of one year ago. Running in circles around a pile of belongings, tail thumping in contentment as his bark resonated through the morning air. There had ensued a momentary tug of war as he'd retrieved one end of a belt from Max's jaws, then he'd crouched down to discover a small gold ring half buried in the sand beside a pile of clothes now wrinkled through with sandy paw prints. He had turned full circle in search of another person, and found a woman jogging towards him, breathless but smiling, with hair slapped in sodden streaks over her face. She was wearing nothing more than a silk slip, soaked through by her swim in the sea. She'd apologised for the confusion, laughing about how it must have seemed to a man who was simply walking his dog and discovered a pile of abandoned belongings.

She had introduced herself as Catriona, her hand small and chilled inside his own. A hand he would go on to hold many times as the two of them walked Max each morning, before she returned home to the granddaughter he'd never had the chance to meet, until now.

Part of him wanted to walk away, to continue with his morning as planned — a stroll across the beach, followed by a strong, black coffee, croissant and newspaper at the nearby café, then home to continue work on the raised beds in the back garden.

But another part of him knew it was folly to ignore a dying woman's wishes. A woman who had chosen him because he understood that Emily's world was about to be turned upside down.

Max nudged his master's leg, pulling him back to the here and now. The garden was still: petals sleepy under the advancing sun; bees going in search of a late breakfast; a robin perched atop the handle of a garden fork, with a worm held tight in its beak.

The dog barked, and the bird took flight as the front door opened. A young woman dressed in a pale green T-shirt and denim shorts appeared in the doorway. Her skin held the beginnings of a tan, all except for a large stretch of scar along her jaw. Stood barefoot, the nails of each toe painted a glossy

15

red, she watched Mr Thomas from under a heavy fringe that stopped just shy of her hazel eyes.

There was something unsettling about her gaze, Mr Thomas thought. The way it drew him in to look at her a moment more, to recognise the curve of lip so like her grandmother's, and the freckles across her nose.

'Are you Emily?' he asked.

A single nod of reply as she bent down to rub behind the dog's ears, a smile that broke through the scar when she was rewarded with a lick.

'I have something for you,' he said as he held out the envelope he'd kept safe for six long weeks. 'It's from your grandmother.'

She considered the offering a moment before taking it, then turned to walk back inside, a small wave of her hand inviting him to follow.

The dog pulled free of its lead, trotting behind the woman who disappeared into a room at the rear. Inside, the cottage was cool, its stone walls clinging to the remnants of night, with a small living room to the left and a narrow staircase straight ahead. A cuckoo clock ticked away in the corner and he was forced to duck his head to avoid a beam as he passed through to the kitchen. The scent of toast and coffee drew his eye to a table by the back door, where an empty plate and cup sat next to a sketchbook open to a blank page.

Emily was stood by the butler's sink and he watched as she turned the envelope over in her hand, looking at it from one side then the other. She held it up to the light, then tossed it in the sink, where it landed atop a slowly disintegrating tower of bubbles, dark tendrils of ink beginning to soak through the paper.

'Ah yes,' he said, with fumbling fingers that betrayed his exterior of calm. 'There's also this.' Out of his pocket came a fountain pen, with bottle-green marbling and gold lid. Emily took the pen, held it in her palm, then suddenly cried out, bashed her fist against the porcelain and slipped down to the floor.

'Are you OK?' he asked, rushing to her side, only for her to dip her head, try to hide her tears. 'I'm so sorry,' he continued, reaching out a hand, then bringing it away. 'Do you know what this means?' Catriona hadn't told him. Asked him only to deliver the letter and pen.

Emily nodded, then shook her head, a low moan escaping her lips. Max came over and lay a paw on her leg. The dog seemed to understand her pain, emitting a soft whine as she wrapped an arm around his neck and buried her face in his fur.

'Is there anyone who can help?' Mr Thomas asked, looking around the kitchen for some kind of sign of what he was supposed to do. His eyes skimmed over the obvious, the everyday items so commonplace to all. A laptop, a coffee machine, a collection of keys hanging from a row of hooks on the wall, two pairs of wellington boots stood side by side by the back door. A framed cover of a children's book, written by one of England's best-loved authors.

Emily was still sat on the floor, one hand absently stroking Max's ears, the other turning the pen over and over.

All of a sudden, he felt the full weight of his intrusion. Of witnessing something he should not, and it made him agitated, annoyed at his decision to come here, to play the hand of fate when it really was none of his concern.

'I really am so very sorry,' he muttered as he took hold of

Max's collar and lifted him away from the woman. 'Please accept my apologies for barging in on you like this. It wasn't my intention to cause you any distress, only I made your grandmother a promise and, well, it's not something I felt I could ignore.' He was rambling, a nervous habit of his, all the more obvious in a room so silent, apart from the tick of a clock and the click of Max's claws on the floor as they left.

She gave him no more than a cursory glance as he left, and it wasn't until he closed the door behind him that he realised, for all his blathering, for the shock of what he had passed on, she hadn't said a single word the entire time he was there.

3

MAGPIE

Pica pica

The man was gone. The dog too. It made Emily feel sad and relieved all at once. To have someone give her a message from the grave was so very typical of her grandmother. Planning it all down to the person who would deliver the news, with a dog no less, as if that might somehow soften the blow.

She picked up her cup, around the rim of which were tiny paintings of turtle doves, and poured herself another coffee. Cradled the warmth in her palms and tapped her pen against the side, tried to think when her grandmother could have taken it. Perhaps she had hidden it away in the pocket of her cardigan, or inside a packet of tobacco, knowing it was somewhere Emily would never look. Emily had searched all over for the pen, tossing cushions aside, even removing books from the shelves in the study and going into the greenhouse to see if it had mysteriously ended up next to the tomatoes.

'Look for the signs,' her grandmother would always say.

'Don't forget to look for all the clues and miracles tucked away in every corner of the world.'

But what sort of clue was this? Emily unscrewed the lid, raised the nib to her nose and breathed deep. It always made her think of the tube of Germoline, all pink and sticky, sitting at the back of the cabinet above the bathroom sink. A left-over cream from childhood with such a distinct smell. The pen had been a present from her grandmother, something to help Emily have confidence in herself, her drawings. Told her she shouldn't ever think of rubbing something away, that all the images she created were there for a reason and she should treasure them all. Ever since, Emily always sketched in black ink, never pencil.

A long sigh, because all of the memories only served to remind Emily that she was alone. She closed her eyes, tried to remember the look on her grandmother's face the last evening she had been alive. Tried to recall the exact words spoken before she had kissed her goodnight and Emily had turned back to her work, away from the sound of footsteps on the narrow stairs. The creak of floorboards overhead as the old woman settled down to sleep.

Emily blew into her cup, let the steam rise and cover her face. Felt tears on her cheeks, grief tangled up with anger at being left all alone.

There was a sudden cackle of magpie and Emily opened her eyes, sought out the culprit sat in the apple tree at the edge of the lawn. Two sharp whistles and the bird swooped down from the branch, hopping across the grass, then in through the door and up onto the kitchen table.

'Hello Milton,' Emily said in a small whisper.

The bird pecked at the toast crumbs on offer, then went

over to tap at a biscuit tin placed high on a nearby shelf. Emily reached up to bring the bird back down, leant in close to whisper a reprimand, which made Milton cock his head in response.

Two black eyes regarded her for a moment, then he leapt over to the sink. Head down, tail up, the magpie went, its beak investigating a saturated envelope that Emily snatched away and dropped on the table.

'No,' Emily whispered, a slam of cup on wood before she stormed out to the garden.

She couldn't look at it. Certainly couldn't open it, or read her grandmother's final words. Because that would make it real, make this more than just a passing distraction from the monotony of life. Make her grandmother's threats and promises come true: that one day soon Emily would be on her own.

If she read the letter, she had the strangest feeling that everything would change, and she wasn't ready for that. Not yet.

Toes on grass, curling through the damp to feel the earth below, and the tiny stems of daisies scattered all around. Daisies she used to make into chains, then drape over the outstretched branches of all the trees that ran around the garden's perimeter. A shield to stop the outside world from looking in.

Always looking, always staring. Always wanting to know about the famous author and, perhaps even more so, about the silent child.

Emily leant against the rough trunk of the apple tree, looked down to where Milton was waiting at her feet. He had been joined by a robin, who sang out his greeting, then fluttered up to land close to her ear.

A soft breeze stirred the feathers at his breast, bringing with it the scent of honeysuckle and spun sugar from the vicarage next door. The vicar had a notoriously sweet tooth and Emily would sometimes sit with him as he wrote his sermons, accompanied by a plate of biscuits or Danish pastries that his wife would bake. Perhaps she could pop in, let him read the letter instead?

No matter who read it, she would need to admit that her grandmother, and her legacy, were gone.

But admitting was impossible. Admitting would make it true.

Her throat began to close as the truth settled in her heart and she let out a low sob that pierced the garden's calm.

Milton shook his head, then scuttled back across the lawn. The robin sang out his own note of remorse and Emily imagined a chorus of birds landing in the apple trees at the back of the garden, a mismatched group of magpies and wrens, crows that perched up high, and swallows that dipped and turned through the brightening sky.

She knew she was doing it again – escaping inside her own imagination, never allowing herself to acknowledge the reality of what she had lost. Because she had lost so much and she didn't want to have to start again.

Emily took a long, slow breath, wiped her eyes and went back to the kitchen, where Milton was pecking at the last remaining crumbs on the breakfast table, her grandmother's letter unopened by his feet.

'OK,' she sighed as she slipped her finger through the seal. Out came a single sheet of paper embossed with her grandmother's neat, black script:

No more, no less. Just a few letters on a page. Was it some sort of breadcrumb trail she was expected to follow?

Emily tore the paper into ever smaller pieces, as one by one they fell to the ground, and she scuffed them away with her feet, wanted them gone.

She had no need to keep the piece of paper intact to find the source – Emily knew the address by heart. It's what was waiting for her there that made her hesitate. Made her look to the table, where her sketchbook lay waiting, offering up an alternative.

As she smoothed the pages flat, Emily traced her fingers over another drawing she had been working on, of a girl now grown, cycling through the countryside, with all the possibility of life right in front of her. A girl she had created in this very room when she was no more than a child herself. When she was battered, broken and unable to talk, but who found another way to give voice to what was inside her soul. Pictures of a tiny heroine who had been stitched into the imaginations of millions of children all around the world, accompanied by the extraordinary words of her grandmother. A girl whose adventures only existed in the mind of someone who was gone. Really gone, leaving behind nothing more than some stupid clue.

But if she didn't go, if she didn't follow the demands her grandmother had left, she could pretend it wasn't so.

Except for the man who'd delivered the letter. He would know. Before long he would figure it out. She had seen the way he looked at her. His mind processing the physical similarities between her and her grandmother. He had seen the framed cover of the first edition, a cover instantly recognisable the world over. It wouldn't take long for all those dots to be connected.

Once more her grandmother had pre-empted how Emily would react, knew she would try to hide, to protect herself from the reality of what had happened. She'd made sure there was a witness, who would eventually force Emily's hand.

In those last days before she died, her grandmother had spoken of something left behind from long ago. A secret kept safe, that she wanted Emily to find. It was a game of sorts; a hide-and-seek puzzle so beloved of Catriona Robinson. Follow the clues to find the prize. A chocolate egg, or a tiny wooden door nailed to the side of a tree that she claimed belonged to a fairy. Except this time Emily wasn't sure if she wanted to play.

The magpie tapped his beak against the biscuit tin. He seemed to be waiting for Emily to make up her mind. Either that or he simply wanted another treat. A swift roll of eyes, a final slurp of caffeine, then back outside Emily went.

Leg tossed over the saddle of her bike, bare feet on pedals, she rode through the village as the wind whispered secrets through her hair. Tiny speckles of pollen touched her skin as she sped along the road.

She felt them staring, heads turning as she went. The bird lady. The silent one. The stranger in their midst, who stood at the back of the church so no one could hear her sing.

Overhead Milton flew: her chaperone, her minder, a streak of black and white who seemed to know where Emily was headed. To a bookshop in the neighbouring village. Not the main one, sat in the centre of the High Street, surrounded by hairdressers and charity shops. This particular shop was

24

hidden away down a side alley, a chalkboard sign hanging above a painted door. Emily had spent much of her childhood there, protected by the make-believe words of people she had never met. Including those of her grandmother, who wrote stories about a girl named Ophelia whose only friend was a pale, grey duck. The two of them travelled all over the world in search of fairy tales and adventure. They had been adventures Emily had never dared to know in real life.

As she cycled close, Emily saw that the door was open. The air around its frame speckled with light that trailed to the floor then seeped inside. It was Thursday. The shop would normally be shut up tight, all a-slumber. Only today was not a day like any other – Emily could sense that now.

With her bike propped against the wall and Milton keeping watch, she crossed the threshold, felt the air settle on her skin as the door swung to, sealing her in.

The space was both familiar and strange. Every surface was covered with books. Shelves that stretched to the ceiling, side tables and chairs that sagged under the weight of all those words. The comforting scent of paper and ink hung in the air.

But there was something else as well, something Emily couldn't quite put a name to. At the far end of the shop, a trio of steps led down and through an archway to a small space dominated by an ancient leather chair. On either side stood a tower of books that looked sure to topple if ever they were bumped. Sat still was the bookseller, a paperback open on his lap. His hair was the colour of winter's frost, his buttercup waistcoat undone and one finger traced over the letters as he read, thin lips moving in silent recognition.

His head raised only a fraction as she approached.

'Ah, Emily,' he said, blinking through the smudged lenses of his spectacles. 'I was wondering when you were going to show up.'

4

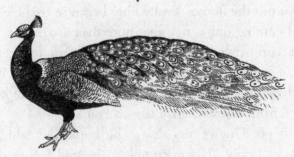

PEACOCK

Pavo cristatus

In her lap, Emily held two documents that the bookseller had procured from a drawer and handed over with a flourish, like a magician lifting the rabbit from his top hat. One was the Last Will and Testament of Catriona Robinson, the other was a letter from her grandmother's solicitor. Both were typed on thick, embossed paper with an elegant signature at the bottom of the final page.

But neither of them made any sense.

'You are the sole heir,' the bookseller said, seemingly oblivious to the way in which Emily's hands were shaking. 'All you have to do in order to inherit your grandmother's estate in its entirety is follow the clues.'

'The clues,' Emily whispered, looking back down at the pieces of paper, thinking of the envelope delivered by a stranger and his dog.

'It says so right there,' he pointed to the Will, to a paragraph that Emily had read twice already but was having trouble understanding. 'The books, the rights and every single item within the house.'

'But not the house.' Emily's lips began to tremble, the last word coming out as nothing more than a whisper. Because the accompanying letter clearly stated that the cottage in which she and her grandmother had lived for the best part of fifteen years did not, in fact, belong to them but had been rented from a businessman named Frank.

'But good news, my dear,' the bookseller said, smiling across at Emily. 'If you complete the trail before the lease is up, then you will be given first refusal to buy the cottage. And at fair market value.'

Fair market value. Emily repeated it to herself. Nothing about this was fair. Her grandmother had lied to her, let Emily believe she was safe.

'Which means,' the man continued with a swift glance at his watch, 'by my calculations, you have exactly ten days to complete the task.'

His words were forming in the air. Words Emily recognised but did not know how to respond to. Because the letters and sentences that flowed from this man's lips were about a trail, a test of sorts, at the end of which was the prize her grandmother had spoken of before her death.

They're like the notes of a wretched symphony, Emily thought to herself, imagining his words transforming into notes, wishing there was actual music to drown out the sound of his voice.

She began to tap her foot on the ground in sync with the rhythm of his words. Imagined herself spinning around like a dervish, faster and faster, until she disappeared inside one of the books that held up the walls of this ancient shop.

Could see herself dancing through fields and over streams heavy with fish, looking for the scarecrow and a road made of yellow brick.

Emily stood, dropped her grandmother's Will on top of a pile of books and went to the door that led to the small patio at the back of the shop. It contained nothing more than a few porcelain pots and a watering can in the shape of a frog, one of its painted eyes staring up to the heavens.

'This is your first clue,' the bookseller said, holding out a book for her to take.

She knew what it was before he slipped it into her hands. Before she turned it around to reveal a picture of a handsome peacock, his tail spread wide so that dozens of eyes were winking back at her. It was a copy of the book that made her grandmother a household name just shy of fourteen years ago. Reprinted only last year in hardback, with a peacock replacing Emily's original drawing of a little girl and her duck.

Emily had first sketched the bird last spring, during a visit to a National Trust garden. Her grandmother had wandered around the gardens, chatting with the gardener about what best to plant in her garden in order to attract more butterflies. Emily had watched the proud bird strut along the edge of the croquet lawn, as if it were master of the house.

They don't start growing their fancy tail feathers until they're three. Emily had picked one up off the lawn, spun it between her fingers and watched the colours blur. The head gardener had commented on how, despite their beauty, peacocks actually tasted pretty foul. Her grandmother had laughed at his terrible joke whilst all Emily could do was muster up half a smile, turn away and back to her drawing.

The garden. Her grandmother's garden. What would happen to it if the cottage were sold? It's what had provided Catriona Robinson with comfort, especially in the last few months when the pain was too much for her to venture even to the village. It was what kept Emily grounded, connected to her grandmother somehow, whenever she felt the sadness lurking. That and the birds who came every morning for their breakfast crumbs and would sit with Emily whilst she sketched in the late summer sun.

What would happen to all those memories if the cottage were to be home to someone new?

And what about me? Emily suddenly realised. Where was she supposed to go?

The idea of starting again was terrifying. So many years spent in one place, with one person, only for it all to be taken away from her at once. The books they had written together had been her constant, her way of coping with the life she had been dealt. The partnership forged between an unlikely pairing, which gave them both so much joy. The letters and pictures sent by readers from all over the world, telling them how much they loved the books with all the secrets hidden within each picture.

Clues Emily and her grandmother would come up with together, laugh about the strangeness of some, talk about the links back to folklore or simply an object from her grandmother's life, before.

'Open it,' the bookseller said, and Emily noted the anticipation, the excitement, in his voice.

'You,' she replied, handing back the book with trembling fingers. Afraid of what more was about to come.

He regarded her for a moment, then set the book down on

a nearby trestle table and slipped his forefinger inside the first page, easing the spine apart to reveal the dedication.

For Emily.
If you don't try, you'll never know.

Emily stepped closer to peer at the typed words that she knew didn't marry up with the actual dedications in each and every book in the series. Ten in all, written in the back room of her grandmother's cottage, typed up with a clatter of keys through hailstorms, heatwaves and everything in between.

She turned around, walked through the shop to the children's section, to where row upon row of books by Catriona Robinson sat. Emily removed one, flicked to the dedication page, saw the same two words as had always been – *For Emily* – then put it back again. She took out another, this one whose cover had a picture of a girl swimming under the sea, a bright pearl clutched tight in her hand.

For Emily.

Another, with the same little girl soaring on an enormous swing through a starry sky.

For Emily.

Each and every dedication was the same – apart from the one she had just been given.

It was a clue. A clue to the next part of the puzzle her grandmother had put together in secret, that she'd kept hidden from her. But why?

'The first one is my favourite,' the bookseller said, pointing at one of the books Emily had discarded on the floor. 'The idea of a magical atlas, transporting a little girl with a disability all over the world. Teaching her about people and places she could never hope to know. I only wish I had that kind of imagination.'

The stories had been their way of escaping, of pretending that the real world wasn't there, if only for a little while. But life, Emily knew, had a way of creeping up on you, even when you were doing everything you possibly could to pretend it wasn't.

'I can't,' Emily whispered, leaning against the bookcase and closing her eyes. She could see herself as a girl of thirteen, sat in a wheelchair beside a lake. Her legs were wrapped in a tartan blanket with tassels she liked to twist into plaits. Her face was bandaged tight so that only her nose and one eye peeped free, and, overhead, nightingales called out their evening song. By her side, just like every night since the accident, was her grandmother, with a flask full of hot chocolate and a red leather notebook, open on her lap.

Would it have come to this if not for that twist of fate, when her grandmother's publisher had come to visit and asked if she had been working on anything new? Emily was sat in the back garden, quietly reading, and Catriona had decided to show her friend the outline of a children's book, along with Emily's illustrations. If she had never discovered the book, would Emily still be stood in a tumbledown shop, being asked from beyond the grave to complete a ridiculous treasure hunt in order to claim her inheritance?

The scent of tobacco, laced through with vanilla, pulled Emily from her thoughts and she opened her eyes to see the bookseller drawing deep on a curved wooden pipe. Tendrils of smoke made their way up and out of the back door, mixing into the sky without a trace. He looked like a character from one of her grandmother's books: all waxed moustache and twinkly eyes.

Emily allowed the scene in front of her to shimmer at its edges, began to imagine the world in which such a character would exist, or at least the world they would have created for him. A grassy hillock hidden deep in the forest, where he lived with only the trees for company. Or an underground network of caves, ruled by a dastardly gang of moles, who paid him to keep the humans away.

Emily could see it all in full technicolour: the perfect shade of emerald green for his front door; a rocking chair in which he sat and smoked his pipe in front of the fire when the winter's evenings closed in; circular miner's lamps worn by all the moles as they excavated a kingdom underground. A whole world no one knew anything about, until a little girl and her pet duck came knocking one day, seeking shelter from a storm.

'She said you would know where to go next,' he said, with a small nod in Emily's direction. 'She said all the clues were right in front of you.'

Of course they are, Emily thought. Her grandmother had always taught Emily to look closer, to see what others would not. But what was it she wanted Emily to see? And what if she chose not to?

'How many books?' Emily spoke slowly and with care, her mouth stretching over each syllable.

'I'm afraid I have no idea,' he replied. 'Nor if all the clues will be books.'

Ten, Emily thought as she bent down to collect an armful of books and began to place them back on the shelves. *Surely she can't be sending me off to find them all?*

'What if I say no?' Emily sighed with the effort of all the words at once, turned her face away so the bookseller couldn't see the clench of her jaw, the flushed skin on her neck.

'Well,' he replied, drawing deeply on his pipe. 'There was no mention of what would happen were you to refuse. But, well, I for one would be rather disappointed if you didn't find the rest of the story.'

'What story?' Emily turned to see the bookseller holding out a red leather notebook, identical to those her grandmother had always written all of her ideas and early drafts for each story in.

'She brought it to me a couple of months ago, along with the other book and documents,' the bookseller said, a clear note of excitement in his voice. 'Told me to keep it a secret, which, I must say, has been particularly difficult ever since that newspaper interview was published.'

Emily opened the notebook to the first page, recognised it as the beginnings of another story about Ophelia, but one that her grandmother had never quite been able to get right. It was about the ghost of a boy who was asking Ophelia for help to solve a crime he had witnessed, but Catriona had been concerned the topic was too dark for the children it was aimed at.

Flicking through the pages, Emily's eyes scanned the mind maps, random words and snippets of conversation that often made up the opening pages of her grandmother's notebooks. But then the pages simply stopped, because someone had ripped them from the spine, leaving behind thin lines of paper, like crocodile teeth grinning back at her.

'She told me she hid the rest,' the bookseller said as he stepped closer and pointed to the missing pages. 'Somewhere only you would be able to find it.'

But, as far as Emily was concerned, Catriona Robinson had never finished this book. Or had she? Because the months before she died were spent in her study, supposedly setting her affairs in order, and Emily had naturally assumed this was the case. Could it be that this is what she had spoken of before her death? Had she spent that time writing another story, one that Emily was now being sent out to find?

'Why hide it?' Emily muttered, looking from the notebook to the rest of the books on the floor. Bending down, she picked them up one by one and put them back on the shelves in chronological order.

As she went to return the last book to its rightful place, Emily paused, the words of the new dedication swirling through her mind and bringing with them the memory of that very first story. A reminder of what happened to the little girl and where she discovered the magical atlas in the first place.

'No,' she gasped and the book she was holding dropped to the floor with a soft thud, its cover facing up to show a little girl and her pet duck skipping through a snow-covered forest.

'Emily?' The bookseller looked over to see Emily's face riddled with panic. He moved towards her, but she backed away, hands raised.

'No,' she said once more, turning to flee from the shop, not stopping to collect either legal document or her grandmother's book. The spokes of her bike wheels blurred as she disappeared along the street, wind whipping back tears from her face, a magpie following in the sky.

Emily wanted to scream. She wanted to rip the thought from her mind and go back to before, to when all was as

35

it should be. Too many memories. Too much she didn't want to remember hidden within those walls. And yet it was exactly where her grandmother was trying to send her back to.

It felt so unfair. Like a cruel, manipulative trick that Emily wanted no part of. Perhaps she could simply stay at home and refuse to give in to her grandmother's demands? After all, it was not as if Catriona could force her to do anything any more. But the curiosity in her had already been aroused. Emily understood this was exactly what her grandmother had wanted – had predicted would happen. She felt something in the pit of her stomach then – the strange idea that today had only just begun. There was something about the twitter of birds in all the trees she cycled past, as if they knew something she didn't.

The scent of summer rain hung in the air, and church bells called out the hour as Emily came to a halt at the edge of the path which led to her home. Propped up against the garden gate was a young man wearing oxblood cowboy boots, a tan leather jacket, frayed jeans, with a guitar looped over one shoulder. The same man who, as a boy, was too afraid to duck his head under the water on their shared holidays, who she had eventually teased and cajoled into jumping from the jetty into the icy blue.

'Tyler,' she whispered as she watched him lift his head and smile as she approached.

5

PELICAN

Pelecanus

He was in her kitchen. Opening and closing cupboards, helping himself to some ham and cheese from the fridge. As if it were the most natural thing in the world for him to be there, with her.

Tyler was now perched on the end of the table, where her discarded breakfast and sketchbook still lay, chatting to her about how sorry he was not to have made the funeral, that he always loved how chaotic and free Aunt Cat was.

Was, thought Emily.

'So, are you all packed?'

Emily looked over to see Tyler wiping at the corner of his mouth with a linen napkin, the edge of which was embroidered with tiny stars. The last time she had seen him was at her twenty-first birthday. A mismatched gathering of lost souls who were connected to her somehow, yet none of them had seemed to know her at all. He had been out in the garden, over by one of the apple trees, smoking a cigarette and frowning at the vicar as he tried to explain the merits of cross-country skiing.

'Packed?' she asked, hating the way her tongue got caught around the middle syllable. It didn't matter that she had known Tyler all her life, nor that he understood where her speech impediment had come from, the blush on her cheek was just as embarrassing as always.

'The train leaves in just over an hour,' he replied, opening the biscuit tin and peering inside before taking out a handful of custard creams. 'I assumed you'd be ready?'

Emily gave a shake of her head, eyes darting around the kitchen as if somewhere was hidden a clue, a hint, as to what he was talking about. The bookseller had said she would know, that she would understand.

Surely not. Emily thought as she began to pace around the room, looking over at Tyler, then across at the clock hanging above the sink, then back at Tyler again.

Although sending a chaperone would be exactly the kind of thing her grandmother would do. Her way of ensuring Emily would go through with the task at hand. Not hide away under the cover of ignorance. Just like sending that man and his Dalmatian, she had decided to send Tyler. But what Emily couldn't figure out was, of all people, why him?

'No, as in you're not packed?' Tyler asked as he watched Emily's frantic pacing. 'Or no, you're not coming?'

Emily stopped. Leaned her head against the wall and closed her eyes. She was no longer a child in a wheelchair who needed doctors and adults to decide what was best. Now she was a grown woman, yet apparently still deemed incapable of making her own choices.

38

Tyler kept talking as she escaped into her grandmother's study. He followed her into the small, dark space that was dominated by a wall of books and a mahogany desk positioned by the back window, an old-fashioned typewriter sat neatly in the middle. Emily approached it and tapped a steady beat of two keys, which she struck over and over. Tyler came up to peer over her shoulder.

'NONONONONONONONONONONONONON...' he read out loud and Emily turned around to face him. She opened her mouth as if to speak, then realised she had completely forgotten whatever it was she was about to say, or even if she had intended to speak at all.

Images swam in her mind; memories she did not want to recall, including one of the way he had looked at her the first time they met after the accident. With a mixture of fear and pity, he'd clearly tried not to stare at the huge gash across one side of her face, or the metal structure which held her skull together but also prevented her from speaking. At the wheelchair that held her captive whilst her spine tried to heal. She remembered how he had stood, half-hidden behind his mother, hands shoved deep in pockets and one foot scuffing the ground. Then turned and ran to the other end of his garden, scaled the ladder hanging from a low-slung branch, up into a tree house where the two of them used to play as kids, and refused to come down, even when called in for supper.

Emily knew how hard it was for anyone to look upon her, strapped into a chair with a face contorted and bruised. She had known it every day since, even when her body had healed, her scars faded to silvery pink. She knew he could still see her the way she used to be, before the accident, and part of her hated him for it.

'You can't stay here, Emily.' Tyler placed a hand on her shoulder, only for her to swat him away. 'Mum told me that Aunt Cat's instructions were really specific.'

'She knew?' Emily grappled with the words and idea all at once. To think that Tyler's mother, her own godmother, had known of her grandmother's intentions yet said nothing.

'Well, yes, of course she did.' Tyler frowned, then gave a small shake of his head as he saw the way Emily's fists were clenched tight and her shoulders raised. 'But you didn't, did you?'

He sank into the desk chair, picked up a glass paperweight in the shape of an apple, then put it back down again.

'I know what you're thinking.' He started to sway back and forth on the chair, opened one drawer, then closed it again. 'And, yes, you're right. I didn't come here out of my own free will. Call it a favour, of sorts.'

Emily looked at him with raised eyebrows, and crossed her arms.

'The thing is, I need this trip as much as you do. So, why not call a truce? Help one another out?'

Emily laughed at how revoltingly obnoxious he was, then turned to walk out of the room, but felt his hand on her arm, asking her to stay. Instinctively, she wanted to pull free, but something stopped her. She considered the weight of him on her, the warmth spreading from skin to skin. And then up to the dusting of freckles across his cheeks, half-hidden by stubble.

'No.' Emily stomped up the stairs, heard him call out after her.

'There is something else,' he said.

She paused on the landing.

'I have a letter. From your grandmother. Only I'm not allowed to give it to you until we're on the train. Which, by the way, leaves in fifty-five minutes.'

Emily slammed the door to shut him out, sank onto her bed and stared out of the window to the garden beyond.

A letter. Another clue? She had to consider her options. Could she steal it from him? Negate the need to even leave the house? Only she didn't know where the letter was hidden; perhaps in his guitar case, or his pocket?

She rolled over and looked under the bed, saw nothing more than a pair of moccasin slippers she never wore, even on the coldest days. No suitcase, but then again she couldn't remember the last time she had needed to pack an overnight bag, nor indeed if she even owned one.

Out onto the landing she went, then pushed the door to her grandmother's room wide, a line of sunlight cutting the space in two. The bed was stripped of all linens, but there remained a hand-stitched quilt folded at its foot. In her last few months, even when the evenings remained bright and warm, Catriona had needed the extra layer. Emily had often sat with her, reading aloud until she fell asleep, the role of adult and child reversed.

Emily wandered over to the bed, then lay on top of the mattress that dipped in the middle, pulled the quilt over her shoulders, closed her eyes and breathed in the scent of lavender that used to follow her grandmother wherever she went.

She hadn't been in the room for weeks, not since emptying the contents of her grandmother's wardrobe and nightstand. Sorting through what could go to charity and what held too many memories to throw away, including a vintage compact and lipstick case, a music box with filigree key and a carriage clock that chimed out each hour.

Other items Emily had never seen before, but held the suggestion of her grandmother's past – items that Catriona apparently couldn't bear to part with, instead hiding them at the back of her wardrobe for so many years. There was a pair of handmade velvet shoes, the soles worn thin, that made Emily think of nights dancing in the arms of a handsome man in uniform whilst the band played on. A copy of *A Room with a View*, tucked inside of which was a crumbling rose, its petals papery and flattened by time, and a photograph in a tarnished, silver frame, of her grandmother as a baby held in her mother's arms, wrapped up tight against the bitter, Scottish winter.

Emily had carefully wrapped each item in between thin layers of tissue paper, placed them inside a cardboard box and then made a list of absolutely everything her grandmother had possessed in a notebook, in the hope that she might not forget a single thing.

Except there was so much she still didn't know. Emily rolled onto her back and stared up at the ceiling, watched a spider spinning its web in the corner above the wardrobe, on top of which was a battered, yellow suitcase. The same suitcase her grandmother said she had taken with her all over Europe, when Emily's mother was just a baby herself.

Where did they go? Emily wondered, because she couldn't remember the names of all the places her mother had been taken as Catriona Robinson went in search of inspiration and adventure. She knew only how her mother had said she much preferred being at home, with her family. Had always told Emily she had no need of adventure when her entire world was right there in front of her.

There was so much more she hadn't been told, and Emily realised she had been too foolish to ever ask. It was as if Catriona had deliberately kept her past a secret because she knew one day it would come in handy.

So many secrets all tangled up together, or perhaps it had simply been too painful for her grandmother to remember. They had hardly ever spoken about her parents since their deaths. Even now, Emily felt her mind shut down whenever she thought back to before the accident. During her recovery, she had been told to focus on the present, to take one day at a time, and her grandmother always said looking back brought nothing but regret, which itself was just a waste of emotion.

Emily sat up and pushed the quilt away. Climbing onto the chest of drawers, Emily stretched up to grasp hold of the battered, yellow suitcase, tossed it onto the bed and opened it wide to discover a porcelain figure of a pelican. The very end of its beak was missing, but its eyes were still painted bright blue.

'Hello,' she whispered to the bird, running her finger over the three holes in its head as she wandered back downstairs, the suitcase held tightly in one hand.

Tyler was sat at the kitchen table, scrolling through his phone. He stood up as she entered the room, upending his chair, and the resounding crash bounced around the silence that hung between them.

'Changed your mind?' He gestured at the suitcase.

Emily shook her head as she dropped it by the fridge, then reached up to take another porcelain bird down from the shelf next to the sink. This pelican had just one hole in its head and thin little eyelashes surrounding its blue eyes. Emily stood the pair together on the window ledge, beak to beak, and tried to remember where they had come from.

'Hoopla,' Tyler said as he picked up the fallen chair, placed his dirty plate in the sink and looked at the salt-and-pepper-pot birds.

''Oopla?' Emily replied, clenching her jaw in irritation at the lost consonant.

'Don't you remember? The fair on the Common?' Tyler turned on the tap, squeezed some washing-up liquid into the sink and swirled his hand through the growing mountain of bubbles.

We went every year, Emily thought, watching tiny rainbows appear in each perfect sphere, and pretended not to notice how comfortable Tyler was in her presence, how easily he had slotted himself into her day. It was like some sort of bad joke, her past appearing out of nowhere and carrying on as if nothing had happened over the intervening years.

'It was the one thing I could beat you at,' Tyler said as he flicked bubbles at her and she turned away so he wouldn't see her blush. 'Your aim was terrible.'

But Tyler had given her the prize anyway, handing the birds over with a deep bow, then lifting his head to reveal a wide grin as she stomped her foot and pretended to be mad.

It was the same every year, the fairground that seemed to appear overnight, with bumper cars, candy floss and row upon row of stalls with brightly-coloured lights, enticing you in, asking you to try your luck and win a prize.

The birds had been carried home in the pocket of her pinafore dress, each step bringing with it a corresponding *ting* of china that made her stop every so often to check neither of them were broken. Salt and pepper pots that stood proudly on the kitchen table of a house that once was her home, used every time she and her parents sat down for tea. Emily's mother would tell her husband off for covering his food with pepper before he'd even taken a mouthful. He would respond with a shrug and a wink at his daughter, then deliberately add some more.

Emily wandered into the living room, sank down into the chair by the fire and looked around at all the knick-knacks her grandmother had collected over the years. Emily now realised she had no idea where they came from, what the significance of keeping them was.

Did she hide the pelican on purpose? she asked herself, taking out the newly-returned fountain pen from her pocket and turning it through her fingers. *But why?*

Everything was done for a reason, as far as Catriona Robinson was concerned, especially when it came to her treasure hunts. Every clue, every stepping stone to the next part of the adventure, was carefully and meticulously planned, just like the books that she wrote. Nothing was left to chance, and Emily was beginning to realise that this call from the grave, this test, was no different.

'Bit warm for a fire, isn't it?' Tyler stood in the doorway, drying his hands on a tea towel as he looked over at the stacks of letters next to the fire.

'I was ...' She was going to burn them. All those individual messages of kindness that didn't belong to her.

Tyler went over to the fireplace, picked up a handful of letters and collapsed onto the sofa by the window. Part of her wanted to snatch them back, to tell him to keep his hands off things that didn't belong to him, but instead she found herself sitting forward on the chair, watching him as he read. He tugged at the collar of his shirt and in doing so revealed to her a thin silver scar across the back of his left hand. A scar she, in part, was responsible for.

She was always making him do things he didn't want to do. Such as climb over a fence to explore the garden of the creepy old woman who lived next door, just to find out whether she was, in fact, a witch as Emily so believed. Tyler had tripped over a tree root and cut his hand open on a broken pot, but he had refused to tell his parents where they had been, or whose idea it was to go off exploring in the first place.

Is this why you sent him? Emily thought as he looked up at her and she saw a shadow of the boy he used to be.

'I don't blame you for wanting to get rid of them.' He tossed the letters aside and stretched out on the sofa, hands behind his head in a pose of utter relaxation. 'What is it like?' He turned his head towards her. 'To have all those people asking something of you, wanting to know about you and Aunt Cat?'

All Emily could muster was a sigh and a shrug.

'She wouldn't make you do any of this without good reason,' he said.

'Perhaps.'

'Seriously, Em. I've never known you turn down a challenge before.'

Except she had been a different person back then, someone she barely remembered.

'What will you do instead? Where will you go when this place is sold?' Tyler eased off his boots and Emily smiled when she saw that, even as a grown man, he still wore mismatched socks.

'The one decent piece of advice my dad ever gave me was "don't quit until you're done".'

'I don't un...' Emily's tongue got trapped trying to sound out the letter 'd' and she pushed herself up from her chair, strode back into the kitchen and out to the garden, where she stared up at the sky. She stood, head tilted back as she scanned the various shades of blue, picked out a couple of swallows that were on the hunt for their supper and followed them until they dipped and turned too far for her to see. She heard Tyler come up behind her, felt him take a breath and could imagine him deciding whether or not to reach out and place a hand on her shoulder.

'Don't let this ... quest, or whatever you want to call it, decide. Make sure *you* decide when to stop.'

He was right, but that didn't make it any easier to digest the enormity of what he was asking – of what everyone seemed to be asking – her to do.

'I can't,' she said, daring a look at him. For as long as she could remember, she had wanted to be left alone, for no one to ask her about her scar, or her silence. But here he was throwing up reminders of what her life used to be like and, as much as it irritated her, she was grateful she wasn't being left to deal with things by herself.

He regarded her a moment, then scratched the back of his head in a gesture so familiar, Emily felt as if she'd been thrown back to 2003.

'I'm hungry,' Tyler said with a yawn. 'And pretty knack-ered, too. So here's my suggestion. We eat.' He took out his phone and started scrolling down the screen. 'Surely even out here we can get a delivery. You still like spicy food?'

Emily nodded as she bent down to pull up a stray weed

from in amongst the rose bushes. It made her think of the crushed rose her grandmother had kept, made her wonder if someone special had once given it to her and, if so, why Catriona had never spoken about them.

'Done. Should be here in half an hour.' Tyler shoved his hands in his pockets, rocked back and forth on his heels as he looked over at Emily, then around the garden. 'If it's okay with you, I'll crash here tonight as it's too late to head back to town.'

Emily sighed with relief that the journey was, at least for now, delayed. It would give her time to think, to consider what it was she wanted to do.

'I'll take the spare room, or the sofa, or whatever,' Tyler said. 'You know I can sleep pretty much anywhere.'

Emily nodded in agreement as she remembered Tyler curled up asleep on the floor of the overnight ferry back from France. He was the only one oblivious to the thunder that had ripped through the sky, unaffected by the sickening tilt of the boat.

'And I promise not to try and force you into any kind of decision. I mean, it's your life, who I am tell you what to do with it?'

Emily walked around the garden, occasionally reaching out to deadhead a bush, listening to all the words that spilled from Tyler's mouth as he followed. He was still talking to her when she went into the greenhouse to open the vents, about the time she stood up to a playground bully, punching him square on the nose when he dared to call Tyler a 'pussy'. It had always been the two of them, all the way through childhood and into adolescence, when it was Emily who had been the daredevil, the leader, the inventor of games.

Because I don't know you any more, she thought as she looked across to see a scrap of paper, marked with black handwriting, caught on the branch of an apple tree. She only knew the boy from before.

Inside the house, in one of the boxes she had so carefully packed away, was a photo album from long ago. One she had opened, then shut away quickly, because she knew it ended after her thirteenth birthday. It remained half full of blank spaces where all her memories should have been, key moments in life that she had once assumed would include Tyler and his family. But even though his face filled so many of the pages in that album, and his laugh, his willingness to please, were in so many moments from Emily's past, there was so much more that he hadn't been a part of, and that was what she was finding hardest of all to forgive.

Later that evening, when the dishes were cleaned away, and the sofa bed laid out, on which Tyler was perched, quietly picking out a tune on his guitar, Emily sat once again at the kitchen table.

I'll decide in the morning, she told herself as she tidied away her sketchbook and pen, tried not to think of the half-finished cockatoo.

She stood and whistled into the dark, waiting for Milton to come for his supper. When he failed to make an appearance, she put a plate of broken pieces of naan bread on the lawn and slid the bolt across the bottom of the door, before climbing the stairs and slipping into bed. The window was open and Emily watched the clouds drift past a moon that was so very nearly full.

New beginnings. Emily remembered what her grandmother

had always said when the moon was round and ripe. The chance to start over, to set new intentions, to begin anew.

But what if she didn't want to start again?

Emily turned from the moon and all its false promises, wrapping her palm around the locket she couldn't quite bring herself to take off that night.

Emily had lain awake half the night trying to decide what to do, tossing all the possibilities around in her mind until they blurred into one giant knot of confusion and frustration.

I can't stay here, she thought, sitting up in bed and staring across the garden, beyond the church spire to where she knew the tide would be slinking across the beach. Across to a stretch of ocean that wrapped itself around the globe, connecting all the dots of land her grandmother had once been so desperate to explore.

I don't want to leave. Emily sighed to herself as she went into the bathroom and stepped under the shower head, let the steady flow of water camouflage the sound of her own doubts. Slowly massaging shampoo into her scalp, as if in an attempt to knead the tension away. Stood at the sink, not bothering to wipe away the condensation on the mirror, she rough dried her hair, then padded across the landing and back to her room.

I could go with him, just get on a train to London. She scanned the contents of her wardrobe, taking out a random assortment of clothes and stacking them on the bed. Simple as that, no need to actually do anything more than pretend to go along with the idea, at least until she figured out another way to stop herself from being evicted.

She could get on the train, take the letter, then get off at the next stop, come back again.

Emily bit back the idea that if she failed to complete the task, in less than two weeks, there would be no home to come back to.

Only it didn't feel like her home any more. She had sensed it from that very first moment after returning from the funeral four weeks ago, and then every morning, every evening and all the hours in between. There was no clink of silver spoon that stirred sugar into her breakfast tea, no scent of frying bacon or lavender shampoo and no hushed words as her grandmother spoke on the phone to her doctor whilst Emily sat in the next room, pretending not to hear.

It was the absence of her that screamed loudest of all.

Emily traced her fingers over the frame of a photograph taken before it all began. Or ended, depending on your point of view. Three generations of women, all in a row. Her grandmother caught mid-sentence, with mouth open and hand pointing to the sky. Next to her, Emily's mother with her head thrown back as she laughed, one arm draped around the shoulder of a little girl dressed in a bathing suit and cape, goggles obscuring all but a wide grin.

Once there were three, now it was only her. Where else was she supposed to go other than on a crazy adventure with a boy who she used to know?

Tap, tap, against the windowpane and Emily turned to see Milton on the ledge, watching her from outside. She let him in, watched as he hopped inside the suitcase and she shooed him away.

'You can't come.' She opened the top drawer of her dressing table, took out the passport her grandmother had dutifully renewed when Emily turned eighteen, but had never been used. Was there even any point in taking it? She looked up to see the bird stood with a golden chain caught around its foot and Emily lifted him gently, fastened the necklace around her throat. Then she picked up a silver brush, pulled it quickly through her hair and tossed it into the case. It was half of a vanity set from long ago, the matching mirror buried at the back of a drawer.

How many years? She thought of all the mornings when someone else would brush her hair, and then again before she went to bed. How quickly time catches up with you when you're not paying attention.

A red dress on a hanger, asking to be chosen. Emily's fingers hesitated, then moved along to take down a simple, blue shirt. She zipped the case closed, looked around the room to see her grandmother's gold compact and lipstick on the bedside table. A slick of red on lips, a touch of powder on the nose: Catriona Robinson was always so well presented, putting her best face out on show. Emily pressed the waxy colour to her mouth, her hand hesitating for a second before she put the make-up back where it belonged.

'One more clue,' she whispered to Milton. 'Then I'll be back.'

The bird fluttered its tail at her, hopped back to the window and flew away.

'Oh, what would you know?' Emily said and banged the window shut.

Back downstairs, searching the house, trying to decide what a person takes on a trip to who knows where. Her sketchbook, her pen. Twenty-eight years old and all of her life contained in one place. She'd never needed to go anywhere before, never had any real desire to leave.

Emily paused in the doorway of her grandmother's study, saw Tyler hovering by the front door, asking her to please hurry up. She ran her fingers over the shelf filled with red leather notebooks, each of them containing the beginnings of an idea that eventually became a book. She looked but did not see a gap at the very end, thought there was no time to count them all, to see if one of them was missing.

Is this just another story? Emily wondered as she let the door swing shut behind her. She put her key in the lock and tried not to think about whether she would ever be allowed to return.

6

SPARROW

Passeridae

There was a man, sitting on the station platform feeding a gathering of sparrows. He was whispering to them, but what he was saying wasn't important. It was the way he spoke, the tone of voice, the pitch and volume and all the nuances in between – it all told the birds he was safe, that he could be trusted.

His torso was bent low over his knees and the sleeves of his striped, blue shirt were rolled up. At his feet rested a leather briefcase, a thin umbrella on top. His suit jacket was on the bench beside him and a paisley tie was tucked into one of the pockets.

Sparrows are adaptable, Emily thought, watching the scene through the window of the train, sketching it in her mind. *They can feed on over 800 different types of food.*

She was trying to commit to memory the exact speckles of dark brown on each sparrow's breast. The shadows that fell at an angle from the man's legs onto the platform. She wanted to imagine what it was that brought him to that place, at that moment, because the story behind the picture was what always brought it to life.

As the train pulled out of the platform, the birds scattered and Emily turned her head, her body, to count them, to follow them until they disappeared from view.

Catriona had told her that sparrows in the Old Testament were associated with loneliness, that they can swim under-water and live for up to fifteen years. She had taught her so much, and yet Emily couldn't help but feel there was so much more she never had a chance to share.

'When was the last time you were in London?'

On the seat opposite, across from the table that separated them, Tyler was shrugging off his jacket, then taking out his phone, along with a small, black notebook and a pair of enormous headphones. He simply dumped them all on top of one another, and Emily resisted the urge to line them up, neatly and in order of size.

He was relaxed, or rather, relieved. Emily could tell by the way one ankle was crossed over his knee, the tightness at his jaw gone, and his eyes no longer darted from her scar to her mouth and away whenever he looked at her. Which meant he was invested in this little trip more than he wanted her to know.

Except she knew. Just as she knew he was impatient to get back to London, because he had glanced at his watch and the clock above the sink more than a dozen times whilst he watched her busy herself about the kitchen, checking for locked windows and that the gas was turned off.

The fact she made him nervous, no matter the reason why,

made her smile a little, despite her own reservations, her own fears, about where exactly they were headed.

Instead of replying verbally to his question, she held up her hands, fingers and thumbs splayed.

'Ten years?' Tyler gave a low whistle as he scrolled through his phone. 'It's changed a bit since then.'

Haven't we all, Emily thought as she stared at him. Willed him to give up something of himself, something she could use to figure out what was really going on. She wanted to ask him why he was there, and what had happened to make him agree to accompany her on such a ridiculous quest?

'You still listen to rock music?' he asked without looking up from his phone.

Emily nodded as she tried to remember which CDs she had shoved into her suitcase. Crossing and uncrossing her legs, she fiddled with her hair, sat on both hands and tried not to look at the line of light that fell across his face. Tried to dampen the urge to ask him to turn a little more to the left, because then the light would cut straight across the bone at his cheek.

'Guns N' Roses?'

'Also Foo,' Emily said, allowing him to fill in what she didn't trust her tongue to be able to pronounce. Along with Chopin, Miles Davis, David Bowie and Adele. Her grandmother was the sort of person to try anything and everything at least once, so Emily had been taught to appreciate them all.

Her days and nights had been filled with sounds from every era. She had been told to listen for the soft crackle of vinyl before the needle found the first note, or the faintest intake of breath before Miss Simone opened her mouth to sing. To hear the story each artist was trying to tell.

But not opera. Never opera.

'I used to think you were so cool.'

'Ha.' The laugh left her mouth before she knew it was even there.

It used to be for fun, the music. The drums. The way the throb and pulse of it would fill her and make her move. Then it served a different purpose. To block it out. To block everything out.

'I don't have anything in your kind of league,' Tyler said as he turned his phone around to show her the playlist he'd been considering. 'But I could download something and we could listen to it together?'

Emily looked at the screen.

'I like Country,' Tyler said with a smile and a shrug. 'Doesn't make me a bad person.'

She knew he was trying to placate her. Trying to work that effervescent charm of his because it was probably always that easy. A smile, a token gesture, and women simply lapped it all up.

'Letter,' Emily said as she held out her hand, watched his smile fade away.

'I'm assuming you know where we're going? Once we get to London, I mean?'

Emily nodded, waiting for him to rummage through his bag; to take out a crumpled envelope much thicker, more promising, than the one she had been given by the stranger at her house yesterday morning. But a part of her wished she could pretend that she had no idea where her grandmother was leading her back to.

'Hatchards,' she said, stumbling a little over the word.

'Where Ophelia found the atlas?'

'Yes.'

'That was nice and easy. I half expected a complicated riddle, or a puzzle box, with us running all over London trying to figure it out, like in *The Da Vinci Code*.'

She stared at the letter Tyler was holding. There was time, surely? Even if she got one of the clues wrong, there would be time to solve it, because for her grandmother to set an impossible task, with so much at stake, would surely be too cruel. Perhaps the letter was an apology, a note of contrition, telling her it was all just a huge misunderstanding, that she could get off the train, go back home and forget this day ever happened.

'Emily?'

Her hand was poised, ready to take the letter, but now she hesitated, as if she was stuck in limbo. Because what if it told her something she didn't want to know?

Emily swallowed away her fear, looked out of the window, at the world rushing by. A green, lazy landscape that blurred like a dream, making her feel as if none of it was quite real.

'Do you want me to open it for you?'

'No.'

'Fine. Suit yourself,' Tyler said as he dropped the letter on the table, sat back and put his headphones on. One last look passed between them before he closed his eyes.

Emily placed her palm on the table next to the envelope with her name written on it. There was no clue as to what lay within.

She glanced at Tyler, allowed herself to examine the way his body moved gently to the beat of whatever song he was listening to. Part of her wanted to sketch him, to use the feeling of pen on paper as a way of delaying what had to come.

Running her fingers across the cover of her sketchbook, she thought about drawing that man and his sparrows, the birds taking flight to weave in and out of the shadows, up and over the train.

'Okay,' Emily said as she sat a little straighter, puffed out her cheeks and blew away the doubt. She turned the envelope over and broke the seal.

The pages she took out were of the palest blue and thin, not quite as delicate as tissue paper, but not so thick as to prevent the light from passing through. They were covered on both sides in a looping hand that barely resembled the usual neatness Emily had expected of her grandmother. In places, the letters were smudged, or the tail of a 'Y' elongated, as if her grandmother had been disturbed, or nudged, as she was writing.

But it wasn't a letter at all; it was part of a diary. And, given the date at the top of the entry, it was written long before Emily had been born.

7 April, 1965

*'When you are imagining, you might as well
imagine something worthwhile.'*

I'm on a train, a dog-eared paperback of Anne of Green
Gables *tucked into the front pocket of my suitcase, with its
worn-down pages, my eight-year-old scribbles on the inside cover
and all my favourite parts underlined. Because I couldn't leave
without it. Without the book that made me fall in love with
storytelling, made me want to be something more. Without this
quote, which pretty much sums up how I am trying to feel right
now.*

*It's raining. Which is a completely unimportant detail
to include, but I feel that I need to write down absolutely
everything I can think of until I figure out what sort of diary this
is going to be. Because I'm here, or there, or nowhere at all, but
the point is I have left. I am gone from that tiny little seaside
version of hell that my parents like to think of as home and I'm
heading towards London.*

*Except I don't want to just stop there, I want to go anywhere
that fate decides to take me. I want to see it all, and not just
because Dad says I shouldn't (although, let's be honest, that's a
massive part of the reason why), but also because I can. I have
absolutely no idea what the future might bring, but it has to be
better than staying behind like Violet and Bess (who both think
I'm crazy and should go ahead with the wedding as planned,
but please, I mean, Henry is lovely and kind and has a 'great
future ahead of him', but in ten years' time, I'd be knee-deep*

in children, he'd be having an affair and I would be completely miserable and wishing I'd left when I had the chance).

Anyway, I digress, or am waffling, or using a thousand words when one will do, as Miss Hamilton always liked to remind me during English class. But that's just it — I want to write, I want to explore, I want to feel something more than just the day-to-day. Because all great writers go on adventures. They actually do something: live, cry, dance through the rain, kiss handsome men on station platforms — I did not do that, but wouldn't it have been amazing if I did? Just kissed someone without even knowing their name and then run away into tomorrow? Leaving them wondering their entire lives who I was.

Of course, there's always the risk that this goes horribly wrong and I have to head back home and grovel to Dad, but it's worth it, surely? Regret the things you do, not the things you don't. That's going to be my motto, my rule, to live by from now on.

In fact, I think that, from this very second, I will be that person. I will take risks. I will embrace everything the universe has to throw at me. I can be whoever I want to be, because to the world I am just another stranger, sitting on a train, heading who knows where, to do who knows what.

Just like that man over there with his top button undone, looking a little flustered as he reads a copy of Ulysses *without anyone staring and thinking him crude — I wonder if he's got to the bit in the brothel? I imagine he has a sweetheart waiting at home for him with a glass of sherry and slippers that have been toasting by the fire. Or perhaps he lives alone, with a dog who he takes for hikes on the moors at weekends. And he writes poetry that he recites to women before making love to them under the stars.*

Then there's the woman sat neatly in her tweed skirt and silk blouse. Hair lacquered into a chignon and a cluster of pearls around her slim neck. No doubt she is someone's secretary. Perhaps a Government minister or company director. That's what Mum always dreamt of for me. Sitting in an airless, soulless office somewhere, taking dictation and making endless cups of tea. She thought it would be a stepping stone to something more, to meeting an influential man who might one day become my husband.

Does this woman, with not a smudge on her shoes or hair out of place, have a sweetheart, a man (or perhaps a woman?) who she is pinning all her hopes on? Thinking that there is nothing more hopeless in this world than never finding someone to love? Or does she have secret longings to be a chorus girl, like those who dance each night at the Moulin Rouge in Paris? Does she sing in the bathtub and once dreamt of swimming in a sea so clear it was as if you could simply reach in and scoop up a handful of sand from the ocean's floor?

Mum told me once about how she'd been offered a job during the war, but her own mother made her turn it down. Said she needed her at home, not off gallivanting around Whitehall. When she told me, she was stood by the back door, cup of tea in hand, simply staring out at nothing. Or maybe she was thinking of what her life could have been if only she had dared to say yes.

Everyone has their secrets, their private stories they dare not to tell. But I want to tell them all. I want to create worlds within worlds. Have people talk about my books, rip them apart, try to understand the motivations behind what I've written. Love them, hate them, but make them remember me for something, anything. I have no desire to live an ordinary life.

Somewhere in this carriage a baby is crying. I can hear his little sucks of breath, the softer shush by his mother. I saw them when I first alighted the train. He was all milky newness, with tufts of blonde hair and blushing cheeks, one hand stuffed into his mouth, the other wrapped tight around his mother's curls. She looked exhausted and confused. As if she'd woken up one day in someone else's existence.

I think that's what happened to Mum. I never got the chance to ask what she used to dream of when she was young. Before she got married. Before I was born. I don't want to end up like her. Staring out of the window, with my hands covered by the bubbles in the sink, wishing upon wishing that I had lived a different kind of life.

Has she found the letter I left? Propped up against the teapot on the kitchen table where it would be seen as soon as she came in to start Dad's breakfast. She knew, at least I think she must have suspected, when she saw my yellow suitcase tucked under my bed. Or when I refused to talk to Henry, his mother, anyone at all, about wedding plans. When I argued with Dad about wanting to be more than someone's wife, someone's mother. That I would rather be poor and happy than rich and alone, trapped by the misery of boredom.

I want to live a different life, write a different story. I'm still young, I can be someone other than who my parents expect me to be. There's still time to change my world, my future. Nothing more than my passport, this diary and a pocketful of hope to help me along my way. And I will not stop until I have a whole lifetime's worth of memories to keep me going when I'm old and grey.

The sun is at last appearing over the horizon, bleaching the sky and waking up the world. I feel so awake and ready. Part of me is terrified, but a whole lot more of me can't wait for what happens next. To steal the words of the Bard himself, 'Come what come may, Time and the hour runs through the roughest day.' So I shall lay myself down in front of the hands of fate and embrace every last second of this so-called life. This is me, Catriona Mairi Robinson, eighteen and counting . . .

CMR

7

PIGEON

Columbidae

People. Everywhere Emily looked, there were people. Walking, talking, zigzagging through and around one another. Like worker ants, busy, busy, all with somewhere important to be. The sound of so many footsteps, voices on phones that expanded and retreated over and over. Station announcements of platform changes, train departures and safety procedures. Music from dozens of brightly-lit shops selling things that no one really needs.

So she stopped, placed her suitcase on the ground and looked up to see the latticework of steel overhead, interspersed with sections of sky. Pigeons marched up and down the long lines of black, and if she listened carefully, she liked to think she could hear their coo-cooing communication.

Birds are constant, she thought to herself. *Pigeons will be here, long after humans have expanded and destroyed everything all over again*. It provided a token of comfort to go over something familiar, stopped her heart and mind from racing even more.

They swooped down, one by one, to perch on the train's roof. One of them looked at her, head cocked as if recognising an old friend, then came to land by her feet, walked full circle around her, pecked at her shoe once, twice more.

'Hello,' she crouched down, held out her hand and waited for him to come close, then ran the very tip of her finger over his head before he gave a soft coo and fluttered away. One of the villagers, a Spitfire pilot named Fred, always sat next to Emily on the back row of the church and told her stories about how homing pigeons were used as messengers during the World Wars, saving lives by carrying messages across enemy lines.

Emily had liked to think of those birds wearing tiny little helmets, carrying guns or dropping bombs on the enemy as they flew across the Channel, back home. Now she thought of home, of Milton, and whether he would be sat by the back door, waiting for it to open. For her to share her slice of cake, or scrap of cheese, and she wondered if the birds really cared for her at all?

'Emily?' Tyler was walking back towards her. He picked up her suitcase and gave her no more than a token glance before turning around and heading towards an escalator, all the while scanning his phone.

'Wait,' Emily called out to him, but he was gone. Sucked up by the never-ending stream of people that appeared from all sides. She could turn around, get back on the train and disappear into the countryside. Return to Norfolk, her village, her home. The vicar would take her in, surely, look after her, provide her with shelter until she figured out what to do.

It was an indulgent fantasy. A momentary glimpse of 'what if?'. But Emily knew it would be pointless, because there was nothing she could do. Not without her grandmother's money, which was all tied up in a trust until she completed this ridiculous task.

Then there was the letter, or rather diary entry, she had been given, from when her grandmother was barely more than a child. When she had left a whole life behind to pursue a dream, a wish, a folly. It was a part of her past she never talked about, and Emily had never questioned why.

By showing her a piece of her history, Catriona had opened up a sort of longing, a curiosity, in Emily that would not leave her be. A puzzle like no other she had ever been given.

Emily watched stranger after stranger brush past her. Not a single one of them stopped to ask if she was okay, to question why she was stood, alone, in the centre of a bustling station. No one stared at her, or wondered about her scar, because here she was another random person, just like them. One more stranger in a sea of millions; all too busy to pay attention to the finer details of everyday life.

One more clue, Emily told herself. Just one more clue and then she could decide if it was all too much.

At the top of the escalator, she could see Tyler turning full circle, knocking into someone with his guitar, holding up one hand in apology. A frown between his eyes as he sought her out, then relief, then frustration as he beckoned her onward and upward.

One step onto the metal grooves, one hand resting on a faded black plastic handrail, and Emily felt the slightest of lurches in her stomach, as she rose like one of those penguins on a toy she used to have. Penguins who would climb a ladder, only to be sent spinning around a circuit and back down again. Over and over, with nowhere to go.

'You okay?' Tyler was there, right in front of her, pulling her away from the escalator and out, into the stifled air of London.

Am I okay? Emily repeated the question as she trotted behind, then down some steps to wait next to a stack of newspapers. *Where's the teller?* she thought as she saw someone pick one up, then walk on without leaving any money behind.

Outside, the noise, the light, was intensified. Bright red double-decker buses, black taxicabs, drills and cars and people, everywhere there were people. The ground was slick with early rain, the sky overhead heavy with cloud.

To her right, a cylindrical tower of brown with slits of glass rose from the pavement, more people spilling from double doors at its centre, heading in all directions, never stopping, never straying from their path. Beyond this was a building that resembled a New York warehouse, so out of sync with the pale, grey Regency buildings that lined the streets. Straight ahead the horizon was littered with cranes, like metal giraffes stretching their necks to the sky, only with no trees to feed from.

It had been so long since last she was here that everything looked like the shadow of what had been. London seemed to her like an old master painted on top of a forgotten, discarded picture, and her mind tried to reconcile her memories with the reality she was now stood before. Nothing looked the same, nor as she remembered, apart from the ivy-clad building on the opposite corner, with the perennial Union Jack hanging above the main door and Victorian gas lamps either side.

'Emily, where are you going?' she heard Tyler shout as she crossed the road.

Stood outside the Railway Tavern, she looked up at the metal sign depicting an old steam train, which was swaying a little, as if it had been up drinking all night. The scent of stale beer drifted out of an open window, showering her with the memory of her father.

'Good idea,' Tyler said as he held open the door, waited for Emily to step inside. 'I think we could both do with a drink.'

It was just like any other traditional pub in London. Stripped wooden floor, large square windows looking out onto the street, a collection of mismatched tables and chairs, and a long bar with a brass pole running around the edge.

Only this was the pub her father used to come to. Every Friday after work, for a quick pint and a smoke before heading home. His office had been in the building opposite and once, just once, she and her mother came to meet him here before getting on the sleeper train up to Scotland, to visit old friends.

'What can I get you?' A rather plump man stood on the other side of the bar, one shirt button stretching over his stomach and Emily could see a curl of hair peeping through. He was chewing something that smelt akin to liquorice and regarding Emily with bulbous eyes that skimmed over her scar then across to Tyler.

'Pint of Guinness and...?' Tyler waited for Emily to reply.

'White wine spritzer, perhaps?' The barman gave a patronising wink, then reached up for a glass.

'Whisky,' Emily said as she pointed at the row of bottles stacked on a shelf up high. 'Dalwhinnie.' The name came out all wrong and she saw the bartender's eyes flicker back to her scar.

'Single or double?'

'Double.' Her tongue got stuck on the blend of 'b' and 'l', made her jaw clench in irritation as she retreated to a corner table.

Emily watched Tyler share a joke with the bartender, envied the ease with which they simply swapped words without the embarrassment of having to try, of pre-empting the way the words would sound. If she were a foreigner, no one would judge or comment on her pronunciation, think it endearing, or simply accept all the strangeness. But it was a physical problem, one that would always catch people unawares and make them look, make them intrigued as to what had happened to the woman who, apart from the obvious scar, seemed just like anyone else.

Tyler slipped into the seat across from her, took a long sip of his pint, then licked away the thin line of cream from his top lip.

'Didn't have you down as a whisky drinker.'

Emily swirled her drink, watched the liquid as it clung to the sides of the glass.

'Mind you,' he said with a chuckle, 'Aunt Cat used to drink tequila straight from the bottle. I remember one Christmas Eve when she brought one all the way from Mexico, then bit the worm in half, just to piss off my dad.'

Emily could picture the scene so vividly. The look on Mr Montgomery's face as her grandmother picked out the worm from her glass, tilted back her head with deliberate extravagance, then placed it neatly on her tongue before biting the creature clean in two. She and Tyler had screeched with delight, before being ushered upstairs by their mothers and told to go to sleep right that minute or Father Christmas wouldn't leave them any presents.

They had spent every Christmas in the Montgomery mansion, overlooking the park. The rooms were filled with the scent of citrus, nutmeg and roasting meat. The sound of jazz mingling with the pop of champagne corks and crackling fire as she and Tyler weaved through the party in their pyjamas, begging to be allowed up for a few minutes more.

On Christmas morning they would tumble down the stairs to drink hot chocolate in the kitchen with the resident housekeeper, waiting and waiting for their parents to brush aside their hangovers and come downstairs. Later they would feast on goose, chestnuts and pudding set alight with whisky, the blue flames dancing as it was brought with a flourish to the table.

Each and every year was spent together. Two families entwined. Until one summer's day ruined it all.

'As I recall, she did it at your christening too.' A voice so familiar interrupted Emily's thoughts and she looked across to where a middle-aged woman approached. She was wearing dove-grey leather trousers, black stilettoes and a cream satin blouse with pussycat bow at her neck.

Tyler's mother. He must have texted her, told her where he and Emily were, which meant she knew both that they were coming and about her grandmother's plan. She bent down to kiss Tyler lightly on both cheeks, then leant across to pull Emily into a hug.

'Emily, my darling, you look so pale. I do hope my son has been taking good care of you?'

Four weeks had passed since Emily had last seen her

godmother, Adrianna Montgomery. Four weeks during which she had known of her grandmother's plan yet said nothing, leaving Emily alone, with no one there to see her through the day-to-day, as she had tried to collate Catriona's life into cardboard boxes now stored safely in the loft.

'You're mad at me, I can tell,' she said, placing her handbag on the seat next to her. 'But I promised, you see, and you and I both know how persuasive, how stubborn Catriona can be.'

'Could.' Emily let the word tumble out as she took another sip of her drink. Felt the burn at the back of her throat, coating the frustration she knew she dared not speak. It was infuriating, having her sit there and pretend that the last fifteen years hadn't happened. To assume that Emily would simply forgive her godmother for ignoring her all that time.

'Could,' Adrianna gave a small smile. 'Of course. She really was a remarkable woman. She helped me mend my first broken heart. Told me no man deserved my tears, especially one who cheated on me with a so-called friend.' She let out a small laugh, absent-mindedly stroked her hair. 'Got your mother and I drunk as skunks on cheap wine from Tuscany. Said it had helped her on more than one occasion.'

When did she have her heart broken? Emily wondered. The idea of Catriona Robinson being vulnerable was so strange. Even more so the image of the three women, intoxicated and bonding over the disadvantages of men. It made Emily want to go back, to know them all when they were young.

'Like the time you fell asleep and forgot to pick me up from swimming?' There was a distinct note of bitterness in Tyler's voice, one that he didn't even bother to try and conceal.

'I seem to remember Emily being the one who taught you

to swim,' Adrianna replied, fixing her son with a look.

'Hardly.' Tyler took a long drink, looked absently out of the window.

'If she hadn't been diving under the water and calling out for you to jump in, you never would have had the nerve to try.'

'Says the person who refused to ever go in the sea for fear of ruining her make-up.'

It was like some banal game of tennis, watching the two of them try to pick points off one another. What had happened between them, or was she forgetting that it had always been that way?

'How Margot and I laughed at the sight of you two with your bottoms in the air like little ducks.' A stray tear made its way from the corner of her eye and she tapped at it gently. Almost as if she were grateful for its presence. Almost as if she wanted Emily to see that she still grieved.

Emily let her mind wander back to her own memory of that day. When the sun was high, the sky empty of clouds and the water just cold enough to make you gasp when it hit your skin. Tyler had stood on the bank, watching her with a mixture of hate and admiration, eventually giving in to her calls of 'chicken' along with the promise from his mother of an ice cream if he dared to jump.

It was the same day she had been thinking of only yesterday morning. Could it be as soon as that? It seemed like a lifetime since Tyler had arrived. Years rather than hours since she had shut tight the front door and walked along the lane to the station. If she were still at home, she would be thinking about bringing in the washing left dancing on the line. Or picking some tomatoes from the greenhouse to have with her lunch. Or tucked up on the sofa with a cup of tea and a slice of Battenberg, going over sketches or finishing the copy of *Magpie Murders* sent to her by her grandmother's publisher.

Yet here she was, sitting in a pub across the road from where her father used to work, with two people who used to be such a huge part of her childhood, only to disappear as soon as tragedy struck. Nothing more than a token letter, or a gift sent through the post from afar. As if Emily had only ever been important when attached to her mother.

'I assume you've solved the first clue?' Adrianna smiled at Emily, only it didn't quite reach her eyes.

'Hatchards.' Emily nodded as she sipped her drink and tapped her fingers against the underside of the table in sync with the beat of her heart.

'I thought as much. Margot always said you spent more time there than you did at home, which is why, I suppose, Catriona put it in the very first book.' She reached across to put her hand on Emily's knee, pretended not to notice when she moved away. 'Is it true she was working on another one before ... You know?'

'Before she *died*, Mum.' Tyler drained his pint, banged the empty glass on the table. 'She won't crumple into pieces just because you mention it.'

Adrianna narrowed her eyes at her son, then turned her attention back to Emily.

'It's rather exciting, this treasure trail, this puzzle you need to solve. Everyone keeps asking me about the book. It's been all over the press, as I'm sure you know.'

Emily ran her fingertip around the rim of her glass, waited for the vibrations to take hold, to transform into one, pure note that echoed in the air.

'No doubt your phone has been ringing off the hook with demands from the press. But remember, we're here for you if you need anything. Anything at all.'

'Thank you.' It seemed like the right thing to say, when really there was nothing she could say that could possibly explain how furious she really was.

Emily's finger continued its circle around the glass and she stared at it, let the repetition dampen the sounds of the room. If she could somehow cloak them all, with all their subtle insinuations of *normal life*, perhaps she could forget about the one she used to have.

Adrianna put her hand on top of Emily's and held it there firmly, cutting off the note. 'Charles sends his regards,' she said. 'He's very sorry he couldn't make it today.'

'Since when does Dad apologise?' Tyler pushed back his chair, a cigarette ready and waiting between his lips, phone pressed tight to his ear as he yanked wide the door and stepped onto the street outside.

Adrianna watched him go. Sucked in her bottom lip, then picked at an imaginary piece of lint on her trousers. 'He's not been the same since, well ... I'm not even sure that you know about what happened with his job?'

Emily had always found that people responded to her silence in one of two ways: with indifference, meaning they chose to say barely more than a few words before turning away to find someone more interesting to talk to; or, as with her darling godmother, they tried to fill the silence with babbling. Quite often, they would find themselves revealing things they otherwise might keep to themselves, as if Emily was some sort of confessional.

'Charles didn't handle Tyler's little embarrassment nearly as well as I'd hoped he would.' Her fingers twirled a thick band of diamonds around and around her finger. 'There was all sorts of talk about cutting him out of his will, but I managed to convince Charles to give him a second chance.'

Emily pursed her lips to stop herself from smiling at the idea of Tyler not being as much of a Prince Charming as he'd have her believe. She glanced out of the window to see him talking to someone and gesturing madly in the air with his cigarette.

'I thought this trip might be a good way for the two of you to reconnect, as well as having someone to help with whatever tasks Catriona has set.'

Emily felt her fingers tighten around her glass, saw the knuckles begin to turn white. She wanted to point out the obvious: Catriona died. Her parents died. Everyone dies, so why bother dredging up the past when Tyler was only doing this as a way of trying to redeem himself with Daddy dearest?

'You really do look just like her.' Adrianna reached out to stroke Emily's jaw, but she turned away. 'Sorry, I forgot. It's just ... I mean. I really don't know what to say.'

Emily wished she knew how to reply, that there was something she could say to make her godmother understand.

I'm used to being alone, she thought as she rose from her seat, picked up her suitcase and left the pub.

Tyler was leant against the wall, scratching at his head, the cigarette still lit, with embers burning too close to his hairline. He was staring at his phone as Emily strode past, so it took him a moment to realise who she was. A moment more before he ran back into the pub to grab his own bag and guitar, to chase her down the pavement and onto the back of a No.11 bus.

He laughed as he looked back to see his mother staring after them. 'You know, you really shouldn't just leave her standing on the street like that.'

Emily flicked her wrist over to look at her watch. Nearly two o'clock. Where did all the time go?

'Do you have any idea what the next clue might be?' Tyler peered out of the window and Emily followed his eye, watched as all the sights of London trundled past.

'No.'

8

CANARY

Serinus canaria domestica

Peppermint green, with a touch of duck-egg blue, and gold leafing around the windows, on the other side of which an elaborate staging of the Mad Hatter's tea party could be seen. With gilded plates, sticky buns and fairies hidden amongst silhouetted trees. Emily remembered pressing her face up against the glass as a child, wishing she could jump inside the make-believe worlds recreated for everyone to see.

Just as her grandmother had done with that very first book. When little Ophelia was taken to Fortnum and Mason for a slice of red velvet cake to celebrate her tenth birthday and told to take a bite, because if she didn't try, she'd never know how delicious it was. The same cake that had been delivered, in real life, year after year up to Norfolk, which they shared with a mug of tea or, as Emily got older, a glass of chilled champagne.

'Aren't you going in?' Tyler asked as Emily moved from window to window, tilting her head to watch a sleepy dormouse emerge from out of a ruby red teapot.

'No,' Emily replied as she walked on by. Because it wasn't there that the atlas was discovered. It wasn't in amongst the shelves of shortbread, delicate china cups and hordes of tourists that the story really began. No, that was next door, in Hatchard's, England's oldest bookshop.

As soon as she went inside, it felt like stepping back in time; back to all those mornings spent devouring the words of Roald Dahl, Enid Blyton and more. All the days when she would run up the curved wooden staircase to the second floor, eyes bright with anticipation, then seek out a new delight to be read, curled up on a green leather sofa until she was told it was time to go home.

'Isn't that Aunt Cat?' Tyler was pointing at a collection of photographs on one wall, including Bette Davis, Anthony Hopkins and, indeed, Catriona Robinson. Photographs of when they had come to sign their bestselling books, the moment captured and framed for all to see.

Emily gave a small nod, then walked on without looking. It had been taken the last time she was here, when Emily was just sixteen and with all the insecurities of youth, hating the way excited readers crowded around her grandmother. And hating even more the way they stared at her scar.

Only ten minutes ago she had stepped off the bus and into Trafalgar Square, marvelling at how different it all seemed, yet somehow exactly the same. They had sped past St Paul's, the Old Bailey and Covent Garden, where Emily went every year at Christmas to watch *The Nutcracker*, before ice-skating at Somerset House.

Her grandmother would have known where the train would end up, which bus Emily would have to take to get from the station to find the next clue.

Did it mean she wanted Emily to remember, to not to hate the memories, but to embrace them for the happiness she once had? But all of the good was stitched together with all of the bad, and it was remarkably difficult to separate the two.

She could sense Tyler watching her as she made her way up to the second floor. So many of her memories were tied up with him, and it made her wonder if he had been chosen for this very reason. To force her to look back.

'Crikey,' Tyler said as they came to stop in front of an entire wall dedicated to *The Tales of Ophelia and Terence*. 'It's like some kind of fairy tale shrine.'

Row upon row of books, flanked at either end with giant cardboard cut-outs of a girl and a duck. There was bunting hanging from the ceiling, decorated with favourite characters from the books. In the window nook there was a forest scene, with a silver tree around the trunk of which a Chinese dragon was curled, and a mermaid sat on a swing made out of seaweed, hanging from one of the branches. At the very centre of it all was an atlas, with each of its pages edged in gold. On either side, the shelves were filled with board games, and pencils, notebooks, and mugs. Anything and everything you could possibly think of, emblazoned with the images Emily had herself created.

It felt like an invasion of sorts – an explosion of all the pictures she had ever painted, back in their cottage by the sea. The characters brought to life with a few strokes of a brush, immortalised on the side of a cup, or recreated as a soft toy to be taken to bed and cuddled through the night.

'I ...' Emily began, then looked behind the counter, past the monogrammed boxes wrapped in brown paper and tied up with striped ribbon, to where a birdcage still sat. Inside of which remained a trio of yellow canaries. Without thinking, she went around the counter and up to the cage, opened its door and stroked the breast of the nearest bird.

Once upon a time, Emily had come here with her grandmother, asked if the canaries were real and why would someone put them in a cage? Her grandmother had told her about how canaries were used in mines as warnings of poisonous gas leaks. That if they stopped singing, the miners knew death was trying to sneak up on them. Emily had cried herself to sleep that night, thinking of those birds and wishing she could somehow rescue them all.

'Can I help you?'

Emily turned to see a young man stood in the archway that connected the children's section of the shop to the storeroom at the back. He was wearing a black shirt with a badge, stating that his name was Chris and he was here to help. He was also carrying a stack of books whilst staring at her with both annoyance and intrigue.

'You're not supposed to be round there,' he said, waiting for Emily to remove her hand from the cage and step aside. He dumped the books onto the counter and made a point of checking the till.

'We're here to collect something,' Tyler said as he stepped forward with a smile.

'Ground floor.' The shop assistant began to sort the books into smaller piles.

'It's for her.' Tyler nodded in Emily's direction. 'From Catriona Robinson.'

The assistant's head jerked to attention as he looked from Tyler to Emily, to the display behind him, then back to Emily once again. He began to hop from foot to foot and wiggled his fingers in the air as a slow grin emerged on his face.

'Oh my,' he said, clasping Emily's hand and shaking it with might. 'Oh my,' he repeated as she pulled her hand away and folded her arms tight across her chest. 'This is just way too exciting,' he said, taking a step towards Emily, his eyes darting about her face, resting momentarily on her scar. 'We were all told this might happen, but is it true? Are you her granddaughter? Are you really *the* granddaughter of *the* Catriona Robinson? I mean, you must be, right? Otherwise why would you be here? I'm such a fan of your work, by the way, both your work and hers, God rest her soul. Amazing. Extraordinary. I can't believe this is happening, my friends are going to be so jealous.'

Emily backed away from the enthusiastic assistant, noticing as she did so that a couple of other customers were now looking in their direction.

'Do you have it, or not?' Tyler asked, a note of boredom in his voice.

'Sorry?' The assistant seemed to have forgotten Tyler was there. All his attention was on the young woman with eyes as bright as pennies, who was tapping the fingers of her left hand onto the counter top, over and over. 'Oh, right, yes. The package,' he said, watching the repetitive movement of Emily's fingers, seeing the way her lips were moving but no sound was coming out. 'It's right over here, next to the birdcage.'

Emily's fingers stopped their tapping as she saw him go over to the cage and pick up a small package, identical to all the others on the display apart from a sticker in the top right-hand corner. A sticker of a little grey duck wearing a spotty bow tie.

Why didn't I see this earlier? Emily wondered, noting that Terence was stood next to a pair of wellington boots with silver stars dotted all over them. The same boots she had worn as a child and first drawn for the girl named Ophelia. Later the boots were changed to being pink, with a purple flower on the side. The original version had never made it into final print.

Everything about Ophelia was what Emily had imagined her to be. A little smaller than average, with curly dark hair that she liked to wear in pigtails, or in a knot on top of her head. Eyes of green that sparkled when she was excited, a button nose and a lopsided grin as wide as her face. What she hadn't been able to draw, not at first, was the fierceness of her anger when someone had been wronged. Or the way her fingers would wriggle with excitement when she and Terence would open up the atlas to discover where it would take them next. Or how she would lay awake at night, wishing upon wishing she had been born with someone else's legs.

All of that came from her grandmother. She was the one to weave her magic with words, not Emily.

'That's why I was so worried when I saw you looking.' The assistant held out the package to her, then took his phone from his back pocket and quickly snapped a photograph.

Emily blinked, then looked around, past Tyler, to where a crowd was beginning to gather. A collection of faces and phones, all pointing at her, documenting the event, ready to be shared with people all over the globe. Millions of likes and comments on social media, wondering about what the package contained. Whether it could be the infamous last manuscript of the late, great Catriona Robinson.

The screens lit up, over and over again, and Emily stared at all those strangers, all those people who thought they had a right to know. Just as they always had, asking questions, wanting to know about her grandmother. Wanting to know about her.

She was still clutching tight the parcel when she felt Tyler's hand on her arm.

'You want to go?' he asked and she nodded, allowing him to escort her through the shop as she tried not to look back, to where those people were following, watching, whispering.

They were sat in the kitchen of Tyler's family home, a house much like all the others on a treelined street in Primrose Hill. It was a room Emily had once spent so much time in, but she had never imagined she would be back there, with him, sharing a simple meal. Bread and slices of salami; cheese that was making an escape from the wooden board; grapes and pickles and sun-dried tomatoes ripe with garlic. There was a clattering of plates onto the table as Tyler put down a fistful of cutlery and glasses. Emily ate each offering in turn, washed it all down with another tumbler of whisky and ice that clung to the side of the glass.

'Any more?' Tyler asked as he stood, went over to a marble sink and turned the copper tap, ran each plate under the stream of water before placing it in a dishwasher neatly hidden behind a panel of painted wood.

Emily watched him as he tidied away the evidence of them being there. No mess, no disturbance to the picture-perfect kitchen so changed from when last she was here, yet somehow still the same. Sleek, modern lines with oversized cabinets and soft upholstered chairs. Fabric on the walls and chandeliers overhead. But the sight of him, backlit from the window, as he slid onto the bench next to her, felt the same as all those years ago. When they would chatter over bowls of pasta or ice cream, bare feet tucked underneath legs dirty and bruised from the day spent outdoors.

It was so hard to reconcile then with now. To realise so much had happened to him, as well as her, none of which she could bring herself to talk about.

Instead, she looked across to the package now open on the tabletop. Another book, another dedication different to all the rest.

For Madeleine – thank you for believing in us all.

'How do you know we have to go to Paris?' Tyler asked as he flicked through the pages of a book about a girl who wanted to paint but always compared herself to others. She had taken Ophelia riding bareback across the open fields, wind whipping through their hair and eagles flying overhead and in return Ophelia had taught her that being afraid to fail was never a good enough reason not to try.

Emily pointed at the name on the dedication. 'I know her,' she said quietly, the face of her grandmother's friend swimming into her mind as her gaze fell onto a white envelope that was tucked inside the book's cover. They had met, at the funeral, when Madeleine had cried on her shoulder and told Emily how much Catriona was loved. But she had said nothing of the puzzle, the task her grandmother had set, even though she must have known.

The envelope was identical to the one Tyler had given her on the train. An envelope that, no doubt, contained another diary entry from her grandmother's past. Another clue, another insight into whatever message it was Emily was supposed to be grasping hold of but felt as if she was simply flailing about in the dark, completely ignorant of why she was being sent to Paris, to a woman she had only spoken to once.

'Why this book?' Tyler picked it up, turned it over as if seeking out a clue, and Emily frowned at the question. 'I mean, why would Aunt Cat choose this book, if it's not set in Paris?' he said, peering closer at the front cover, looking from the depiction of Ophelia to Emily and pausing. 'What's the connection? The first book actually has Hatchard's in it, it's where Ophelia first finds the magical atlas, but this one's set on a ranch in California, so why aren't we going there?'

'Because it's not real.'

None of it was real. Catriona had made up stories as a way of showing Emily the world. It was her way of teaching Emily about life, about fear, about everything she thought her granddaughter needed to know.

'I get that, but surely there's a connection between the books, other than the obvious fact it's all about Ophelia? There has to be, otherwise it's all so random.'

Nothing was ever random as far as Catriona Robinson was concerned. Each plot point, each detail in every book was meticulously planned before she ever started writing the actual story. Which meant the quest, the treasure trail, would have been planned just as meticulously. Nothing would be left to chance. There was a meaning behind each and every clue. Each and every book chosen for its own, specific purpose.

'Google,' she said, pointing to Tyler's phone.

'You want me to Google the significance of why she chose these two books?' he asked with a frown. 'Emily, all that's going to come up is a whole heap of photographs of you looking scared whilst stood in the middle of a bookshop.'

Emily snatched his phone away, opened up the internet and tapped in the name of a painting that hung in the Louvre, behind what some would consider the most famous portrait of them all.

She showed the picture of *Marriage at Cana* to Tyler.

'I don't get it,' he said, then waited as Emily began to type something on his phone, looked closer to read out the words that contained her explanation. 'This is the painting that hangs on the wall opposite the *Mona Lisa*,' he read. 'It depicts the first miracle of Jesus, when he turned water into wine. It's a masterpiece, but no one ever goes into that room to look at it.'

She couldn't stop watching him as he spoke, at the way one of his bottom teeth stuck out, just a fraction.

'Grandma took me there once,' he went on. 'Then decided to put it in her story.'

He was looking at her, waiting for her to say something, but her mind was struggling to remember what it was they were talking about.

'Look,' Emily said out loud as she shifted a little away from Tyler, then flicked through the book they had discovered in Hatchards, to the very last page of the story. She pointed to a picture of the girls stood in an art gallery filled with abstract paintings. In the corner was a tiny, cartoonesque replica of the *Mona Lisa*.

'Everything we added was for a reason.' Emily began to

type again, trying not to register the warmth of his breath on her neck as he read. 'Just as with every other book, there is a list at the very back, asking the readers to find each and every item that is of importance. This book isn't just about a girl in a wheelchair named Ophelia getting to ride a horse, it's about teaching children not to follow the crowd.'

Her grandmother always told her not to care what other people thought. Emily looked away as she felt the weight of Tyler's eyes on her again. Tried not to imagine his mind working through all the possible reasons someone would need to teach their grandchild such a lesson.

Emily wondered if he would connect the dots, realise the book was written shortly after she went back to school, when most of her physical scars were healed. It was when she found out how cruel children could be to anyone who didn't quite fit in, no matter the reason why.

'You are allowed to talk to me, you know.'

His words surprised her, given how he witnessed first-hand the extent of her injuries. Knew how long it took her to learn to talk, to walk again, to do all the things she once took for granted.

'I can't.' She didn't talk to anyone. It was a habit she didn't know how to break, because modern technology, the dominance of email, texts and the Internet, meant she never had much reason to speak to anyone, other than her grandmother and the birds.

'Can't?' Tyler said, watching as she drained her glass. 'Or won't?'

'Please,' she whispered, turning her face away.

For a moment he waited, hand resting on the table between them and she couldn't help but think of how it would feel if he were to put those hands on her. Then he sighed, shifted his weight and she felt him lean away.

'Paris it is, then. First train leaves St. Pancras International just after 5.30 tomorrow morning, but personally I'd rather not drag myself out of bed at such an ungodly hour.' He stopped. Saw the look of horror on Emily's face. 'You want to go now?' He exhaled slowly, shook his head as he looked at his watch. 'I assumed you'd want to at least rest for a bit, but I guess we could go today if there are still seats available.'

She was shaking her head, over and over, willing him to comprehend what she was so scared about. What she knew she could not do.

'Emily?' Tyler put both hands on her shoulders, tried to get her to look at him. 'What's wrong?'

She couldn't willingly go into a tunnel underneath the sea. A long, dark tunnel with no light and no air and all that water pressing down from above. She would be trapped inside a tube of metal with no way out. Just like before.

'Mum?' Emily barely breathed the word and it came out caught in a sob.

'Shit,' Tyler edged closer, wrapped his arms around Emily and drew her close. 'I'm sorry, Em, I just didn't think.'

'Mum,' Emily whispered again, shaking her head against the bundle of disjointed images she couldn't quite make sense of, didn't want to make sense of. A car, the world flipping in and over itself, a flash of black and the dull thud, thud, thud of pain all the way along her spine. She knew the feeling would pass. But all she could do was sit, trapped in her own fear, unable to claw her way out of the darkness and back to reality.

So she let him rock her gently, to and fro. Breathed in his

words of comfort, kept her eyes tight shut and waited for her heart to calm.

Then the sound of a message sent, an urgent ping, calling out its demand to be heard and pulling his attention away. Up he got, muttering an apology, saying he would be right back. She was left alone in his parents' kitchen, with nothing more than a book and another memento from her grandmother's past. A memory she wanted to discover but was frightened of where else it might lead.

Blue-black clouds hung in the sky as Emily looked out of the window, watching dusk approach. This was when it was hardest not to cry. Not to remember summer sunsets with her mother singing, her father smoking a cigar as he taught her all the constellations or sat waiting for a shooting star. Wishing upon wishing they were somewhere in the world, watching the passing of another day.

When it was quiet, she could still hear their laughter. The low rumble in his belly, the softer trill at the back of her throat. The way they spoke to one another as if no one else was in the room. Sometimes she believed they were still with her, or perhaps it was just her imagination.

Which was why she always had to cover up the silence with music, needed it to drown out the pictures, the memories in her mind, in order to stop her from painting what she missed most of all.

Opening the window, she heard the whistle of a bird somewhere high in a tree. A bird that called out to her, told a story through song. Perhaps he had yellow feathers and had flown free from his cage to soar up and through the sky. Maybe he had come to try and help cover some of her pain, if only for a little while.

Because she had lost so much more than her parents, and being back in this house, this home, only made her feel it all over again. He had been her best friend, and then, quite possibly, something more, something still to happen. So many firsts experienced with him, then suddenly gone, as if she had imagined it all. Two years spent in a rehabilitation clinic, during which her godmother had never visited, simply sent letters that Emily's grandmother would read, telling of all the things Tyler was achieving, so many hopes and dreams that should have included her.

Turning the envelope over and over between her fingers, she sat, then took out more sheets of pale blue paper that contained another snippet from her grandmother's past, lay them flat on the table and began to read.

8 June, 1965

'Be not inhospitable to strangers,
lest they be angels in disguise.'

*Paris, c'est magnifique! This city is just exhilarating and
exhausting in so many ways, I'm not sure I could ever capture
them all and find a way to put it down on the page.*

*The quote at the top is written above the doorway in the
bookshop where I am now living, yes living! Something taken
from the Bible, apparently, but meant as a motto for all who are
lucky enough to stay. In exchange for working during the day,
myself and five other aspiring writers/artists/creative souls are
allowed to stay here and experience everything that Paris has to
offer.*

*How did this happen? Me, a girl from the wilds of Scotland,
in Paris, where so many creative geniuses once hath trod?
James Joyce actually stayed here, in this very shop. So too did
Hemingway, Kerouac and Mr Fitzgerald. Not to mention all
the streets around here, virtually impregnated with the pain
of Monet, Picasso, Van Gogh, crikey, just about everyone
who ever lived in this ridiculous city, once upon a while ago.
Someone told me that Picasso used to trade his paintings for
food when he first came here because he was so poor. There's a
house up in Montmartre, near his studio, that was sold recently,
only for the new owner to discover one of his canvasses in an old
trunk in the basement. How incredibly pissed off would you be
if you'd sold that house???*

To think this is where they all started, all those years ago.

And who else has passed through, who else is still to come? Will I be one of those people? My name synonymous with books that line the shelves all over the world? Will people one day come here to think about me, about how I once slept on a bed and came up with an idea for a story that inspired them to follow my dream for themselves?

This place is the stuff of legends, of stories and experiences passed down through generations, but I feel strangely possessive of it. As if it's too good to share. As if this is my own, private discovery that would only be spoilt if others knew about the magic contained in these crumbling walls.

I said there were five others staying here with me, but so far I've only met three...

Charlotte, who hails from West Berlin and is sharp and bright and smokes like the veritable chimney. She's also at least a head taller than I am and has legs that go on forever, so part of me hates her already. But only because of how fabulous she looks in her teeny-tiny skirts.

Next comes Gigi. French, gorgeous and I am completely obsessed with her. I get the feeling she's filthy rich and running away from her heritage, or an arranged marriage, or something in between. But she has the dirtiest laugh and looks at me in a way that makes me know we will be friends forever.

She flirts with everyone, and I mean everyone, which means nobody is capable of leaving the shop without buying at least three items, so she's definitely the favourite employee.

Is it the eyes, or the hair, or simply the way she makes you feel as if there's nobody else in the room whenever she says your name? Bright red lips that catch on the end of a cigarette, long, slender fingers that always seems to be touching you, ever so lightly, somewhere on your body, pulling you into her space, her world. And curves that cling to her pantaloons, her blouse unbuttoned just the right amount.

I wish I had that self-assuredness of who I am. I hope she can teach me what it is that makes French women just so, so sexy. I want to be sexy. I want someone to think I am sexy. Not just a wife-in-waiting, a dutiful woman who will do as she's told. I want to meet someone who will push me to the very limits of my persona. Who will challenge me as much as they adore me, and make me rock with frustration and desire.

Then there's Noah. Oh my. From California no less. With a voice that melts inside your soul and a smile that melts everything else. He's quiet. He's broody. He's probably going to destroy me, but I do not care. With stubble that I want to run my fingers, my lips over, skin the colour of milky coffee and jeans worn low. The way he says my name, as if it's the beginning of a song, makes me fizz. I feel like a silly girl stood next to him, all flustered thoughts that do not know how to behave.

Last night we all sat around the piano, most of us drinking French (of course) red wine, and some of us smoking deliciously fragrant cigarettes that make the whole world spin. Talking about literature and art, music and love. So much to learn from these strangers, brought together under one dilapidated roof. Purely by chance, or, peut-être, fate had a hand in it as well? Either way, I don't care, because I feel more alive, more accepted, here than I ever did at home. Nobody to tell me what to wear, to eat, to think! Here I can be whoever I want to be. No restraints, no past, and the future is entirely down to my choosing.

There are bunks dotted around the shop, so that when the customers go home we all camp out in our makeshift castle, in amongst the words of the greats, hoping that some of their ability will rub off on us poor, hapless novices.

This is it. I can feel the beginnings of a wonderful adventure. These people have already seen more of the world than I have even dared to imagine. Noah hitch-hiked his way across America, can you believe that? Past the Grand Canyon, through the desert, over the plains and then caught a boat from New York to Ireland. He has no idea what to do with his life, I'm not certain any of us do, but he doesn't care. He doesn't care that he isn't doing what his father wants. He doesn't care that he barely has two francs in his pocket. He doesn't care that tomorrow the sky might fall on his head, because today is the only day worth living.

Oh, and did I mention he is a cowboy? A bona-fide cowboy who grew up on a ranch, with the swagger to match. Be still my beating heart!

As I said, he will be my undoing, of that I am sure.

Gigi, on the other hand, has been seducing me with her own stories. Stories all about the colours of France. Of lavender fields in Provence that she danced through naked with a farmhand she cannot quite remember the name of, but says everything else about him she will never, ever forget.

She told me about the light on the Atlantic Coast, so gentle, so subtle, compared to the darkness that drops over Paris like a stone when the day is done. About a man she met, with skin as dark as a conker, who fed her seafood fresh off the back of his boat, then took her skinny-dipping under the stars (and then they did all sorts of other things that I feel myself blushing about as I write). She is most definitely not a good girl from back home – Mother would have a fit if she knew!

Gigi says she wants to be a chef, to discover all the tastes

the world has to offer. To find inspiration for her food in all the
people she meets (and loves) along the way. To write a book
that makes people think about food as more than just a necessary
part of their day. To see it as art, as pleasure, as indulgence.

She is leaving in a few weeks and wants me to go with her,
all the way to the Mediterranean, and then who knows where?
But Paris is bubbling over with possibility, with ideas, so I
don't know if I shall. Because I need to write my own story, to
find my own raison d'être.

Tomorrow I shall go exploring. I will walk along the banks
of the Seine, stand under the Eiffel Tower, eat pain au chocolat
and simply drown in all the absolute magnificence of this place.
I'm hoping my muse will show up, somewhere along the
way, proceed with an idea about what to write. Because at the
moment all I have is the picture of a place in my mind. A house
at the edge of the sea, where an old woman lives, trapped by her
memories, too scared to go outside.

CMR

9

SEAGULL

Larus canus

Emily wanted so badly to go home, to have it all return to how it once was. Her week used to be shaped by a long-practised routine, not least waiting for the sound of milk bottles being left on the doorstep and post sliding through the letter box. The whistle of kettle, the clunk of cupboard and the ting of spoon as her grandmother stirred her morning cup of tea.

Now she was on a ferry, headed for France. Utterly terrified. Trapped between two worlds, neither of which she really wanted to be a part of.

Last night she had feigned tiredness, asked to go to her room, only to sit up re-reading her grandmother's diary, and flicking through her sketchbook, seeing if there was anything from before to give her an idea as to what the final story could be about. If she could somehow figure it out, there would be no need to travel any further. Trapped within the fold were a few crumbs from the biscuits that were her everyday staple, which she would usually toss outside for Milton and his friends. It had made her sad, to think of them there, without her, and she could not remember when at last she fell asleep, with curtains wide open so that dawn would wake her.

There had been no time to think about, to truly process, what it was she had been asked to do.

'Are you drawing me?' Tyler opened one eye to accuse her, then dropped his head back against the seat.

'In a way,' Emily replied, the words coming out more easily because he wasn't watching. Her sketchbook was still inside the front pocket of her suitcase. She hadn't been able to draw anything since leaving home. Something was stopping her, but she wasn't yet sure what it could be. So instead she had been watching, storing up all the images she wanted to collect for later, when she was ready to start again.

The space around him blurred as she assessed every part of his face. As always, the real world slipped away as she gave in to the images forming inside her head.

What would life have dealt her instead, if that one day had been different?

It was an impossible question to answer; one Emily had tried, unsuccessfully, not to think about. But now she found herself also considering what could have been for her grandmother, if she had stayed in Scotland, done what was expected of her, instead of travelling across this same stretch of sea, long before it was commonplace to do so. Before women were given such freedoms as to be able to live alone in a bookstore in Paris.

Is that why you chose him? Emily thought as she watched Tyler sleep. Because he somehow reminded her grandmother of Noah?

Noah. It was the name of a man she had never heard her grandmother mention. He was clearly someone who had made a remarkable impression on a young Catriona, along with the four other people mentioned in her diary. But Emily only knew who two of them were.

Charlotte, or Charlie, as Emily called her, was her grandmother's editor. The dear friend who stumbled across the story of Ophelia and Terence when she came to visit one spring night. Who saw the potential, who convinced Catriona to try and publish it. To put aside the adult fiction she had toiled with for over twenty years. A woman who fought for Emily's drawings to be part of the very first publishing deal they both signed. She had been there for every book, every tour, every proposal, and always understood their need for privacy, despite the whole world begging for more.

Did she know? Emily wondered. *Is she a part of this too?*

But that made no sense, because Charlie had called only yesterday, asking once again if Emily knew anything about the existence of a new manuscript. If the rumours swirling around the newspapers were true.

Charlie down. Four more to go.

Gigi had to be Virginia, with whom Catriona travelled across Europe. The person who had bought her closest friend, the sister she never had, a locket when they parted ways. The same locket Emily wore around her neck, inside of which was a photograph of the two young women, taken somewhere in Rome. Two young women with the rest of their lives ahead of them, but who had met again only a handful of times before Gigi died, which was long before Emily was even born.

So not her either. Which left just three, but for the moment it was Noah she wanted to know more about. Because the dates matched. The dates from the diary entries were just under two years before Emily's mother was born. And Catriona had never told, never revealed, who the father was.

Could it be that the secret, the mystery, her grandmother hinted at before she died had nothing to do with the manuscript after all? Could it be that Emily was being sent to find her grandfather, wherever he may be?

'Seriously.' Tyler sat up and yawned once more. 'Stop staring at me. It's making me nervous, all that thinking you do.' He stood, stretched his arms high, revealing a line of skin between T-shirt and jeans.

'I'm going outside for a smoke,' he said with a grin. 'You coming?'

Outside, the morning sky was inky, thick with damp and the promise of more rain. Emily followed Tyler to the back of the ferry, leant over to watch the trails of frothing sea that stretched all the way back to England. Overhead, a gaggle of seagulls flew, every so often pitching down to grab at a fish upset by the boat's engines.

Back home, more often than not, Emily would sit at her bedroom window, staring up at the sky and counting all the birds that flew through the blue. More and more, she would think about that freedom, that sensation of tilting up and over the ever-changing seasons. Of going wherever the wind took you, never staying in one place for too long.

Now she looked at the seagulls, always on the wing, always searching for food, and felt sorry for them in a way she couldn't quite explain. As if the freedom she perceived was in fact false, that they were tied to this world by the same rope as she.

Seagulls can drink salt water. Emily watched one bobbing

along the surface of the sea. Just the same as they did off the Norfolk coast. *They're clever too, using breadcrumbs stolen from humans to attract fish, and tapping on the ground with their feet to make worms think there's rain up above, tricking them to the surface. They're survivors.*

'What's that?' Tyler nodded at the envelope Emily was fingering, one of its corners beginning to fray.

'Her diary.' Emily found herself handing it over to him and wondered how she would feel if he used his cigarette to set it on fire, or simply tossed it out to sea.

'You've never seen it before?' he asked, opening the lip and peering inside.

'Nope.' Emily had no idea her grandmother had even kept a diary. There had been nothing in the cottage, which meant Catriona must have moved it before she died.

When had it all been planned? Emily had been so wrapped up in her own day-to-day, along with trying not to think about how frail her grandmother was, how much she was slowly slipping away, to notice what she was really up to.

'And you don't mind me reading it?'

Emily tilted her head to the heavens, shut her eyes and sucked in great lungfuls of salty air. 'Knock yourself out.'

'Maybe later.' She heard him give a low chuckle, then the shift of foot and quiet rustle of paper. She imagined him tucking the envelope into his back pocket of his jeans, thought of reaching in her hand to check.

'You're rather chatty this morning.'

'So?'

A pause, followed by a slow exhale. 'What's changed?'

Emily shrugged. She herself didn't know. Perhaps it was the very fact she was somewhere else, with someone else.

Heading towards a place she had not been since she was a child. So many changes in the space of so little time.

'May I?' she asked, pointing at the headphones draped around his neck. The one thing she had forgotten to bring. The one item she should have made a point of putting in her suitcase but which she knew still hung off the back of the chair in the kitchen.

'Sure.' There was an unspoken curiosity on his face, but his upbringing, all that private education and lessons in etiquette, seemed to be telling him not to pry.

'I want to draw,' she said, gesturing over to where a single seagull was perched on the railing, regarding them with eyes like marbles, his long, orange beak curved open.

She wanted nothing more than to draw something familiar, something that had nothing to do with the search. The escapism of drawing a magnificent seagull stood so proud and cocky on deck, waiting to snatch a sandwich from an unsuspecting hand. Like the urban fox of the sea.

'And you need music for that because?'

He was fishing. She knew, and he knew, that the question was loaded with so much more.

Emily considered him for a moment as she took a scrap of paper and her fountain pen from her pocket. Considered whether or not he was someone to trust. Because he was still a stranger, no matter how many times they had pretended to be wizards, or spies, or dinosaur hunters when they were children.

Emily went over to sit on one of the plastic benches screwed to the deck, lay the paper flat on her lap, then dipped her head so he couldn't see her mouth as she spoke.

'She typed with her eyes shut.'

Emily could still see her. Sat at her desk, eyes like narrow slits, fingers bashing away at that monster of a machine. Words spewing onto the paper like liquid letters that were simply waiting to be released from her mind. As always, Emily would be next to her, sketchbook on her lap and pen at the ready, filled with black ink.

'Go on.'

Emily wiggled her jaw, felt the stretch along her scar, sensed the words that were waiting for her to speak. Waiting for her to stop caring how long it took.

'She always said it stopped the doubts.'

'And the same thing happens when you listen to music?'

'In a way.' Because the pictures always had a way of creating themselves and, by drawing in ink, it meant she couldn't change her mind, couldn't undo any so-called mistakes that were really meant to be.

That came before. To block out all the noises of a world she no longer wanted to be a part of.

It began when her speech therapist back at the clinic in Switzerland had played the piano. When Emily was having a particularly lengthy meltdown. She had tipped herself out of her wheelchair and lain on the floor, smacking her fists into the carpet and screaming at everyone. She remembered wishing she had the words to make them see that all she wanted was for them to leave her alone, to stop staring, to stop trying to fix her.

Her grandmother had tried to console her, but all she had done was lash out, shouted even louder. The therapist had ignored Emily, walked over to the piano and sat down to play. At first, the notes hadn't penetrated, hadn't found their way through the fog that still hung inside her mind, the ear that refused to heal because the nerves were too busy torturing her with pain. But then, as the therapist continued to play, the space all around her seemed to vibrate, to slowly trickle over to where Emily lay.

And just like that, the screams inside her head were stilled. All the images she did not want to see, and the frustrations she could not overcome, were forced away by those beautiful melodies.

From that moment on, whenever Emily became restless, or overcome with feeling, she would go into the room that looked over the lake and sit with headphones on, volume turned up. She would sit, calmly drawing all the monsters and demons that would not leave her be. Simply put them down onto paper, then throw them all away.

Emily looked down to see she had been busy drawing the face of someone she once knew: the therapist who pulled her from her darkness and showed her another way.

'Who is she?' Tyler asked as he looked at the drawing.

'Beth. Psyc ...' Emily stopped as her tongue got caught on the word. 'Shrink,' she said, tracing over the lines she had drawn, remembering the way that Beth's mouth would curl up a little more on one side when she smiled. The tortoise-shell spectacles she wore on a chain around her neck, and the earrings made from Venetian glass she once told Emily were a gift from a dear, dear friend.

'What was it like?' Tyler asked as he flicked the butt of his cigarette overboard.

He meant after the accident, when Emily woke up and discovered her world had been split into a million tiny pieces and there was no way she could ever hope to put them back together again.

'Jelly.'

It had been like living in jelly, because everything seemed to be in slow motion and all the sounds were muffled.

Music helped. Both because she could feel the vibrations, but also because it blocked out all the noise, the sympathetic words of people she didn't want to hear. For so many months, Emily had wanted to be able to hear properly, and then when it happened, when she understood what they were all talking about, she wished she could go back to living in her bubble of silence.

Screwing up the scrap of paper, she stuffed it back into her pocket, wiped angrily at her eyes, at the tears that were threatening to fall.

Tyler pretended not to notice, instead took out the envelope containing her grandmother's words and read each page in silence. She watched his eyes dart over the words, wondered what effect they were having on someone other than her.

'Why do you think she's given you this?' He waved the blue paper at her and it caught in the wind, nearly got carried up and away. Emily grabbed at his hand, wrapped her own around the sheet.

'The people she met.' Emily looked down at their names, thought of the people she knew, imagined the faces of those she did not. She could hear their voices, picture the gait of their walk. She could see them all sat on the banks of the River Seine, smoking cigarettes and drinking red wine. Gigi, she knew, was petite, blonde and effervescent, whilst she imagined Noah as being all furrowed brow, with the scent of bourbon clinging to his skin.

But she couldn't picture her grandmother, the young

Catriona so full of doubt. Couldn't get her head around the idea that once she was shy and insecure. She wanted so badly to go back in time, to meet the girl who was no more and ask her what it was that made her change, become the woman who seemed so certain of it all.

'You think you're supposed to find them?'

'Perhaps.'

Perhaps that's what her grandmother wanted. For Emily to understand who she used to be. To discover who and what it was that shaped her, left such an impression on her life that she chose to share those particular months, those specific memories, with her granddaughter.

Only, what would happen if all she did was discover more death? If she were to go through all of this simply to find that none of them, other than Charlie, still existed? It was an idea so sad that Emily pushed it away. Because her grandmother couldn't – *wouldn't* – be that cruel.

Tyler folded the pages neatly in two. Slipped them safely back into their envelope and handed it over. 'Maybe it's not that convoluted. Maybe she just wants you to see the life she once had.'

The wind rushed over to them, sneaking under the hem of her skirt, lifting the hairs on her legs and she stood, turned her back on England, from where they had come.

Back inside, she took out her sketchbook and ancient Discman, felt the familiar weight of them in her palm, then plugged in Tyler's headphones. Sketchbook on the table by the window, she flicked through to a blank page, smoothed the sheets down and readied herself to begin. She knew he was watching, that he was trying to catch a glimpse of all the pages filled with her pictures.

'What will you do after?' he said.

'After what?'

'When this is all over. Will you stay in Norfolk? Mum told me you've been doing some freelance work.' He pointed to the window, to where a trio of seagulls now stood. 'Is that what the birds are about?'

'Sort of.' Emily placed the headphones over her ears and pressed the play button, a button which once had the indent of a triangle but had long since been worn smooth. As the thud of bass guitar drowned out the world, she turned a little away from his gaze and began to draw the familiar shape of a wing.

It had been her grandmother's idea, for Emily to try working for herself, once she decided to turn her hand again to adult fiction. Emily had resisted, said she didn't want to paint to order. But then Catriona got sick and could no longer find the will to write and Emily had needed something to keep her mind occupied, keep her hands busy whilst she watched doctors pump poison through her grandmother's veins in an attempt to rid her of cancer.

They would sit and talk about the books, the characters waiting to be brought to life on paper through Emily's talent. But for Emily it was never the same, because they came from someone she didn't know. For her there was no one she wanted to draw more than Ophelia.

Then her grandmother had gone into remission. The cancer was gone and she could pick up where she left off, begin to write once more. For just over a year all was as it should have been, with Emily watching as a new story began to unfold. She had listened to her grandmother on the phone, talking to her publisher, to Charlie, about how she had an idea for something else. Something other than a little girl and her duck, with more magic, more exploration into what it is that binds us all together.

All was well, the two of them settling back into their hive of creativity, shutting out the world in favour of make-believe. Emily was content in her routine of old, waking each morning to eggs for breakfast, followed by a walk along the beach, then back to work on the next drawing, the next idea. She had been happy to continue freelancing, to wait for her grandmother to share her story.

Until one morning Catriona stumbled on her way back from church, bumped her hip and said it was nothing to worry about, just a bruise. But the bruise had spread and the ache had deepened, and the doctors confirmed that the cancer was back, more furious than before.

That was when Emily stopped painting for other people, and decided instead to create pictures for her grandmother. Pictures from books they had read, classics and comedy alike. Her own interpretation of Elizabeth and Darcy, Romeo and Juliet, Heathcliff and Cathy.

Seascapes, forests and imaginary worlds. Portraits of Golum, Dracula and even Mr Potter. Anything and everything she could possibly conjure from her mind, thinking it was a way to block out what they both knew would eventually come.

What on earth was she supposed to draw now?

Unbeknownst to her, Tyler was sat, watching her draw. He noticed how her features had relaxed, the frown turned smooth, and all the tension surrounding her scar had disappeared. It helped him to remember the girl she used to be, the one who taught him what it meant to never be afraid to try.

10

PARAKEET

Melopsittacus undulatus

Tucked away in the corner of a side street in Paris, there sits a bookshop that has become something of a legend among literary enthusiasts.

Shakespeare & Company has a green façade, battered wooden shelves set outside on the pavement, a chalkboard adorned with quotes and facts of old, and a square portrait of the Bard himself, hung above the door.

Does it still look the same? Emily wondered as she crossed over the threshold, breathed in the comforting scent of books. Felt the weight of all those words, some new, some ancient, that filled the minds of people from every part of the world.

She wished she could ask her grandmother how it had felt when she was there – swap notes to see if the stacks of books, strewn higgledy-piggledy on every available surface, the faint smell of peppermint, the brown lino floor, if it was all different, or exactly as it used to be.

'Who do we ask?' Tyler called out to Emily as she passed underneath the sign from her grandmother's diary. She simply shook her head in response.

Not yet, she thought as she negotiated the narrow steps up to the first floor, discovered a trio of girls, their blonde heads bent over a book, huddled in a tiny reading alcove set into one wall.

Emily caught her breath as she spied a grey, plastic typewriter sat atop a makeshift desk. Two of the keys were missing and the rest of it was stuck together with tape.

On the walls around it were pinned dozens of scraps of paper, each adorned with quotes, doodles and outpourings of love. Used Metro tickets, polaroid pictures, a restaurant receipt, all stuck to the wall and one another with sticky tape, pins, even lumps of chewed gum.

As she leant closer, she mumbled through a few of the poems and notes, wondered if ever something of her grandmother's was pinned here. If ever her fingers used the typewriter to begin one of her books, those she had written before Emily was born.

This was where it all began, where Catriona Robinson turned her love of literature into a career, a life. Where she found inspiration, kindrid spirits, a reason to keep going no matter the odds. Which one of them did she confide in, turn to for help, when she was as poor as a church mouse, raising her daughter alone? Did any of them know who the father was, if he was still alive?

From somewhere deep within the store came the sound of a piano being played. Following the notes like a rat to the piper, Emily weaved from room to room, spied a couple of narrow beds, under which more books were stored. At the end of one room was a ladder propped up against the wall, and above this was another bed, fashioned out of a shelf with a faded piece of material used as a curtain of sorts.

Where had she slept? Which bed bore the weight of her? So much about her grandmother was a mystery, but walking in her shadow only seemed to make Emily miss her all the more.

'Emily?' Tyler's voice called her over to where he was stood by the piano, holding a brown paper package, tied up with string.

As Emily approached, the man playing the piano turned his head, nodded his welcome without ever halting the movement of his fingers. He was older, but not old enough to be who she had dared to hope for.

Emily snatched the parcel from Tyler, turned it over to see another sticker, this one of a mermaid with golden hair, playing a harp made from shells. She paused a moment, tried to guess which book her grandmother had chosen to hide within. Would it be the one about a boy who was afraid to put his head under the water, just like Tyler used to be? Someone who Ophelia took swimming with mermaids, down to the bottom of the deep blue sea, and managed to overcome his fear of the unknown.

Part of her wanted it to be the last clue, the last book. But already she felt disappointed because she knew there would be so much more to come.

'Where was it?' she whispered to Tyler, trying not to show the anger in her voice. Trying not to let her feelings pour out all over the floor.

'I asked the woman at the front desk,' he replied, squinting up at the bookshelves behind him.

'It's not yours.' Emily clenched her jaw, registered the spasm that followed, that always followed, when she tried to talk too fast, too soon.

Tyler shrugged, took a book from the shelf, then put it back again. 'I just thought it would save time.'

'Save time?' Emily said, trying not to imagine all the places he would clearly rather be. All the people he would rather be with, because it was starting to feel as if there was something more at stake for him, something other than simply helping her solve her grandmother's puzzle. Turning from him, she undid the knot of string around the package before slipping the paper from the book. One quick glance at the cover, then she opened it up to read the dedication.

For Antoine – thank you for showing me how to capture the light.

'Who's Antoine?' Tyler was peering over her shoulder and she took a step away, tried not to let him see.

'Not sure,' she replied, flicking through the pages of a story about a boy who walked barefoot to school. A child who was gifted a pair of magical boots so he could soar higher than all the people who thought he was less worthy because he was poor. 'Where is it?' she muttered, holding the book by both covers, turning it upside down and giving it a gentle shake.

'She said to come back tomorrow.' Tyler looked back towards the front of the shop. To where an assistant with a sharp, black bob was passing over a bag filled with books to a man and his three girls were all twitching expectantly, their blonde pigtails jiggling. 'Apparently Madeleine wanted to give it to you personally, along with something else.'

'What?'

'She didn't know. But she did give me these.' He held out two small rectangles of plastic, in the corner of each was a tiny, metal square. Hotel keys.

'A hotel?' She had no desire to go to a hotel. It felt clinical, yet seedy, the idea of being ushered to a hotel with him. Was this part of the plan?

And yet it couldn't be, because Madeleine had something more. Something her grandmother may not have known about.

'Apparently it's just around the corner. Same one Aunt Cat always stayed in whenever she came back.'

Ever more secrets. Ever more surprises to bear.

Emily knew her grandmother had travelled when Margot was just a baby. Taken her all over the world, carried her in a sling as she researched her next book. Worked any job she could find to make just enough money to feed them both, buy paper, ink and a ticket to wherever the desire took her next. It was only when Emily's mother was older and needed a proper education, to have what society described as 'stability', that Catriona returned to England. That was when she went to live with an old friend who worked for a large publishing house in London.

But Paris? She had never spoken of Paris.

'I can't do this.' Emily felt the ache along her scar. Not the one on her cheek, but the one that reached all the way around her spine and down her leg. It was too much, too many highs and lows all tangled up together.

'Yes, you can,' Tyler said, resting a hand on her arm. 'It's just one more day.'

For him, maybe, but for her it was forever.

She pushed him away. 'I want to go home.'

'I know, I get it.' He followed her out of the shop, watched as she turned left, then right, then left again. 'It's frustrating as hell to only be given half the clue, half the answer. But you did find it. And the one in London. And you found them really easily, which means this next one will be just the same.'

Emily didn't answer, because she was afraid to admit that she had absolutely no idea who Antoine was.

Marching ahead, the river to her right, Emily barely even noticed the crowds all heading towards Notre Dame. She didn't think about how she was walking through the streets of a city she came to as a child, but had since only ever visited in her mind. A city she dreamt of – the romance, the history, the art – but never thought she would have the courage to come back to. Sometimes she thought she would never again have any courage at all.

'Look, we're both exhausted.' His stride had fallen in with her own; quickened then slowed so that they walked in perfect sync. 'And hungry. Are you hungry? I know I am. Why don't we go and get something to eat? There's a place not far from here we can try.'

'I'm not hungry.'

'You say that now,' he replied with a grin. 'But wait until you try their coconut *moules* and fresh baguettes. Absolute heaven, I promise.'

Emily scuffed the ground with her feet, stared across the road to one of many bridges in Paris dominated by padlocks, a supposed sign of someone's everlasting love. She was still annoyed with him for taking the next clue from Madeleine, annoyed with herself for showing him her sketchbook,

'So what's the book about?' Tyler asked as she strode on ahead.

'You didn't read it?'

'I did. All of them. But what's it really about?'

Emily stopped in the middle of the pavement. Ignored the irritated tuts of people who passed her by and tried to think of when it was the book was written. What it was they were doing when her grandmother came up with the idea.

'Judgement,' she said, looking back at him in expectation.

'Prejudice against being poor?'

A quick shake of her head.

'More.' Never judge a book by its cover.

Emily thought back to the day when they had come out of church to see a homeless man propped up against the lychgate, asleep, with a tiny dog in his lap. So dirty was the poor creature's fur it was more grey than cream. Emily had hurried past, holding her nose, and her grandmother had scolded her for it, told her she had no idea who he was, what had happened to make him so desperate as to sleep on the streets.

Catriona had invited the man and his dog back to their home, then made Emily wash the dog in an old tin bath whilst its owner sat in the kitchen and ate plate after plate of roasted potatoes with lashings of gravy. A dog who licked bubbles from her hands, his little tail wagging so hard it sloshed half the water all over the lawn. Then the two of them were gone, with no more than a doff of threadbare cap and a yellow-toothed smile.

Emily had asked her grandmother why he wouldn't want to stay, why he would choose to go back to such destitution, but she had gotten that look in her eye, the one which meant she was travelling somewhere new. That all the cogs and wheels of her mind were turning faster than she could keep up with.

Catriona Robinson had raced into her study and began to write out the bones of a new story, about a boy from Singapore, whose mother lived in a shed at the bottom of her employer's garden. Someone who had never owned a pair of shoes but walked to school each morning due to an endless curiosity about the world. His classmates teased him about his worn-through clothes, the dirt embellishing his skin, and the fact he was a servant's child without a father or a home. But still he shared his breakfast one morning with an old hag being taunted by the other children in his class.

It was a play on *Cinderella*, with a touch of other fairy tales thrown in for good measure, but the message was clear enough.

'It's about you,' Tyler said. 'They're all about you.'

She started walking, the wheels of her suitcase hopping and bumping with each agitated step.

'Do you think it's a lesson about money?' Tyler asked as he jogged to keep up. 'Aunt Cat could have lived in a castle in Scotland, or on a boat in Monaco.'

'So?'

'Why didn't she? I mean, the cottage is great, but it's small. Really small, and you had enough money to buy whatever she wanted.'

'She didn't care about money.' She wrote because she had to, always told Emily it was in her bones, her blood.

'Most people would have been rich and greedy.' Tyler moved aside to let an elderly lady and her poodle pass. 'Your parents were the same,' he said as he caught up with her. 'Unlike mine, who always seemed to relish in having so much more than everyone else.'

They stood, side by side, waiting for the pedestrian crossing to flash up green, then Tyler rested his hand in the small of Emily's back as she began to cross the road.

'I remember Aunt Cat telling me not to rely on money. Tried to get me to understand that there would always be someone with more, just as there will always be someone with less.'

One summer in the south of France, when they were all staying in some ridiculous villa paid for by Tyler's parents, Catriona had bustled into the kitchen, insisting that she help the staff prepare dinner, because she could never forget how close to poverty every rich man lived.

'St Tropez.' Emily tossed the place name over her shoulder, didn't bother to look to see if he was still following.

'What about it?'

'Next stop.'

'You're sure?' He glanced at her, then took out his phone, began to tap in a message.

She was sure. Because along with being scolded, Emily had also been reminded by her grandmother of all those summers spent in the South of France. When she and her parents had holidayed in extravagant villas, feasting on lobster and sipping champagne, whilst children went to bed with empty bellies and dirty feet. St Tropez was a town dripping with excess, a town Catriona Robinson had first visited, then lived in, when she herself was poor.

But who's Antoine? Emily asked once again as she passed by shop windows displaying beautiful things that nobody really needed but someone would buy anyway. *Is he who she lived with in St Tropez?*

It was where she had written her first novel, about a woman

who fell for the wrong man. A man who could never love her in return, but spent a lifetime trying.

Did she follow Antoine to the south of France? Could he be the man she couldn't love, could he be Emily's grandfather?

With tears in her eyes that blurred all she could see, Emily turned her head from side to side, tried to latch onto something that didn't make her ache with regret, because she had never asked more. Never questioned who her grandmother was, never stopped to think of all she gave up in order to raise her and how everything had changed because she survived.

'If you're sure, there's no reason we couldn't get on a train now,' Tyler said, checking timetables on his phone. 'To St Tropez. If you wanted.' He waited for a reply, for a sign that Emily had heard him, but her attention was elsewhere.

There. A little further up the street. Something familiar. Something she had seen before, but when?

A memory. A smudge in her mind of a memory from when she was still a child; crossing the road wearing brand new red shoes, with buckles on each side that twinkled when they caught the light.

'Where are you going?'

I remember this, Emily thought as she walked towards an art shop with a display of brightly-coloured découpage parakeets in the window. Some were in mid-flight, with ancient, mismatched keys in their beaks, as if they each held the secret to places of old.

She inhaled deeply as she went inside, wax and oil and parchment flooding her senses. It was like an apothecary's, with wooden drawers and glass-fronted cabinets lining every wall. Everywhere you looked was colour – tubes and tubs and bottles of paint, crayons and pencils and stacks upon stacks of paper.

A corner wall was covered in hundreds of squares of white, each one containing a picture drawn by a child that tickled Emily's fingers as she looked at them each in turn. A dove, an angel, a bright purple octopus. She remembered her parents thinking she'd gone missing, when in fact she was sat at the top of the shop, by the easels, trying to draw because she'd seen small square pictures tacked to the walls.

Someone had pointed at what she'd done, told Emily's father she had a natural talent that should be nurtured. It was a sketch of a duck, with long, patchwork feet, and identical to the stuffed toy she took with her wherever she went. He was called Clyde and he knew all of Emily's secrets, all of her hopes and dreams.

Behind her stood a wooden cabinet, divided into equal sections and each containing a thick, cylindrical crayon. They were like lipsticks, wrapped up in cream paper all with their own individual number.

Her father had bought her a box of crayons. Emily reached out her hand, couldn't quite bring herself to touch a crayon of deepest vermillion, was unable to stop her mind from picturing the cardboard box still sat in her dresser at home, containing the last remaining fragment of her first ever gift from this shop. It made her question whether her grandmother had known this is where she would end up in Paris. But did she even know of its existence? Of what it meant to her?

She could still hear her parents' voices, talking to one another about if they had time to go up to Montmartre before dinner. Debating whether it was too far to take her, but then it was a holiday, an experience, after all. She can see the way her father looked at his wife, gave her a slow kiss, as if they had all the time in the world. She could still remember what it was like to have them love her.

A familiar feeling began to take hold as she looked all around, imagined the cabinets moving closer, the crayons and tubes of colour cascading onto her body and burying her deep. The sensation of falling, as her legs gave way. No ground beneath her, no sky above, just darkness and a persistent ringing in her ears.

Emily didn't register the sound of Tyler's voice, nor the concerned looks of other shoppers. She barely heard the rush of traffic or felt the splatter of rain on her skin as he took her away from the shop and all its reminders of the parents, the life, she had lost.

A moment later she was in a café, listening to Tyler order food and wine in French so fluent he could have been native. She was only half aware of the seat in which he had deposited her, of the walls adorned with art deco posters and a giant wooden cockerel standing guard by the door.

She sat with hands cradling her glass as she took slow sips of crushed grapes, felt the acidity catch at the back of her throat. Slowly, the world came back into view, her heart settled and her body relaxed into the padded bench.

A waitress brought a basket of warm bread and two pots, black like cauldrons, curved handles and tendrils of steam that teased her nose. Emily peeped inside, saw a pile of mussels covered in fragrant cream, with wilting coriander leaves and finely sliced shallots. Her stomach growled in appreciation and she rubbed her hands together before diving in. It was salty and sweet, due to the combination of shellfish and coconut sauce that she dipped her bread into. A simple meal, but one that hit the spot.

'I was thinking about what you said about going home,' Tyler said in between mouthfuls. 'About working remotely.'

'Oh?' Emily tossed a closed shell into the upturned lid of her pot and looked across at him. There was a slither of juice running down his wrist, a piece of coriander stuck in his teeth and crumbs all over his shirt.

'I don't think it's a good idea. Only ever communicating with people via email, not in the real world.'

'I see people.'

'The same people,' he said, pointing an empty shell at her. 'From the same village you've lived in for most of your life. People move to Wells to retire, Em, to see out the end of their lives. After they've done all they can, made their memories, had their adventures, broken hearts, wishes fulfilled.'

Emily licked salty droplets from her fingers, ignoring the thinly veiled insult.

'Well?' A drop of juice fell from his chin.

'Well, what?'

'I think you should leave Norfolk.'

'You don't understand.'

'No, I don't.' He sat back, pushed away his plate. Looked down to see the way her hand had unconsciously been moving breadcrumbs into a pattern on the tablecloth. It was the shape of a mouse, with a long tail that curled around her plate.

'You used to make up stories.'

'I did?'

'All the time.' He nodded, then reached out for another piece of bread. 'When we were in the park, or on the bus, or watching some incredibly dull play. You would make up stories about all the people around us. Imagining where they lived, what their secrets were. If they liked Marmite or fudge.'

'Vanilla fudge.' It was like heaven in a bite.

'Chocolate.' He gave her a gentle nudge with his foot, under the table, and it made her smile. 'My point is you could carry on, you know, without her.'

It was the same idea presented to Emily over and over, by well-meaning friends. Her grandmother's friends, people she only knew because of her. On some level Emily knew they were right. Understood she was the best person to carry on Catriona Robinson's legacy. But she also didn't want to do it by herself, because what if Tyler was wrong? What if they were all wrong and she was nothing more than someone who painted the pictures of someone else's story?

'No.'

He was looking at her in that way again. As if she were his own private puzzle that he needed to solve.

'So, this unfinished manuscript.' He sat back, looped his hands behind his head. 'You know how it ends?'

'Sort of.' The truth was her grandmother had never said.

'Are you allowed to tell me?'

Emily leant down beneath her chair, took out her sketch-book and opened it to reveal a picture of Ophelia as a teenager. She was carrying the magical atlas in her rucksack whilst skimming through country lanes on her bike.

Tyler turned the book around, looked at the detail of each strand of Ophelia's hair, the spokes of wheel that seemed to be spinning and the tiny specks of dirt that clung to her skin.

'Where is she going?'

'No idea.'

'Maybe you don't need to know,' he said. 'Maybe all she's doing is giving the atlas to someone else because she's grown up. She doesn't need it any more.'

'But that's so sad,' Emily blurted out. 'Just because you're not a child, doesn't mean all the magic should be taken away.'

'At last she speaks!' he said with a grin. 'I was beginning to think you never would.'

It hit her, square between the eyes, as she realised that, for the first time in weeks, she had spoken a complete sentence, sentences, without taking a breath. Without stopping to think about how her tongue would betray her, stumble over the words, or worse, spit all over the table.

'So is it just me, or do you really not speak to anyone at all?'

'I ...' Emily hesitated, because she hadn't really thought about why, not for years.

'You never used to care what people think.'

Emily took a sip of her drink, then looked away.

Tyler regarded her for a moment more, then pulled the sketchbook close to look at the picture again; at how the atlas seemed to be leaping, rather than falling, from Ophelia's rucksack. He noticed a flock of sheep blocking the road ahead, as if trying to get her to stop, to turn around and see what was hidden within the picture.

He stared at the face of a wizened shepherd, one hand curled around an ancient hook, the other cradling a fuzzy, yellow duckling. Tyler recognised the shepherd, even if Emily appeared not to. It was her father. She was hiding things within her drawings, things even she couldn't see.

'You seem to notice everything.' He rested his hand on

the depiction of someone who taught him how to throw a decent punch, never to rat on his true friends and always, always, stand up for those you love. 'You were always so good at understanding people and their emotions better than they did themselves.'

'I draw what I see.'

'No,' he said with a swift shake of his head. 'It's more than that. There's a story behind the picture. More than any of the words your grandmother wrote. I see it now.' He looked at her, really looked at her, taking in the pronounced cupid's bow, wide hazel eyes and skin like the finest porcelain. 'You're more talented than you think.'

Emily swatted away the compliment, ignoring his kind words because she was so unaccustomed to such attention and had no idea what to do with it.

'What about you?' She had seen the shades of blue under his eyes. The subtle lines that were there, underneath two-day stubble, along with the absence of something that used to be, replaced by a different kind of smile.

'What about me?'

She nodded at the guitar perched on the chair beside him.

'I love music,' he said. 'It's what makes me feel alive in a way that nothing else ever could. But, as you know, I come from a family where everything was decided for me. Which school I went to, which university, which career. No doubt my father even had a list of prospective wives written down somewhere.'

'And now?'

'Let's just say *Daddy dearest* doesn't approve of my life choices.'

Emily recalled her grandmother telling her Tyler had lost

his job. Something about an extramarital affair and recreational drug use. She remembered thinking it couldn't have been easy for him to tell his parents and wondered what made him throw away his career, or in fact why he had decided to stay for years in a life that clearly didn't make him happy.

She felt sorry for him, and this surprised her. For so long she had hated all those letters from his mother that told of how he had been chosen as Head Boy, become captain of the swim squad, won a place at Cambridge. Emily would scoff and pretend not to care when she heard of how he had travelled all over the world, climbed mountains and swum with creatures of the sea. More than anything, she resented him for making her so incredibly envious of what she once thought could have been her life too.

'You hated it.'

Tyler nodded in reply. 'All of it. The drugs, the affair, it wasn't me, it was the lifestyle I pushed myself into, without actually wanting it. That's what pisses him off more than anything, the fact I don't want to be like him.'

His face was closed, shutting away the rest of his response behind a door. But there was a crack, a clue in the way he fiddled with his fork at the table, tapping it against his glass, letting the note sing out. Emily imagined bubbles of sound, inside of which were all his secrets, all his pain. Bubbles that floated through and over Paris until they burst amongst the clouds.

'The first time I heard Johnny Cash play,' he said as he called the waiter over to pay their bill.

'Sorry?'

'I remember it so clearly. We were driving back from my grandparents' and "Ring of Fire" came on the radio. It was a physical reaction. My entire body sat a little straighter and I asked my mum to turn it up.' He looked across at his guitar. 'All at once I knew what it was I wanted to do.'

He had been given a guitar one Christmas. Emily remembered his excitement that year, perched on the end of his bed and asking her if she thought that even if you no longer believed in Father Christmas, would you get what you hoped for most of all? They were so young, so full of hope. It was the last Christmas Emily ever dared to wish for something, the last time she still believed there was magic in the world.

'Have you ever felt that way about something?' He put some money on the table, pushed back his chair then came around to hold hers out as she stood.

Emily smiled as the cover of a favourite book floated into her mind.

'*Matilda*.'

'Who?'

'By Roald Dahl.' It was one of the first books she had ever read by herself, in her head, without help from anyone to decipher all the words. It had made her truly understand the power of those words, how they could transport you to another world. More than that, the sketches of that tiny, little girl had made her want to draw all the pictures she had carried around in her mind for as long as she could remember.

Tyler had been given a guitar that year, but what she had been given seemed to be so much more. A leather-bound sketchbook, embossed with her initials, and a wooden case filled with crayons, each wrapped up in cream paper with a number stamped on the side.

Crayons bought here, in Paris, by her parents. No doubt when she was still sat at the top of the shop, gazing at each of those white squares in turn, wondering if she would ever be so lucky as to be able to recreate her imaginary worlds.

'What do you do for fun?' Tyler asked.

'Fun?' Emily replied with a frown.

Tyler looped his arm around her shoulders as they walked and Emily could smell garlic on his breath.

'We're in Paris, one of the most incredible cities in the world, and given what Aunt Cat was like, I'm sure she would have wanted you to at least try and have some fun whilst you were here?'

He was waiting for an answer, but she had no idea what to say because 'fun' wasn't something she had exactly had her fill of ever since her life was ripped apart by one, stupid mistake. One split second when everything became altogether dark and decidedly un-fun. Not just for Emily, but for her grandmother too, and they had simply had to carry on regardless, find joy in the simplest of things, such as a bird who learnt to trust her enough to come each morning and share her breakfast. Or getting lost in the world of imagination, trying to convince themselves that happiness could be created, as long as you didn't allow yourself to remember the people you most wanted to share it with.

'I only have eight days.' Eight more days until she had absolutely nothing left.

Tyler waved her disdain away. 'I know, I know, there's a ticking bomb set to go off somewhere in the not too distant future, but Madeleine won't be back until tomorrow morning, and some of the people from the bookshop asked if we wanted to meet up with them later?'

'We?'

'Let's pretend, just for today, that we are in Paris for any other reason than finding a lost manuscript, or saving your inheritance, or simply doing what Catriona Robinson has demanded. What's the worst that could happen?' The last part was said with a wide grin, one that Emily remembered from years ago. A grin that told her he was on her side, that he wouldn't let anything bad happen to her, at least on purpose.

11

LITTLE OWL

Athene noctua

It felt like being inside a storybook, as if she were momentarily living out the life of a character dreamt up in the mind of someone she did not know. An afternoon spent in the company of a half-stranger, who told her it was impossible to choose between all the galleries and museums Paris had to offer and so instead took her cycling along the Canal Saint-Martin and then walking the old railway line of the Promenade Plantée. They had explored artisan shops under the arches that housed glass blowers and violin makers, then snacked on coffee and macarons as they sat surrounded by greenery and simply watched the world go by.

All that time, Tyler hadn't pushed her, hadn't asked Emily questions about her choice of lifestyle, instead filling the moments with stories from their shared past. He had spoken about sandcastles, snowmen and fireworks that you could still see when you closed your eyes, and Emily had been perfectly content to listen, to remember all the good bits, without ever allowing her mind to drift into the parts she had so carefully chosen not to ever think of.

Hours later, when her feet were throbbing and her mind was stuffed full with images of just one afternoon, Tyler convinced her that what she needed most of all, instead of a bubble bath back at the hotel, was a cocktail.

They came to a stop in front of a bar, outside of which people were sat in bright yellow chairs next to palm trees in oversized planters and there was a pink neon strip light above the entrance. Inside was just as trendy, just as intimidating, with parquet floors, recessed seating and ivy trailing the full height of one wall. A bartender was flipping bottles over his shoulder, a long line of liquid pouring into a row of tall glasses, and every inch of the space was filled with young Parisians enjoying what, for them, was a night out like any other.

For Emily, it was altogether other, because this was the first time she had ever set foot in such a place. It made her feel like a tortoise without its shell, desperate to hide away, to retreat into a space that was small, quiet and familiar.

'Come on,' Tyler eased her close to his side, slipping his arm around her waist and guiding her through the crowd to perch on a velvet chair at the bar.

Emily scanned the menu for something to focus on other than how completely out of place she felt.

'What do you want?' Tyler had to bend close in order to be heard and Emily felt his breath on her cheek, found herself shaking her head as she leant away.

Tyler looked as if he was about to say something but then turned to the bartender and began a conversation Emily couldn't have followed even if she had been able to hear it properly. A few minutes later two bottles of beer were slid across the bar, along with a couple of shot glasses containing luminescent blue liquid.

'What's that?' Emily picked up one of the bottles and used it to push the shot glass away.

'Dutch courage,' Tyler shouted over the music, then picked up both glasses and handed one to Emily before swallowing his drink and screwing up his eyes as the alcohol hit the back of his throat. 'Come on.' He gave her shoulder a gentle poke and Emily surprised herself by raising her own glass to her lips, then pouring its contents down her gullet.

It was like fire and ice, all at once, along with a nose full of seawater that made her eyes sting. She blinked rapidly as a shiver ran right through her core, wiping at her eyes as she spied two more shots had somehow appeared in front of her.

'No,' she said, but the word didn't quite ring true and her fingers reached out to curl around the glass and bring it once again to her lips. When her eyes came back to the horizon, Emily noticed a young woman had appeared at Tyler's side, with jet black hair cut in an asymmetric bob and a mouth painted a deep shade of red. She was curling herself around him like a cat, two dark eyes that swept over Emily then turned back to their prey.

'Emily,' Tyler said as he stepped away from the bar and took hold of Emily's arm. 'This is Agnes. She works at Shakespeare & Company.'

'Pleased to meet you,' Agnes said in heavily accented English, although her face seemed to be anything but pleased at discovering Tyler had not come to the bar alone. 'What are you going to sing?'

'Sing?' Emily cursed herself for lisping the 's', hated the small twitch of lips as Agnes looked a moment too long at her scar.

'*Oui,* why would you come to a karaoke bar if you do not sing?' Agnes collected a tray of drinks from the bar, the various glasses chattering together as she went to walk away, then turned back to Emily with a challenge. 'Or perhaps you cannot?'

'Let's just go and join the others, shall we?' Tyler handed Emily a beer and she scratched one fingernail around its neck as she followed him to the back of the bar and down an industrial staircase that led to a corridor with three doors on both sides. Above each of them was a lightbulb, five of which were shining red, but Agnes stopped outside the one with a white bulb overhead and kicked the door with her shoe. A moment later it opened and another young woman stuck her head out, this one with long, peroxide-blonde hair, whose gaze moved past Agnes to Tyler, then Emily. She said something to Agnes, then came forward to kiss Emily on both cheeks.

'*Enchant*é,' she said with a smile that reached all the way up to her eyes. '*Je suis Clementine.*' Emily liked her immediately, not least because she was wearing a vest top and jeans and had paint underneath her fingernails. It made Emily feel a little less self-conscious about her own khaki shorts and plain white T-shirt, a little less aware of how polished, how very French, Agnes was.

Clementine introduced herself to Tyler, then stepped aside to let them into the private karaoke box. Emily had been expecting some kind of padded cell, but the space inside was like a very small, windowless living room, with green seating wrapped around three of the walls, low-level lighting and an enormous screen next to the door. There was a man fiddling with the control panel just below the screen, muttering to himself. He was wearing tight leather trousers and a shirt emblazoned with flowers, unbuttoned nearly to his navel and showing off the edge of a tattoo. He looked up as they entered, with a frown that turned to a smile as his attention fell on Emily.

'*Agnes, tu ne m'as pas dit que tu m'apportais un cadeau,*' he said with a bow as he took hold of Emily's hand and kissed it slowly, then escorted her to the corner of the room and sat her down.

'I don't...' Emily said, vaguely recalling that *cadeau* was French for 'present'. She looked across to Tyler for an answer, only to find him glaring at them.

'Ignore Frederic,' Agnes said as she shut the door. 'He flirts with everyone.'

The soft thud of wood, the decisive click of a lock and Emily's heart jumped back and forth as she tried to breathe, tried not to panic.

You're fine. Emily began to tap her fingers against her thigh. *You're fine,* she repeated to herself as she stared at the door, at where a moment before there had been a line of sight to a staircase but now there was no window, no light other than the artificial glare coming from a TV screen.

'You OK?' Frederic sat down beside her, but any attempt Emily would have made to reply was lost as the tune of 'Single Ladies' blasted from surround-sound speakers and made her ears pulsate. Agnes came into the centre of the room and began to sing in a powdery voice aimed directly at Tyler. Emily couldn't help but watch as Agnes started to writhe, her body transforming in Emily's mind into a serpent that was coiling itself around and around the room, wrapping them up tight and squeezing out all the air.

Emily gave a sharp shake of her head, dipped her chin and tried to focus instead on the way in which she had earlier watched as a man blew into molten glass, turning it over and over to create a sculpted vase that looked as if it had a rainbow running through its centre. She took a breath, waited for the music to do what it always did, make it possible to ignore the real world.

'Do you want to try?' Frederic was sat too close and the way he was looking at her like some kind of delicacy to be sampled made Emily shift to the side, place a cushion on the space between them.

'Non, merci,' she said, taking a sip of her drink and looking over to where Agnes was shimmying and writhing, all for Tyler's benefit, but he seemed more interested in watching how Frederic was edging ever closer to her. It was surreal, like she had fallen down the rabbit hole and woken up in an alternate reality.

The music stopped and the room fell still with nobody speaking, each of them waiting for something to happen. Agnes sauntered over and held the microphone out to Emily, one eyebrow raised in silent question.

'Elle a dit "non",' Clementine took the microphone and offered a sympathetic smile to Emily.

Agnes yawned then helped herself to another drink, stirring through the Martini with an olive on a stick. 'So you are just an illustrator, not like your grandmother?'

Just. One simple word thrown into the mix, so innocent, so deliberate. Then Emily realised what it was Agnes had said. 'You know?'

'The whole world knows about you and your little quest,' she replied. 'Why else would he keep you so close?' Agnes looked over at Tyler, then back at Emily's scar.

It was a challenge. Something Emily had managed to avoid for most of her life but at one point would have risen to without a moment's hesitation. Perhaps it was the alcohol firing her spirit, or even the very otherness of this day which made her stand up, snatch the microphone from Agnes and go over to the screen. Or maybe she was just fed up with the way Agnes was looking at her, with a mixture of pity and amusement, that had Emily scrolling through the list of songs, trying so very hard not to let her mind overthink what it was she was about to do.

'You don't have to do this,' Tyler said as he came up beside her and bent his head close.

Emily didn't dare look up at him, knew that if she did all her bravado, all her crazy impulsiveness would simply disappear.

'Yes, I do.'

As the opening bars of 'Heart of Glass' filled the small room, Emily closed her eyes and imagined everyone else around her being spirited away. Her hand gripped the microphone as she felt the pulse of bass guitar, allowed it to fill the space inside of her and she opened her mouth to sing. In that moment, there was nothing but her and the song, nothing but the way that music always made her free and completely detached from her fears. Her voice was soft, but powerful, each word wrapped up in rich tones that escaped from her throat without getting caught around either her scar or her doubts.

The song came to an end, a moment's pause as the world fell back into place and Emily opened her eyes at the very same time Frederic, Clementine and even Agnes leapt to their feet and began to holler their response.

'Wow. Just, wow.' Tyler pushed his hair from his face and stared at Emily. She handed back the microphone and bit down on the inside of her cheek to try and stop herself from smiling, but it did nothing to quell the flush of emotion that spread from her cheeks and all the way down her neck. Bringing her hand up to cover her scar, she started when Tyler pulled it away and squeezed it tight.

'That was amazing,' he said with a slow shake of his head.

'So it's not true?' Agnes asked with a frown.

'What?' Emily replied as she placed one hand on the wall, aware of how the earlier two shots she had drunk were now spinning through her veins.

'That the accident left you unable to speak properly. Because you can sing, so you must be able to speak.' She held out her phone, showed Emily a photograph taken of her inside Shakespeare & Company along with a headline in French that Emily didn't manage to translate before Agnes pulled the phone away. 'Is it all a lie, for the publicity?'

Emily wobbled, fell back onto the sofa as she tried to get her brain to put together something vaguely resembling an intelligent response.

'Singing is different.'

'Agnes,' Clementine tugged at her friend's arm. '*Laisse la tranquille.*'

'The books are *incroyable,*' Agnes said with a pout. 'But it is wrong to lie if there are no more.'

'You may have lost an idol, someone you admired from afar,' Tyler draped his jacket over Emily's shoulders and

136

helped her to her feet. 'But she lost her grandmother, so leave her alone.'

'It was good to meet you, Emily,' Clementine smiled as she held the door open for them both, gave a small shrug of her shoulders as she glanced back at where Agnes was now sitting on Frederic's lap.

'Come on, Cinderella,' Tyler said to Emily as they climbed the stairs and he escorted her back through the bar. 'Let's get you home.'

'Home,' Emily mumbled as they stepped outside, and for a second she felt her mood drop back down from where it had been balancing, if only for a little while, precariously close to happy. Then she breathed in the scent of a city she did not know, remembered the sound, the sight, of a group of strangers who had invited her into their world, and it made her smile. A real smile, one that pushed along her scar and beyond, one that made her believe, for the first time, that coming here, with Tyler, wasn't a mistake.

The moon was low and bright, casting dappled pieces of light on the puddles that had appeared whilst they were inside, singing about love, loss and all the fractious hope that Emily had told herself not to believe in. Once more, it was as if she had stepped inside someone else's life, an existence that didn't belong to her, that had never before been within her reach. For so long she had assumed that the future she once thought she could have had would never be. Years had passed since she had done anything other than follow a routine, a script of the day-to-day that never changed because it was safe, it was secure. But now she had been shown the other side, seen what was waiting for her if she dared to step through the door and into the secret garden that she had ignored for far too long.

'We could wait for a taxi?' Tyler said as he lit a cigarette, then blew a couple of rings into the sky.

Emily shook her head as she wrapped her arms around herself and looked both ways before crossing the street.

There was something inside of her that seemed to be trying to set itself free. A feeling, or a memory of a feeling, that, up until now, had seemed nothing more than an impossible dream. Emily still couldn't wrap her mind around the idea she was walking the streets of Paris, with Tyler by her side, away from everything she thought she needed, what she thought was all she could ever have.

Is this what her grandmother had wanted her to find?

She looked up again, began to count the stars that were blinking back from the heavens.

'I'm moving to Nashville.' Tyler was staring at a street performer on the bridge as they passed. A man with a dark, wiry beard and pink cheeks that swelled as he played on a burnished trumpet.

'Why Nashville?' Emily couldn't think of anything better to say, because she couldn't figure out why a man who used to trade stocks and shares, making rich people richer, could suddenly decide to pursue a career in country music.

'To collaborate. To breathe it in. To wear it like a favourite jumper, have it cocoon you, nurture you, protect you from all the negativity.'

Just like Catriona had when she came to Paris and met five strangers who became her closest friends.

'There's a romance to it all,' he said, taking her arm and guiding her across the cobbled street. 'Drowning yourself in music, and country has all that heartache, all that pain, wrapped up in such beautiful melodies.'

Emily thought of the notebook he carried around with him. Wondered what was hidden within, and if he would share it with her, the way she had shared her drawings.

The hotel staircase was old and narrow, with a metal cage for a lift that ran up its centre. Room 304 had a brass door knocker in the shape of an owl.

A group of owls is called a parliament. Emily looked along the corridor, saw a line of little brass owls, their beaks peeping out from every door. *And their ears are asymmetrical so they can pinpoint the exact location of their prey.* She began to tap the owl's head against the door, softly softly, over and over.

'I'm sorry.' Tyler was stood beside her, holding out a key. 'About what Agnes said earlier.'

'Forget it,' Emily replied, letting go the owl to fiddle with the chain of her locket.

'I didn't want you to find out about that stuff on the internet.' He was leaning against the door frame, the very tip of his boot touching her shoe.

'It's OK.'

'No, it's not. It's not fair that everyone gets to have an opinion on what you're doing here, when you don't even know yourself.'

Everyone had an opinion on her, they always did, only now Emily couldn't ignore it because if she did, if she gave up and went home, there might not be anything to go back to.

'Goodnight, Tyler.'

'Goodnight, Emily,' he said as he leant towards her and

gave her a gentle kiss on the cheek, but she didn't flinch, didn't back away from his touch as she would any other.

He smelt the same. Of leather, hair gel and mint. It snapped her back to her childhood, up through to the beginning of adolescence and the first time they looked at one another in a different way.

She was stood in the hall of her old house, ready to go to a performance of *A Midsummer Night's Dream* in Regent's Park. With her hair down and wearing a tea dress made from the deepest green. The doorbell rang and she opened it, saw him before her in jacket and tie, with hair slicked back and a look of disbelief on his face.

Thirteen years old and on the cusp of a life most extraordinary. Two children still to grow into adults, catching a glimpse of how they were changing into something more.

He pulled back and looked at her in the exact same way as he did that summer night, fifteen years ago. As if he was only seeing her then for the first time, looking beyond the scar and all the damage her body had endured.

For a second, for just a fraction of a moment, Emily forgot all about the absolute bombshell her grandmother had dropped. But as he walked away and she closed the door to her room, Emily realised she felt a little disappointed; that somehow he had managed to brighten her mood, and without him all seemed duller, less interesting, than before.

So she did what she always did when the pain began to creep close, she sat by the window, opened it wide to breathe in the night, slipped on the borrowed headphones and began to draw. But this time the lines that appeared were of someone new. A man who ambled as he walked, a guitar thrown over one shoulder and a curl of hair at the nape of his neck.

She drew him in the middle of a field draped in midnight, with trees that turned to listen as he played. A long line of notes escaping from strings gently plucked. Notes that flew up and over his head, one by one transforming into a swarm, a miasma, of hundreds and hundreds of birds on the wing.

12

BLUEBIRD

Sialia

The woman sat across from Emily wore her face like an apology for getting old. She was stirring her coffee and eating tiny forkfuls of cake, waiting for Emily to finish reading another excerpt from her grandmother's past. Emily herself was trying to ignore the symphony of accents coming from the other side of the café, from where a group of six people were huddled around a table, discussing the previous night's adventures in broken English, one of whom had a dark bob.

Agnes was part of the next clutch of hipster twenty-somethings living out their literary fantasies by sleeping in the upstairs library next door. Apart from when they were exploring the delights of Paris, and one another, from what Emily could make out, on a summer's night just gone. It made her jealous, to think of all that life they still had yet to live, that someone like Agnes was following in her grandmother's footsteps when Emily had never had the chance to do so herself.

'Catriona used to write to my mother, even when she no longer ran the shop.' Madeleine was staring at Emily's scar. She could feel those eyes on her as she carefully folded her grandmother's words, tucked them away inside her bag. 'She used to send us an advance copy of all her books, even the ones from before she was famous.'

Before, Emily thought. It always came down to before. As if her grandmother was only worth remembering because she had stumbled upon an idea, a character, that had touched the lives of so many. She always found it insulting that all of her grandmother's published works up until that point were only considered of worth because of what came next. Fame and fortune, the perennial dream.

Emily yawned and took a final sip of her coffee. She hadn't been able to sleep again last night, tossing and turning in the unfamiliar bed as she tried to draw, but found her mind full of questions, too many reasons to disappear back to England. In the end, she got up, slipped a note under Tyler's door and walked through Paris, searching for more clues about her past, waiting for memories to appear.

Just before dawn, she found herself outside the bookstore café, already lit from within, the scent of coffee and croissant spilling onto the street. A woman was stood behind the counter with auburn hair, flecked through with grey, who looked up as Emily stood in the doorway and the two of them paused a moment, to drink each other in.

Madeleine had gestured towards a table by the window, with a view of the world slowly waking, then brought coffee, dark and strong, along with slices of almond and cherry cake because the croissants were still in the oven. After she sat down, she slipped a plain, white envelope over the tabletop towards Emily without a word.

Emily looked across at the hipsters and wondered what it would feel like to be a part of something so uninhibited, so raw. If she would have been a person brave enough to embark on such an adventure, had her life turned out differently.

'I'm sorry for keeping you in the dark.' Madeleine followed Emily's gaze, watched with her as the group ambled out of the café, and Agnes nodded in their direction whilst saying a curt *bonjour*.

Emily envied them their closeness, the bond made through shared experience. The ease with which they moved around one another, the scent of desire stuck to their clothes, their skin. 'You knew.'

'About the treasure trail?' Madeleine picked up her cup, set it down again. 'Yes, but I promised not to tell.'

Promises and secrets, all tangled up as one.

'Who's Antoine?'

Madeleine smiled at the mention of his name, then used her fork to gather the crumbs of cake into a small pile.

'Antoine was – *is* – a force of nature. Strong, handsome and intelligent. A lethal combination in any man, more so in one who could recite the entire works of Shakespeare, even after two bottles of wine. My mother told me they were all in love with him, in one way or another. Even I had a crush on him, as a teenager, despite realising he would never be interested in someone like me.'

'Where is he now?' *He's alive.* Emily felt a murmur of anticipation.

'You tell me. Isn't that the point of all this, to make you figure out the clues yourself?'

Emily wished she knew what the point was, and if Antoine was the real reason she was there.

'Come.' Madeleine stood. 'Let me show you what it is I asked you here for.'

They went to the back of the café, climbed a tight, winding stair to reach a cluttered attic space that seemed to be part office, part storeroom. Madeleine began to search through stacks of books, then clambered onto one of the desks and moved aside dusty cardboard boxes from a top shelf.

Emily went over to the window, leant out and looked down to see an internal courtyard where someone was sat, reading. Balconies and rooftops of Paris were dotted as far as the eye could see, and if Emily stood on tiptoe she could just about discern the tip of the Eiffel Tower on the horizon.

'Ah, here it is.' Madeleine dropped something onto the desk, then clambered back down, wiping her hands together and sending tiny particles of dust spiralling through the air.

It was a photo album, filled with snapshots of the past. Emily recognised Gigi first of all, pouting at the camera with one foot kicked out behind her whilst stood on an upturned crate, stacking shelves in the shop next door; then another of her sat in an oversized chair, drawing on a cigarette, all of her concentration on the book in her lap.

There was also one of Charlie, arms thrown wide as she danced in the courtyard, surrounded by fallen leaves and candlelight. Another of a man with hair that reached his shoulders, smiling at the camera with eyes that seemed to see inside your soul.

'Noah?' Emily asked.

'How did you know?'

He had that look about him. Dangerous but alluring.

She turned the page to find a group shot of six people, young and full of hope. They were huddled together outside the front of the café, arms draped through and around one another, no space between them to let the light through.

Emily recognised them now. Her grandmother, front and centre, holding Gigi at the waist; Noah on her other side, his arm draped over her shoulder, but with fingers wrapped into those dark curls. Next to him was Charlie, just as tall as he, even in bare feet, who was shouting something at the photographer, brow furrowed, hand waving. No doubt as commanding a presence back then as she was now.

On the other side of the group were a pair Emily hadn't ever seen before. A man and a woman who seemed a little detached from the rest of the group. Her head was dipped to the ground, hair falling down either side so that Emily couldn't make out her face. Next to her was an angelic figure of a man, with delicate features and light blonde hair. He was stripped to the waist, wearing tight jeans that flared at the bottom. He had broad shoulders, taut muscles and a wide, relaxed grin with a gap between his two front teeth. He had to be Antoine.

Emily couldn't help but stare at the sight of all that beauty in one person, smiled at the idea he could have been someone her grandmother once loved. She looked a little closer, tried to determine if any of his features were akin to her own, then glanced again at Noah, but found no obvious similarities on either man that might have given her a clue as to whether she shared DNA with one of them.

Below the photograph someone had scribbled a quote from *Alice in Wonderland,* along with a smiley face and the date.

'It's no use going back to yesterday, because I was a different person then. 12 July, 1965.'

Did you write this? Emily wondered as she followed the loops and kinks of the inky script, stared at the happiness on her grandmother's face, at the ease with which she held herself. When did it all change, and which one of those breathtaking men broke her heart in two?

Turning the page once more, Emily stopped when she saw a photograph of her grandmother stood at an easel by an open window. Her hair was mostly pinned on top of her head in a haphazard bun, with a few loose curls at the back and around her ears. The painting was of a pair of bluebirds, perched on a branch and sharing, or fighting over, a worm. A painting that hung in the study back home in Norfolk, but Emily had never before known it was painted here, by her.

'This is the last one I have of Catriona,' Madeleine said as she perched against the desk. 'Before she left.'

'With Antoine?'

'With Antoine.'

'Not Noah?'

Madeleine gave a wry smile. 'Seems you don't need anyone's help to figure it out after all.'

'Why did she leave?' Emily wished she could make them all come to life somehow, or that she could dive into the past, experience what it was like to be her grandmother, just for a day. The beginnings of an idea, of a picture, wavered at the edges of her mind, and she automatically looked around her for a pen.

'I don't know all the details. But my mother did say that Antoine and Noah never did get along. She often spoke of those six like they were her own children, she was so proud of them all, more than any other group before or since. But the two men were at constant odds with one another.' She looked carefully at Emily, at the curve of her lip, the brightness of her eyes that never rested for long on any one thing. 'Not surprising when you look at the woman they were fighting over.'

'Can I keep these?' Emily seemed not to notice the way her tongue lisped over the last word as she flicked between the two photographs. So preoccupied was she with the images from her grandmother's past, she didn't give herself time to understand how much more easily the words were now falling into place.

Madeleine took a deep breath, hesitated before replying. 'It's just ... they belonged to my mother.'

The picture in Emily's mind was gone in an instant, replaced by the image of a metal ladder swung down from a hatch in the ceiling of her upstairs landing back home. A square of black into which she climbed, over and over.

'It's OK.' Emily understood, because she wouldn't have wanted to give anything away either. Which is why the loft of the cottage in Norfolk was fit to burst with boxes filled with her grandmother's belongings. Items that Emily had no need for but couldn't bring herself to give away or sell. Along with dozens more she was certain contained things that once belonged to her mother. Things Catriona had clung to but never looked at.

The memories of people hiding away in darkened spaces, collecting dust, collecting nothing but time.

'Why did you show them to me?'

'I thought it might help, with the treasure trail.'

Emily's eye fell on another box, half open, containing dozens of pages stapled together along one edge. She lifted the top copy out, saw a name and date written on the first line.

'Celine Dubois, 1979,' Emily read aloud, skimming the rest of the page but understanding only half of what was written there in colloquial French. She turned to the next page, saw another name, date and collection of words, then looked at Madeleine with an unspoken question.

'Everyone who stayed here had to leave something behind. Usually a short autobiography, but sometimes more.'

'More?'

'Before you ask,' she said, putting the pages back and closing the lid to the box. 'Hers is missing. She left a whole notebook behind, apparently. Filled with poems and snippets of a story. But my mother tidied it away somewhere for safekeeping when she realised how valuable it was and then couldn't remember where she'd put it.' Madeleine sighed, looked around the room at the stacks and stacks of boxes. 'I suppose it could be in here, for all we know. Or she gave it away. Or someone stole it. I guess that's the curse of being famous. Everyone wants a piece of you.'

They had always wanted more. But Catriona had been so very good at keeping Emily away from that part of her life. Kept her hidden from view.

'*Maman* told me Catriona and Gigi were always playing tricks on people, how Catriona refused to allow any customers to buy what they claimed they wanted. Said she had a knack of understanding what it was someone wanted, or needed, to read. That they always left here believing it had been their idea all along.'

Catriona Robinson was always so very good at persuading people to do her bidding. Even, it would seem, when she was no longer alive, she had the ability to make everyone run around doing exactly as she had planned.

'So many people have come back, telling their stories about the day she sold them a copy of *Animal Farm, A Room of One's Own* or *The Grapes of Wrath*. One man claimed he left here carrying a copy of *Pride and Prejudice,* despite him arguing with Catriona about how Austen was nothing more than a load of sentimental nonsense. Apparently he met his future wife on the way home, who saw the book and commented on how much she adored the Bennetts.'

'What was her story?' Emily wished upon wish it was there, that she could read it, discover the very first one she ever wrote.

'Quoi?'

'The one she wrote here.'

Madeleine smiled. 'It was about a woman who lived at the edge of a forest, trapped by her own fear of the outside world. But at night she turned into a bird and soared high above the earth, looking for her long lost love. Do you know the story?' Madeleine asked as they went back downstairs.

'No,' Emily replied, seeing that the café was now half full of people, most of whom were stood by the door, listening to the sound of someone singing. The tone of voice was like butterscotch, sweet but with a bite, and it weaved through the air to slip inside of Emily without warning, reaching a part of her that had been ignored and neglected for as long as she could remember.

She found herself moving through the small cluster of early risers who had gathered to listen and went outside to see a man sat on a woven metal chair with a half-drunk coffee on the table next to him.

It was Tyler. His fingers moved deftly back and forth across the strings of the guitar, conjuring up a rather mournful song. She watched the movement of his lips as he played.

The song came to an end and he nodded his thanks to the small audience and their soft ripple of applause, picked up his guitar and ambled over to Emily and Madeleine.

'Are you blushing?' he said, creasing his forehead.

Emily's hand rushed to her cheek. 'What? No, I'm not.'

'It looks good on you,' he said, before turning to Madeleine, placing one hand on his chest and giving a little bow. '*Enchant*é, Madame, you must be Madeleine?'

The two of them fell into an easy conversation, all in French, and Emily tuned out the words. Stopped trying to listen to what was being said, but rather intuiting through the subtle movement of eyes across to her, the dip of Madeleine's face, the slow blush on her skin as Tyler gestured to the shop behind.

Tyler always had been at ease with himself. Charming, with the ability to talk to anyone and, if all else failed, Emily now realised, he had his guitar. His voice did more than simply carry a tune, it was deep and rich and full of emotion, but it was more the rhythm of his fingers, the soft vibrations of sound he created, the concentration on his face and how he lost himself in the song, that made her pay attention. It was hypnotic, and it only made him all the more attractive.

But underneath it all, she could now see a boy afraid of disappointing a foreboding father. Someone who first played to try and make the doubts, the fears, go away. Just like she did with her drawings, losing herself in another world, where her feelings didn't exist.

She looked up to the attic window, tried to remember the moment at which the idea of a picture had first trickled into her consciousness. She was vaguely aware of how the fingers of her left hand were moving against her thigh, drawing the shape of something she couldn't quite picture in her mind.

'You ready to go?' Tyler was talking to her and it took Emily a second to come back to the here and now, to focus on what it was he was saying, and that he was saying it to her.

'Go?'

'St Tropez. Next stop on the magical mystery tour.'

Emily saw he was holding onto her suitcase, along with his own. Which meant he had packed her things, simply tossed them all into a case of yellow, battered leather and brought them here.

Emily made a mental list of all the things he could have seen, all her private things she had no desire for him to lay his hands upon.

The fact he went into her room, without permission, went through her belongings, made her feel violated somehow. But he clearly didn't seem to think he had done anything wrong. Did he not think it would have been more prudent, more polite, to wait until she returned, or at the very least asked if she was ready to go?

Why was he in such a hurry to leave Paris?

She bent down, unzipped the outside pocket of her case and reached inside, then let go her breath as she realised her sketchbook was still there, along with both of the books and diary entries.

'I hope you find what you're looking for.' Madeleine pulled Emily into an embrace, kissed her on each cheek, then pressed something into her palm.

'Thank you,' Emily whispered as she saw the two photographs she had asked for.

'*Au revoir,*' Tyler called over his shoulder as he led Emily away and she turned to look one last time, allowed herself to hope that maybe, just maybe, she would get another chance to come back to this incredible corner of Paris.

Another train. Another journey. It all felt the same, yet each passing second brought something new to contend with, to push into a box inside her mind and try not to think about. Because thinking would lead to remembering, which would lead to nothing she could cope with right now.

They were sat on the top deck – a double-decker train, who knew? – by the window in faux-leather seats that reclined not quite far enough to be comfortable, with an armrest in between. A polished table with fold-down flaps was covered in magazines and a make-do picnic of bread and cheese that Tyler was slowly eating his way through, and there were two more, empty, seats opposite.

Emily looked down at the photograph of her grandmother stood by an easel. It made her think of the finished painting that had always hung on the wall in the study. Along with a chair by the fire, just big enough for two, where Emily liked to sit, listening to an old French fairy tale about a prince who was turned into a bluebird by an evil queen, and a beautiful princess locked away in a tower.

L'Oiseau Bleu. Emily knew there was a copy of the seventeenth-century story in one of the boxes in the attic, but once again she had never thought to question why her grandmother had it. Emily had simply loved the ornate picture on the front, of a girl reaching out for a bluebird swooping down from the sky.

But why would she paint a pair? Emily's eyes blinked back fatigue as she turned all the questions, all the possible answers, over and over.

She knew that bluebirds were only ever found in North America, and the males were possessive, protecting the nest, their mate, from any other suitors. Did it mean there was a link from the book back to both of the men Catriona shared that summer with? A book that seemed to have inspired a painting she kept close, one that she looked upon each and every day.

Emily's head fell back against the seat as the train picked up speed, the constant motion forcing shut eyes that for days had been too anxious to properly close.

As she slept, her fingers twitched in perpetual movement and her mind filled with dreams of pictures both drawn and still to come. Pictures of all the places her grandmother wrote down and asked her to conjure up onto the page, filling blank sheets of paper with colour and light. Memories too, that when awake she could not bring herself to remember. Memories of the two faces she missed most of all.

On the seat beside her, Tyler sat, reading her grandmother's books, scouring the pictures, seeking out the treasures hidden in each and every one. He smiled at the roller skates hung over the wardrobe door, a *Star Wars* poster on the wall or a brightly-painted train set. Details from Emily's childhood, tucked away in the corners of every story. Details even she seemed not to realise were there – the faces of the characters, or the shoes they wore. A sleek, black convertible car that once belonged to Tyler's father, complete with GB sticker on its boot. A car that could never be driven again.

It was as if Emily had painted her past in order to take it from her mind, to free herself from the agony of remembering a life cut short.

He set the book aside and looked over at Emily, at the stillness of her face. Then he waited one moment more before reaching inside her bag and taking out a plain, white envelope, inside of which were more sheets of palest blue.

5 September, 1965

'Yes: I am a dreamer. For a dreamer is one who can only find
his way by moonlight, and his punishment is that he sees the
dawn before the rest of the world.'

Oscar Wilde, *The Critic as Artist*.

*It is late, or very early, depending on how you look at it. Either
way, I am sitting on the rooftop of our tiny one-bed apartment,
staring up at the moon. Thinking of how it is always there
(silly, I know), of how no matter where you are in the world,
you can sit and stare at it and think of someone you hope is
missing you as much as you are missing them.*

*It's been just shy of a fortnight since I left. A week more
since I last saw Noah and there has been no word. Which I
should take as a sign, I know. All the logical parts of my brain
are telling me I should, but I don't want to. Perhaps he doesn't
even know where I am? More likely he is distracted by a bevvy
of Italian beauties and can barely remember what I look like, let
alone my name. I could always go to him. I know exactly where
he will be. On a lake, with his boat and his dreams. Alone, but
free.*

*I can't go to him. That's just too much of a cliché. And
weak. I am not weak, not any more. I will not be the sort of
woman who goes running after a man, simply because he claims
to love her. Although I do so want to see the lake. To sail past
terracotta mansions and shorelines dotted with Cypress trees.
I want to swim in the clear waters, dive as deep as I can, hold*

my breath, feel like a mermaid, like a creature who lives in a magical lagoon.

But it is beautiful here, in the town that is known as St Tropez (sounds like the beginning of a song). I wasn't quite sure what to expect, but there's a simplicity to this place, if you look beyond all the glitz and glamour. A way of life that follows the tide and the sun. Fishermen who have learnt their skills from generations long since dead and buried. Farmers and artisans hidden in amongst all the millionaires who finally seem to be disappearing back to wherever they go once the summer is done.

The light at dusk here is breathtaking. A muted rainbow of pinks and purples that slowly fade to grey, dipping beneath the horizon and mixing with the constant movement of sea. Crisp, salty air that you can feel rejuvenating you from the inside out. Sunlight that has turned my milky skin golden brown, covered from tip to toe in a crazy dot-to-dot of freckles. Antoine keeps threatening to join them all up, to see what secret pictures there are on my skin.

He is like no one else I have ever met. I feel so at ease, so comfortable around him. He makes me believe I can do, be, anything I want. Tells me I mustn't hide the truth from myself, which is incredible given how much he has to hide.

I know I am here to help him, as much as the other way around. I know my presence allows him to pretend, for appearances' sake, that he is just like everyone else. For we all have secrets squirrelled away in our hearts, and he seems less capable of concealing them here than in Paris.

On the journey south he presented me with a ring. A single, emerald-cut diamond on a gold band that once belonged to his grandmother. He told me that my mouth hung open like a giant grouper fish when he held it out to me. Then the whole bus began to cheer and holler as he slipped it over my finger and placed a kiss behind my ear, whispering that could we please pretend, at least for a little while.

Because the apartment we are renting is owned by a formidable woman named Esmerelda, who carries her rosary beads like a weapon. With hips that fill a doorway and lines so deep between her brows, she is not someone to be trifled with. She stood in the tiny makeshift kitchen that consists of little more than a sink and hotplate when we first arrived, reeling off a long list of rules (all in French, none of which I understood but Antoine said were mainly about no parties and no cats), all the while looking me up and down. Her gaze rested on the third finger of my left hand, before she disappeared with a curt 'bon', followed by a door slammed shut.

Antoine has told me I can stay for as long as I want, or at least until I finish my book. He isn't charging me a penny in rent and sleeps on the sofa, whilst I get the (rather lumpy) bed. All I have to give in return is my agreement to go along with the lie he has told – that we are, in fact, engaged to be married. He says we can have a massive row whenever I feel the time has come for me to leave. That he will accept full responsibility for cheating on me with a woman called Sophia. He is obsessed with Sophia Loren, and often steals my block of mascara to paint flicks on his upper lids, then marches up and down the full length of the apartment (which takes twenty steps at most), muttering indecipherable Italian, which I suspect is nothing more than swear words and nonsense.

I'm not used to such a way of life. With no responsibility, no demands on my time. Free to come and go as I please. To fill my days with long, lazy walks along the seafront. Staring at the mixture of boats – some old, some new, some battered and worn, others pristine and clinical.

Only I'm not very good at doing nothing. Clearly I won't end up a trophy wife, sipping champagne on one of those yachts with a sugar daddy for a husband (Antoine, on the other hand, would slot into that lifestyle without so much as a moment's hesitation). So I've found myself a job, waitressing in the bar of one of the overpriced hotels along the coast. All I have to do is clear away empty glasses, smile at all the wealthy Americans and Englishmen who are holidaying here before heading back to the banks of New York and London. Of course, the work will dry up now the summer is fading fast, but Antoine assures me it won't be a problem as there's always someone here with money to spend.

Part of me is afraid to ask how he knows this. Part of me is afraid to ask about where he goes the nights he doesn't come home. Because I love him, but in a completely innocent way. Like siblings who bicker and fight but then laugh so much it makes my belly hurt.

He has been drawing me. I caught him the other day, watching me as I slept. He told me he's fascinated with the way our faces change when we're no longer trying to hide. When we are back to being our true selves, not constrained by the social niceties we project every second of every day.

He is putting together an exhibition and I fear I'm going to be at the centre of it all, but he won't let me in the studio (it's nothing more than a lean-to out back, which reminds me of my dad's old shed at the bottom of the garden). Says he cannot show anyone until it is ready. In the meantime, he's been charming all the local galleries, trying to find someone to take a chance on the complete unknown.

He did let me in the studio once, when he was working on a commission for some grande dame who took a shine to him in Paris, asked him to send her something fabulous, as long as it wasn't a nude. He painted a group of men playing boules in the small park just behind the harbour. All flat caps, linen shirts and braces, with rolled-up cigarettes between their teeth and a lifetime of memories, of the horrors they witnessed during the war. Said it was his way of putting the truth on her wall, even if she was too rich and privileged to ever truly understand what that was.

I sat and watched him paint, which is like nothing I've ever seen before. The way he allows it to consume him, to become a part of him. Trusting that the picture, the idea, he holds in his mind, will be freed by the stroke of brush on canvas.

It was his idea for me to type with my eyes shut. To push away all the doubts, to allow the muse to flourish. So every night after my shift at the hotel, I have been coming back here to type, with a bottle of red wine, some cheese and a baguette to keep me going. Only there was something about tonight. About the fullness of the moon, surrounded by stars reflected back tenfold into the sea, that made my mind too distracted, too sad, to write.

Part of me knows I came here to try and spite Noah. Because he's jealous of Antoine, and I let it happen, encouraged it even. He so rarely showed me how he felt, let alone said it. All those nights wrapped up in each other's arms. Sharing our bodies, sharing our desires. You'd think that would be how to get close to someone. But more fool me, because every time, every single time, I would wake to find him gone. Discover him the next evening flirting with someone new.

Gigi never liked him. She's arriving next week and has

already written to say she wants me to go with her, back to Italy. She's met someone, a chef who has made her fall in love with food all over again. Claims she's worried about getting fat and him no longer fancying her, but that's such a ridiculous idea and so I told her that if he can't see beyond all her curves and lips, to the incredible person she is, then he doesn't deserve for her to love him.

I don't know if I will go with her. I don't know if I left Paris simply because it reminds me of Noah, or if I have changed enough to be ready to venture somewhere new. I feel so different to the shy girl who stepped off the train in London. The one with eyes like saucers as I looked all around, so naïve, so trusting.

But part of me wants to stay here. To hide my loneliness away in the hilltops with my fake fiancé, books and French wine.

Last night, Antoine cooked me paella, insisting that I would love it, even the strips of squid (they were delicious, and even better when dipped in garlic mayonnaise). He was telling me about how jellyfish change colour according to whatever it is they have eaten – his brain is like an enormous vault of information, even he can't remember where he's learnt it all.

I asked him if there were jellyfish in the paella and he swatted at my hand, told me no, he'd been talking to someone who wants to sponsor his work, his passion, who also knew a lot about the creatures of the sea. Of course I wanted to know who this mysterious benefactor was, and what he wanted in return, but Antoine offered up no more than a sly smile, which told me everything and more.

He needs to be careful. I need to be careful for him. Because the world is changing, but not fast enough, and there are people who I fear would not be so accepting of his ways, even here. Perhaps Gigi and I could stay a while longer, keep him safe from prying eyes and minds. For although he is beautiful, and although he may be quite possibly the smartest person I will ever meet, I know all too well that love can make you do stupid, reckless things.

CMR

13

COCKEREL

Gallus gallus domesticus

'Shit,' Tyler said, looking at his watch, pacing back and forth, staring once again at the 'Closed' sign on the gallery door.

'It's Sunday,' Emily whispered. She couldn't believe they were so stupid not to check whether a museum would be open on a Sunday.

'He might not even be here,' Tyler said, facing her, hands on hips and a look in his eyes she couldn't translate.

'You Googled him.' She pushed at his chest, kicked at her suitcase, was tempted to pick up his guitar and smash it against the wall of the museum, again and again until it splintered beyond repair.

Seven hours, she thought to herself. Seven hours on a train and then another two on a sweltering bus, trapped by the stench of men who seemed to forget what water and soap were for. She should have stayed in Paris.

She could have visited the Louvre, discovered some more of where it was her grandmother spent her first summer away from home. Or gone back to the art shop, bought some supplies, then sat in the Jardin des Tuileries and drawn all that she could see. Why couldn't she have stayed a few days more, walked all the way up to the Sacre Coeur, wandered around Montmartre where so many artists before her once lived?

Because there was an invisible egg timer in the back of her mind. Slowly pouring out grains of sand, each one representing another moment that she would no longer have to get to the end of her so-called adventure.

The idea of it all, that she could even contemplate staying in Paris, terrified her. But there was a small part of her, a voice that had been ignored for oh-so-long, the one that had been trying to get her to pay attention to herself, to her secrets and dreams, which was shouting a little louder. Asking Emily to remember what it felt like to experience something new.

'You're right,' Tyler sighed as he leant against the wall and closed his eyes.

Emily had forgotten about this side of him. The side which looked for penitence even when it wasn't due. The boy who was so adept at making people feel sorry for him, despite all the advantages he possessed.

It's Sunday, she thought again. A day of rest. One for roast beef with all the trimmings, the smell of which would hit them as they opened the back door on their return from church with the bells still ringing clear and true. A day for long walks along the beach, sharp winds in winter to blow all the cobwebs away, as her grandmother used to say, then back to sit and tackle the crossword with a mug of tea and a pile of home-made cookies.

Except they didn't taste the same without her. Nothing tasted, or sounded, or felt the same since she had died. Even before that, when she was given her final diagnosis, decided to forgo further treatment, chose instead to go graciously, whatever the hell that meant.

What were her Sundays now, other than a mess of thoughts she had no idea what to do with? And where did all the days go? How did it come to the end of another week without her even noticing?

'Wait here,' Tyler said and she watched with a tilt of her head as he picked up their suitcases. 'I'll drop the bags at the hotel, then we can go and grab something to eat.'

'I'm not hungry.' Emily heard her muttered response, berating herself for acting like a petulant child. But he was the one who had insisted on leaving when they did. Tyler had been the one to book a train ticket without even asking if it was okay with her. He was the one in such a hurry to leave Paris and now they were here. In another town where her grandmother had once lived, long before Emily was born.

Retracing her steps, Emily followed the narrow street out towards a harbour lined with designer stores and overpriced restaurants. Beyond the super yachts, she could just make out the Maures mountains, thought how much quieter life would be over there.

What made you stay? she wondered as she walked along the quayside, looked up to watch the clouds roll by. She saw a handful of birds that dipped and turned through the blue and followed them as they flew up and over the harbour wall. In the distance she could see a round, stone structure, on top of which was an unflagged ship's mast.

Two rusted anchors were lain together on the rocks that

separated land from sea. The horizon was lined with boats and overhead a plane was leaving a line of white as it headed north. Climbing across the rocks, she sat, took off her shoes and stared out at nothing at all.

Why am I here? she asked all over again as she tried to figure out what it was her grandmother wanted her to see, to understand, about that specific part of her life. Why she sent her pages from a diary that Emily had no idea even existed, instead of simply telling her everything in person, before she died.

She imagined the ghost of a life once lived, somewhere within this place. A young woman with a bruised heart, seeking shelter with a man who loved her in the safest possible way.

It was about him. The thought came to her, pure and simple. The first book her grandmother ever published was about the love between a man and a woman that never quite was.

'Everyone deserves to be loved at least once in each lifetime,' she whispered the first line of the novel, then skimmed through the story in her mind. It was centred around the broken promises of a man who needed to hide his real identity from a society not yet ready to hear the truth. Promises he made to a woman so in need of love, who deserved more than what he offered her. A woman who finally learnt how to let go of the things she could not control.

'Antoine was your muse.' She shook her head at the idea, smiled as she imagined her grandmother living in this place, writing down a story so closely tied to her reality.

It's what her grandmother had always done. Linking real

life to the stories, showing Emily that there was always a way to imagine something more.

'There you are.' Tyler was stood, holding onto one of the anchors, a little out of breath. 'I'd forgotten you have a habit of disappearing.'

'No, I don't,' Emily replied as she got to her feet, slipped back on her shoes and hopped across the rocks.

'Oh, really?' Tyler dropped one arm around her shoulder, bumped his hip against her own. 'What about that time in the Natural History Museum?'

She shrugged herself free from him, went over to peruse the menu from one of the indistinguishable restaurants lining the harbour. Emily barely registered the letters and words on the page as she tried to swallow away the disappointment she could not be rid of.

'How about a drink?' Tyler nodded in the direction of a bar, above which hung a bright green shamrock.

The covered space outside was simple, with a stone floor, a handful of tables and a beer keg in one corner, around which two men were stood, nursing their pints of stout. Inside was more cave than room, with low ceilings covered in shingle, from which hung a line of plastic flags. A wooden bar ran the full length of one wall, on top of which was a machine made from copper pipes fashioned together into some sort of pump.

Emily's eye landed on an old-fashioned jukebox, the kind with vinyl records and strips of rainbow light. The whole space smelt of stale beer, sun cream and a thin layer of fish, accompanied by the low, nasal voice of Liam Gallagher singing about cigarettes and alcohol.

'Whisky?' Tyler asked as Emily climbed atop one of the

stools against the other wall and she nodded her reply, trying not to think of what the vicar would say if he knew where she was right this minute.

A tower of beer mats stacked one on top of the other, resting on the edge of the bar. Tyler smacked the back of his fingers against the underside, sent them spilling into the air and then all over the floor.

Emily spun one between her fingers, saw a flash of red cockerel with each turn, making her think of the packets of cereal in the cupboards back home.

The cockerel is the only bird in the Chinese zodiac calendar, seen as both confident and intelligent. She considered whether or not to tell Tyler the random snippet of information as well as trying to remember how it was she knew it in the first place.

Just like Antoine. A man who was a walking, talking encyclopedia, according to her grandmother, which made her wonder if she had inherited her artistry, her obsessive nature from him?

Except she couldn't quite believe that Antoine and her grandmother had produced a love child as well as a phony engagement. That would have been extreme, even for her.

Tossing the beer mat into a woven basket with a solitary chip stuck to its side, she picked up her empty glass and added it to the collection they had been accumulating over the past couple of hours.

'So who is this Antoine guy?' Tyler asked as he signalled to the barman for another round of drinks. 'Were he and Aunt Cat really engaged?'

'You read her diary.'

'I did.'

'Show me yours,' she said, holding out her hand.

'My what?'

'Notebook. You saw mine, read hers, it's only fair I see yours.'

For a second she thought he wasn't going to comply. Would perhaps claim he left it back at the hotel, but she knew it was in the inside pocket of his jacket even before he reached to where it hung over a neighbouring stool and handed it over.

Opening it to a random page, she frowned as she read, trying to make out some of the words.

'Your handwriting is awful.'

'You sound like my primary school teacher.'

Emily stifled a giggle. 'It's like a drunken spider making its way across each line.'

'If you're going to be mean,' he said, reaching across for the book, but she batted his hand away.

He had written a song about the falling leaves of autumn, likened them to the people of your life, the ones you have to let go. There was another about the cruel hand of fate, that pulls you away from what your heart desires most of all. Not exactly Proust, but the sentiment was clear. Emily could see more, sense what was hidden in between all the letters and words Tyler wasn't quite brave enough to say.

She could see the blame he threw at his parents' feet, for forcing him to be a certain kind of man, to live a certain kind of life. But he always had a choice. He could have said no.

Did she have a choice? Or was she complicit in allowing her grandmother to make all of her choices for her?

'What do you think?' He sat there, waiting for a reaction, a small comment to spur him on. Just as she did whenever she first showed her grandmother her art.

She closed the notebook, tapped one finger on the plain, black cover and imagined what she would paint on it to reveal the person hidden within. A mountainscape, perhaps, through which a river runs. With a waterfall made from crystal droplets of sound, each one representing a part of his soul, a part of the pain he thought he had felt.

'Isn't country music just like church music?'

'I'm offended,' he said, with hand on heart but a smile on his face.

'It is. They both blame someone else for all of life's problems.'

The waiter came over, put down two more glasses and gathered away the empties.

Tyler took several, slow sips, then licked his lips and leant towards her.

'That's a bit deep for a Sunday night, don't you think?'

Emily fished out a cube of ice, sucked away the whisky, then crunched the rest between her back teeth, felt the absence of sensation on one side of her face, where the nerves had never quite healed. She pictured a well, at the bottom of which sat a boy, trapped by his past, by his mistakes. Waiting for someone to throw down a rope and set him free.

'I'm not saying there's no power in music.'

'Exactly,' Tyler said, raising his glass in a toast. 'Think of how much more you feel when watching a film, a TV programme, because of the music. *Psycho* was originally shown to audiences without the infamous score and they weren't scared, not even a little bit.'

Emily gave a small shudder. 'I always pull back the shower screen to make sure there's no one there.'

'Really?' He raised his eyebrows.

It had crept up on her, like a birthday surprise. The way he had covered her sorrow with a web of friendship. Little by little, something new growing from something old that before had never been given a chance to breathe.

'Anyway, music and religion are both about expressing what is too difficult to explain,' Tyler said. 'In fact, isn't that what painting is too? Surely you can relate to that?'

'You can't equate Dolly Parton with God.'

'Yes, I can, Dolly Parton is a genius,' he said, waving his pint at her and sluicing a little over his jeans. 'And I dare you to deny that you know all the words to "9 to 5".'

She could already hear it in her head, and smiled.

'You have a nice smile.'

She looked back down at the beer mat on the table, desperate for a change of subject.

'Did you know that a cockerel's testicles are influenced by the sun?'

Tyler nearly dropped his pint. 'Come again?'

'It's true. They shrink and grow with the seasons.'

He laughed, shaking his head and making the sound bounce off the low ceiling. 'Alcohol clearly loosens your tongue.'

'Maybe it just stops me from caring so much about what people think.'

He was looking at her again, in that way she couldn't quite make sense of. As if she were some kind of anomaly. A person who did not quite tally with the image he had carried around in his head for so long.

'Do you have any traditions?' he asked.

'Like Christmas?'

'More a good luck charm. Or a way of making yourself remember a certain person, a particular day.'

Emily always said goodnight to her parents. She would touch her lips to her fingers, then place them on the window-pane in her room every night before she went to sleep. Gaze out at the heavens, seeking out a star and sending a wish to her parents, wherever they may be. A tiny ladybird kept in a box, in a treasure chest under her bed. Along with a four leaf clover, a bumble bee and a chain of daisies. From a summer long ago.

Traditions? No. Memories? More than she wanted.

'Here.' Tyler reached into the front pocket of his jeans, took out a small paper bag and slid it along the bar to her.

'What's this?' No one ever bought her anything, other than her grandmother, but she didn't really count.

'Call it a reminder of this trip.'

Emily reached inside the paper bag, took out a pair of earrings in the shape of golden stars.

'Thank you.'

'I saw them in Paris and thought they would suit you. Bring out the flecks of gold in your eyes.'

She had no idea how to respond to his kindness.

'I need to tell you something.'

Emily felt her throat tighten at his words.

'There's more than one reason why I'm here.'

Emily swirled her drink around the glass, avoided look-ing at Tyler as he spoke. She heard him take a deep breath, steeling himself for what he was about to say, and she was grateful for his nerves, because it meant that he did care, if only a little.

'Dad cut me out.'

'Your mum said she convinced him not to.'

'Not entirely. At least, not until I can prove to him I'm not a total loser.'

Emily considered his response, allowing the truth to settle in her mind before replying.

'So it's about money.'

'Yes. No. I mean at first, for sure. But I've really enjoyed getting to know you again and Paris was fun, wasn't it?'

She tried to stifle a smile as she found herself to be nowhere near as angry, or disappointed, as she might have been only days before.

What's changed? she wondered. Was it really as simple as sharing a moment, creating a memory with someone new?

'Thank you,' she said, daring a look at him, finding those eyes already on her.

'For what?'

'Telling me the truth.'

He gave a small nod in response and for a moment she thought he was about to say something more, but then the song on the jukebox changed, the soft, full voice of Patsy Cline spilling into the bar, and Tyler stood, held out his hand in invitation.

There was an awakening in every part of her body as he moved closer and she felt the charge between them, tried to capture the moment in her mind, like a photograph she could look at in years to come. The rawness of her emotion was intense, yet invisible, but she knew he could see it, just as she could see his. Then a sudden change of his features, as if he remembered the way he should be behaving, and he pulled away.

The air vibrated with rejection even before he opened his mouth to speak.

'It's late,' he said, glancing at his watch by way of explanation. 'Do you want to go back to the hotel?'

'I'm not tired.' Emily shouldered her bag and walked out of the bar, leaving the echoes of 'Crazy' and all that nearly was contained within its walls.

Everything was wrapped up in the night. Couples holding tight to one another as they weaved through the back streets and kissed in doorways. The constant clink of glasses, laughter and music that spilled from all the bars and restaurants she passed, not stopping to imagine how it could have been her. Nor to breathe in the happiness, the normality, enjoyed by so many. Something that seemed to elude her, to leave her be.

An elderly man was walking his dog, one hand around its leash, the other holding onto a twisted, wooden cane. He stopped at a low stone pillar around which a rope was tied, bent down to ruffle behind the dog's ears, then nodded his head in greeting to her.

A pair of strangers, sharing the night air.

He was no doubt one of those people who always had to work for a living, really work, not just push numbers about on a screen or paint pretty pictures. People who had called this place home for generations, who were here long after the tourists went home. Who filled in all the blanks and tidied up after those too entitled, too rich to notice, were gone.

Emily walked alongside the water, all the boats with their ostentatious displays of wealth, to where a set of steps led down to the narrow beach, slowly being eaten away by the incoming tide.

Toes in the ocean, she stood, thinking of how her

grandmother had spent every summer in various places along the coast of France. Four months from June through to the end of September, renting an apartment somewhere in the seaside towns. She claimed it was because the air was good for her disposition, but now Emily understood it was also because the sea made her happy, that it was a link back to that first summer, when she found what she needed to write.

She gave it all up to care for me, Emily thought, and the idea made her feel so incredibly sad and grateful, all at the same time.

'It smells the same.' Tyler scuffed the sand with his feet, disturbing a tiny crab that scuttled back to the sea. 'It wasn't here we came though, was it?'

'No,' Emily shook her head and pointed a finger west along the coast. She could still picture the villa they always rented: enormous and white, with a pool perched at the edge of a cliff, the water so blue it felt like swimming through a filter. The two families had spent their summers exploring the shoreline on speedboats, lazing by the side of the pool, fattening themselves up on fresh seafood and Tarte Tatin, all prepared by those brought in to cook, all tidied away by maids with frilly aprons who spoke not a word of English.

Emily watched a fisherman sort his nets and ready his boat for another night on the water.

'Do you remember the year Aunt Cat took us fishing?'

'We dove for oysters,' Emily said with a smile as she remembered being shaken awake before the dawn had broken, cycling down the hill, stretching her legs out either side, squealing as Tyler let go of his handlebars, all of them singing ABBA at the top of their lungs. Feeling so free, so alive, and knowing it was a day she would never, ever forget.

'It was a boat barely big enough for two,' Tyler replied. 'But she rowed the three of us out of the harbour, all the way round to a small cove, where a heap of other boats were, all of them empty.'

'Then told us to grab a mask before being the first to jump off the side.'

He was looking at her with amusement, then shook away whatever he was about to say, picked up a stone and examined it quickly before tossing it into the sea, where it skipped and hopped, once, twice more.

'My mother was so angry with her.'

'Why?'

'The smell lingered for days, no matter how hard she scrubbed at my fingers and toes. She even threw my shoes in the bin.'

Emily wondered at what point someone changes. If you're surrounded by money, at what point do you begin to care for it so? Tyler's mother was someone who wore her wealth with pride. Who went to great lengths to project just the right image to anyone who bothered to look. How much of that affected Tyler and the choices he made? How much of anyone's life was determined by the family they were born into?

But it never changed the way her grandmother chose to live, even when all the zeroes began to appear on the bank statements and the royalty cheques tumbled through the letter box. They could have bought half the village and still had money to spare, or moved back here, to where her grandmother wrote her first ever book, and lived an altogether different kind of life.

She had done it for her, for Emily, thinking she was better off, staying in Norfolk.

Emily brushed sand from her feet as she stepped back onto the quay, then looked to the rows of silent boats moored in the harbour, heard the quiet ting of a dozen bells as their hulls were rocked by the approaching tide.

It was so easy for something to become a habit, if you didn't question your life or surroundings. How simple it could be to wake up one day and realise you'd been existing in a halted state, that you allowed it to happen by hiding from the change which allowed experience, to actually live.

'That was my favourite day. The best day from all the summers put together.' Tyler was next to her now, she could feel the heat from his skin through the thin fabric of his shirt and she turned to look at him, saw his attention caught by someone further along the quayside, waving in their direction. 'Emily, I...' He began to speak, took a step away, ran one hand through hair speckled with salt. 'I meant to tell you about her.'

Emily watched a young woman approach. She was wearing a lilac cotton dress that showed off long, tanned limbs, with blonde hair that seemed to shimmer in the evening light. Her eyes were blue, her teeth were white. She was perfect, and she was wrapping herself around Tyler, kissing him long and slow.

14

FLAMINGO

Phoenicopterus

Emily was stood, staring up at a set of iron gates, beyond which she could just about see the roof of a vast mansion. A house which the gallery manageress had informed her belonged to Antoine Marchand and that he would be at home and was expecting her. Emily had declined her offer of a lift, nor did she want her to ring ahead, to let Monsieur know she was on her way.

Instead, Emily had decided to walk. Out from the centre of the town, along the edge of the park, with trees on one side, houses hidden by high walls on the other. It gave her time to think about what best to do next. It gave her time to realise, to accept, that Tyler wasn't here for her after all.

It turned out his girlfriend worked in Cannes, in the bar of some fancy-pants hotel. She had simply hopped in a taxi after her shift to come and meet them. Emily wished it wasn't the same one her grandmother had worked in, didn't want there to be a connection between her and Tyler's girlfriend.

All the excitement she had felt about being here, with him, had fizzled away as she lay on another unfamiliar bed, listening to the sound of the sea and trying not to cry as she thought about how far away from home she was, from everything she had ever known.

The sight of him with someone else was enough to make Emily's stomach turn. The soft hand that reached out to say hello, to introduce herself as Phoebe and she was ever so pleased to meet her, Tyler had told her so much about how they used to be friends, had practically grown up together.

Which was why Emily hadn't bothered to leave a note this morning, to tell him where she was going. Not that he and Phoebe had emerged from their room, even long after breakfast had been tidied away, and she had sat at the table, alone, smiling politely at the waiter when he asked again if anyone would be joining her.

Emily scuffed at a patch of earth in a flower bed by the gates, watching as an ant scuttled out of sight. She wished she could tunnel into the ground below, become a mole, blind to all she could see, all she had seen.

Because she didn't want to see the way they had leant close to one another on the walk back to the hotel, didn't want to see Phoebe gaze up at him with such longing in her eyes when he asked the man at reception for the keys to their rooms. Nor did she want to see them step out of the lift and turn down the corridor, a last-minute call of goodnight tossed over their shoulders out of habitual politeness.

Rubbing her fingertips over the nameplate next to the bell that would call forth the person she had been sent to find,

Emily screwed her eyes shut, tried to block out the picture of Tyler's face.

She hated that she could remember, in intricate detail, the first time he had kissed her. A summer's night, a stolen moment behind the seats of an outdoor theatre. When Shakespeare's words called out to them and he bent his mouth to hers. They were on the cusp of adulthood, hormones and the trick of dappled evening light playing tricks with their hearts. A smile on her lips on the walk home, bumping hips as they went. A hushed goodnight, then back to her bed where she lay awake, wishing upon wish she could go back and do it all again.

The very next day, when all of life stretched ahead of her, every ounce of happiness from that night was crushed beneath the wheels of a speeding truck.

Do I go in? she thought, looking again at the name on the bell. If she did, nothing would be the same and everything was already so changed, so altered, from what she was used to, that she wasn't sure she could handle any more surprises, or disappointments. She was sure Antoine wasn't her grandfather, and yet a small part of her hoped that he might be, that she was here to find some leftover piece of her family, some smattering of normality, whatever it might be.

The idea to turn around and go home was tempting. But if she went home she would spend the rest of her life wondering what if? Sometimes she loved that nothing ever changed, but sometimes the idea of every single tomorrow being the same became unbearable.

Even if she somehow managed to cobble together a life for herself – Charlie would help her, surely? – Emily knew she would never be able to stop wondering what it was her grandmother had sent her to find, and if Antoine was the key to it all.

If only she could talk to her grandmother, have her tell her what to do.

The sound of a small motorbike came climbing up the hill towards her. A soft *phut-phut* of exhaust as the engine began to slow.

'*Ça va?*'

Emily opened her eyes to see someone step off a white Lambretta. She waited as he removed the sunglasses from his face, hand frozen in the air for a few seconds before he smiled to reveal a gap between his two front teeth.

'Emily!' he cried, pulling her close with tears in his eyes and whispering her name over and over.

In any normal circumstances, being hugged by a stranger would make Emily rigid, uncomfortable, but there was something about this man which instead made her wrap her arms around him and hug him back. It was like something out of a corny love story, only he was old and gay and she was young(ish) and anything but beautiful.

'Let me look at you. Oh my,' Antoine said as he stepped back, one hand to his mouth, the other holding onto his bike. 'Oh my,' he said again, tapping a code into the keypad on the wall and the gates slowly hummed to life, opening wide to reveal what lay beyond. 'Welcome to my humble abode,' he said, stepping aside to let Emily through.

Humble wasn't exactly the word Emily would have used to describe Antoine's home. Opulent, gigantic, a little bit ostentatious even, but it was fabulous. Palm trees lined the flagstone driveway, the walls of the house were palest pink with terracotta tiles on the roof and olive green shutters on the windows.

The front door was opened by a woman dressed in a pale grey maid's outfit, who took Antoine's helmet and keys, then promptly disappeared. Inside, there was a crystal chandelier hanging from the double-height reception hall, with a staircase that wrapped around both sides, and in the middle was a view straight out to manicured gardens, an infinity pool and the ocean beyond.

There was also a painting of Catriona Robinson, hanging on the wall right next to where Emily was stood.

Emily became quiet and still, aware of the man next to her, watching her with a mixture of intrigue and excitement. She could tell by the way he kept stepping towards her, opening his mouth as if to say something, then thinking better of it and moving away again.

It stayed this way for several minutes, but Emily couldn't break the silence. Couldn't bring herself to look away from the portrait of her grandmother sat on a padded window seat, reading a copy of *The Picture of Dorian Gray*. Her hair was tied at the back of her neck, a few wayward curls finding their way loose as always. Her lips were parted gently, as if she were reading some of Wilde's words to herself, and her face was at peace, content. It was a look Emily recognised, even on a face that had sagged and folded with age.

'She's beautiful.'

'She looks just like you.'

Emily's hand strayed to her scar, covering it with her palm, and she shook her head in response.

'You painted it, in 1965?'

'She told you?'

'In a way.' She didn't know whether to tell him about all the diary entries. Wasn't yet sure how much she wanted to share.

'It is all because of her,' he said as he nodded at the painting. 'My crazy Catriona, my muse, my beloved. She was the one who inspired such a fury in me, a desire to put that face onto canvas, for the whole world to see.'

'It's incredible.' The way he had captured the light on her face, the look in her eye, with only a few strokes of brush. Emily stepped forward, wanted to try and understand how he had accomplished such detail with so little paint.

'It belongs to you.'

'Me?'

'She bought it many years ago. Sent it back to me on the condition that, one day, I should pass it on to you.'

'I don't understand.'

Antoine looped his arm around Emily, drew her close and placed a kiss on her head. Then he took her chin in his hands, turned her head to the light, exposing her scar, but she didn't pull away, found she didn't want to hide, not from him. He made her feel at ease, the same way he had Catriona. A gift of sorts, one that was impossible to explain or describe.

'I think she wanted you to understand that happiness isn't ever constant.' He cupped her face with both hands. 'That summer was magical in so many ways, but it also nearly destroyed her.'

'You mean Noah.'

'You know about Noah.' It wasn't a question, accompanied only by a small nod of his head as he moved to the back of the house, taking Emily by the hand and walking out onto the terrace.

Two bright ceramic flamingos stood guard by the pool as Emily shielded her eyes and looked across the coastline of Sainte-Maxime, tiny dots of white that interspersed the green. There was the faintest of winds, carrying the scent of the sea and of lavender from the various bushes dotted around the garden.

'Lavender always makes me think of Catriona.' Antoine twirled a lock of Emily's hair through his fingers, then handed over a glass of iced tea from a tray that had miraculously appeared on a nearby table. He took a sip from his own drink, regarding her over the rim.

'Why did she leave?' Emily held her glass with both hands, registered the shiver along her spine in response to the chill.

'Right to the point.' Antoine gave a small chuckle. 'Just like her.'

'Because of Noah?'

'He was an utter bastard. Playing with her emotions, her love, as if it were something she would give to just about anybody.'

'But did they ever...?' Emily left the question hanging, unsure whether or not she wanted to know the answer. To find out if her grandfather was the man responsible for causing so much pain.

'I expect so, but she never did speak to me about him after she left. Knew how much I disapproved.'

He was hiding something. She could tell by the curve of his shoulder, the fact he took another sip of his drink before answering.

'Where is he now?'

'Your guess is as good as mine, my dear. Noah and I were never what you would call friends. Oh,' he said, registering

184

the way Emily's body slumped at his words. 'You're disappointed. Why would you be?'

There was no need to finish the question, because he had seen the way Emily scrutinised every detail of his face when she was stood outside the gates, watching him in silence. He had seen the tilt of her head as she listened to him speak, felt the sharp intake of breath, the tightness with which she hugged him back. All of this and more made him realise what is was she had hoped to find.

'She left because of me.' He gave a short sniff, wiped at the corner of one eye, then tossed his head in annoyance. 'I was stupid enough to ask her to stay.'

'Why was that stupid?'

'She was like a caged animal here. Always prowling, always on the hunt for more.'

'More?'

'Of everything,' he said, spreading his arms wide and nearly knocking over one of the flamingos. 'Of life, of love, of loss. She needed inspiration and there's only so much you can glean from a town filled with nothing but vacuous rich people.'

'And you.'

A small smile as he gave her arm a playful squeeze. 'And me. I was young, in love, and selfish. I thought I could only stay if she was here too, protecting me.'

Emily knew better than to ask for details of something from so long ago. From a man who clearly meant the world to her grandmother, even if they had drifted apart.

'You're Sebastian.' It wasn't a question. Nor was it an accusation, more her way of showing him that she understood, because she had read her grandmother's first book, as well as her diary. She was telling him he didn't need to reveal anything about himself, or the man he had fallen in love with.

'Clever as well as beautiful. Why am I anything but surprised?'

Emily looked up, watched as a pair of sparrows flew down from one of the palm trees, squabbling like siblings as they landed on the grass. She approached them slowly, bent down to avoid startling them and they hopped apart. One flew away, the other regarded her a moment, watched as she took a slice of apple from her glass and held it out.

The little bird jumped forward, took a bite, then jumped back again.

'It's OK,' Emily whispered, breaking the apple into pieces and scattering them on the ground.

'They trust you,' Antoine said, watching her, watching the bird.

'I like birds.'

'Why?'

No one had ever asked her why.

'Their simplicity?' She turned her face to him, saw the sparrow fly up to land on the roof.

'No, birds are anything but simple. Take my friend the flamingo over there.' He pointed to one of the ceramic sculptures wearing a shiny top hat. 'Did you know that they are only pink because of a chemical reaction that occurs in their body due to the specific type of algae that they eat?'

'Did you learn that from the same person who taught you about jellyfish?'

Antoine frowned, then opened his mouth wide as he realised what she was referring to. 'She told you.'

'I've read her diary from that summer.'

'She kept a diary? She never told me, the minx. Am I in it? I suppose I must be.'

'She wrote about why she came here.' Emily realised it was because of Antoine, and Noah, and the way she had felt trapped because of her love for them both.

'I had to hide who I was, for so long.' He looked towards the house, and Emily thought he seemed to be looking back in time. Trying to pick up on a memory, a feeling, that was no longer with him. 'But I never hid from her. She always accepted people for who they were on the inside, no matter what other people thought.' He seemed sad, as if he too understood what it meant to lose someone special, someone who was his whole world.

'I wish I'd known her back then.'

'She was glorious, simply glorious. My late partner, Jean-Christophe, told me she was the wife I never had. Told me I was an idiot for letting her go.'

Jean-Christophe. Someone who wasn't there. Emily could sense the absence all around her, saw the memory of him in Antoine's eyes. She reached out for his hand and he took it, gave it a gentle squeeze. To touch someone, to bridge that infinite divide, was something so uncharacteristic of her, so unexpected, that she didn't realise what she had done until he let go and the air around her skin registered what was no longer there.

'I like their freedom.' She looked to the sky, searched out the birds as was so often her go-to, her escape from dealing with what was happening there and then.

'Do you wish you could be free?'

'I don't even know what it means.'

'Free from this?' He reached out for her scar, then put his

hand on her heart. 'So much inside, so many scars you don't let anyone see. No doubt you learnt that from her.'

Emily felt her insides tighten.

'Do you think she ever told Noah how she really felt? Do you think she ever took the leap of faith that was needed to be happy? Even after Margot was born, she refused to ask for help from anyone, even me. Insisted on doing everything by herself. Said she certainly wasn't going to ask Margot's father for help.'

Emily took a long sip of her drink, tried to swallow the lump in her throat before speaking. 'Noah?'

'I suppose he could be,' Antoine replied as he handed her a silk handkerchief, pretended not to look as she wiped at her eyes. 'But she wouldn't ever say. The point is, don't be like her. Don't lock yourself away for fear of what may come spilling out. Life is too short for you not to be daring, especially when it comes to love.' He paused. 'So what's his name?'

Emily twisted the handkerchief around her hand. Antoine was little more than a stranger, yet somehow understood what she was feeling.

'He has a girlfriend.'

'They always do,' he said, looping his arm around her and taking her back inside. Up and around the staircase that climbed to the sky. 'In my experience, men like that aren't worth the hassle.'

Emily followed him into a turret room with windows on all sides, a glorious view of the coastline stretching out before her.

'My darling girl,' he said, sitting down on a chaise longue and opening a small, glass dish to reveal a sugar-laden stack of

Turkish delight. 'You deserve someone who will treat you like a queen.'

Emily put a piece of gooey deliciousness into her mouth and sucked at the sweetness as she looked around the room. It was a cacophony of objects, none of which seemed to be in quite the right place. Buckets of brushes, stacks of paper, drawers half-open with pastels and tubes of paint all chucked in at random. It seemed to suit him, more than the glitz and polish of all the money back downstairs.

'The money was never mine,' he said, as if reading her thoughts. 'I only inherited it when J-C died, but I'd give it all back in a heartbeat if I could have him instead.'

'I know what you mean.'

Emily walked around the room, noticing there were four easels, all of them faced out, each on a different point of an invisible compass. Three were covered with cloth, but the fourth was on display. It was another portrait of her grandmother, dressed all in white. She was stood in the shallows, with the ocean curling around her feet. Her face was in profile and she seemed to be looking toward somewhere just out of view.

'Where was this?'

'Nowhere. I've found myself painting her more and more, simply from memory. It helps me remember.'

'She always loved the water.' Emily stepped closer, looking at the layers of paint Antoine had used. Tiny brushstrokes to recreate the dips and lines of her grandmother's face. It was a talent she envied, to be able to capture a mood, an expression, of someone that they themselves were probably completely unaware of.

'Did you ever consider going to art school?' he asked.

'Why would I do that?' At one point she had considered it, but was too scared to try.

'You're very talented, I can see that from the illustrations in her books. But untrained. I could train you.'

'That's very kind of you, but...'

'But what? You can make your own decisions, can't you? Live wherever you want to, be whoever you want to be.'

Emily spied a well-loved copy of *L'Oiseau Bleu,* tucked away at the bottom of a pile of magazines and wondered when was the last time it had been read. If he had given it to her grandmother or the other way around. It made her see how much there was she still didn't know, or understand, about her grandmother's life, her past, what shaped her, what pushed her into becoming a single mother, a famous author. So many personas, each worn at a different point in time.

'It's not that simple,' she said, watching as Antoine opened up a large trunk with brass hinges, took out a paper package and handed it over to her.

'No, I don't suppose it is. I guess we're both rather too good at pretending to be someone else.'

'I don't pretend.'

'You're sure about that?'

Sat cross-legged on the floor, on a Persian rug with a cigarette burn in one corner, she pulled apart the paper to reveal an enormous full moon in a starlit sky. Two friends sat on a swing, legs out straight, bodies leaning back as they circled above the earth. The story was about a girl who lived in the mountains with her father. Together she and Ophelia caught stars that were made into two identical necklaces, one of which Ophelia wore and never took off.

Emily's fingers sought out the chain around her neck as she opened the front cover to read the new dedication.

For G – because you never know what's around the corner.

'Gigi's dead.' Emily frowned at the dedication.

'And?'

'How am I supposed to find a dead woman?'

Antoine popped two more cubes of Turkish delight into his mouth. 'Perhaps that's not what this is about.'

'I don't follow.' Emily pulled out a plain, white envelope, turned it over in her hand, then shut the book.

'Perhaps you're not supposed to find a person.'

'This makes no sense.' Why would she be pointed in the direction of someone who was no longer alive? It felt as if she were being deliberately set up to fail.

'Where is it you think she is asking you to go?'

Emily wore a necklace that Gigi once gifted her grandmother, inside of which was a photograph from when they were young, along with one of her parents. Which was why she never opened it, or went anywhere without it.

They had bought matching lockets in a small shop in the back streets of the last city they both spent any time in together; where they said their goodbyes, promised to see one another again soon. But Gigi died only a few years later from a brain haemorrhage and Emily had always hated the idea of her grandmother not knowing that she had so little time left.

'Rome,' she said with conviction, as there was a faint knock on the door and the housemaid entered, telling Monsieur that there was a young couple at the front gate, asking for Emily.

15

GOOSE

Anser indicus

Sat on the terrace, where brunch had been served, Emily found herself unable to eat, to take her eyes away from Tyler and Phoebe, who were helping themselves to Antoine's hospitality. She kept wising she had a magical swing that would take her somewhere, anywhere, but here.

The two of them had come blustering in, full of apologies and contrition for oversleeping, for not being there when Emily had gone to the gallery. Tyler had even gone so far as to blame her for not owning a mobile, then had the clemency to shut up when he spied the portrait of Catriona. Phoebe had gushed about how amazing, gorgeous, spectacular the house was, how lucky Antoine was to live in such a beautiful setting. She hadn't stopped talking since stepping foot inside, her enthusiasm only going up a notch when she saw the pool and the view.

'I can't quite believe it,' Phoebe said, lifting another forkful of smoked salmon to her lips. 'I mean, it's just so incredible when you think about it. A magical treasure trail set up by *the* Catriona Robinson. A secret quest to discover her unfinished manuscript. It's like some sort of film.'

'You told her?' Emily glared at Tyler, unsurprised to find him looking anywhere but across the table at her.

'Tyler told me everything,' Phoebe went on, popping another slither of fish into her mouth. Licked the lemon juice from her fingers as she smiled up at her beloved.

'I wouldn't say that,' Tyler shifted in his chair, took a sip of coffee.

'What would you say?' Antoine stirred his own drink, lifted the cup to his mouth. Emily imagined rays of fire emerging from his pupils, pointed at Tyler, like a recalcitrant superhero. The idea of him strutting around in pants and a cape was enough to make her smile, make her forget how angry she was, if only for a moment.

Antoine was also smiling, aiming those pearly whites at Tyler. To the untrained eye he would appear as nothing more than the perfect host. Welcoming, warm and funny, with an uncanny ability to make everyone around him feel at ease. But Emily had confided in him, only a little, so he knew that the handsome young man sat at the table, eating his food and enjoying the view, wasn't necessarily someone to be trusted.

'I had to explain what I was doing in the South of France.'

'What are you doing here?' Emily asked him, wishing he had turned around and gone back home instead of following her. Instead of taking his responsibilities seriously simply because it suited his own selfish needs.

'Is this the next clue?' Phoebe picked up the book Antoine

had given Emily, without asking, and began to flick through the pages. 'I absolutely loved this one when I was younger,' she said, looking up to smile at Emily, seemingly oblivious to her irritation. 'The idea of being able to soar through the sky on a magical swing. To visit the moon, come back with stars in your pockets. It's just amazing.'

Emily looked down to find Antoine's hand on her own, making her let go of the fork she didn't realise she was gripping.

'Emily thinks the next clue is in Rome.'

'What makes you think that?' Tyler's interest had been piqued, enough for him to actually look Emily in the eye, for the first time since his insipid girlfriend had arrived, unannounced, and put herself firmly in the middle of it all.

'Rome,' Phoebe said with an extravagant sigh, leaning into Tyler and stroking his cheek. 'It's just the most amazing city. Although the Colosseum is a little gruesome. My parents took us when I was a kid and my brother spent the whole time pretending I was a lion and he was a gladiator.'

Emily rolled her eyes, busied herself with tidying away some of the plates.

'It's where Gigi bought the necklace,' Antoine said, ignoring the warning look Emily gave him.

'The one you're wearing?' Phoebe leant across the table, hand outstretched, and Emily pushed back her chair to stand, to get out of her way. 'That's just amazing.'

Please stop saying amazing. Emily closed her eyes, took two long, careful breaths. *Please stop speaking altogether.*

'How do we get there?'

Emily picked up a couple of empty dishes, found them taken from her by Antoine's maid. Instead, she looked around for something else to busy herself with, to try and remove herself from the conversation. Not that she had been contributing much at all. It would seem as if her mouth, her tongue, had become tied into knots by Tyler's very presence.

Phoebe popped a strawberry in her mouth just before Emily snatched her plate away. 'I guess we drive.'

'No.' The word was out of her mouth before she'd even thought about whether or not to reply.

'But, Emily, honey,' Phoebe went on, resting her hand on Emily's arm and simpering up at her. 'The train would take forever.'

'I said no!' She slammed the plate back onto the table, watched it break clean in two before falling to the ground. 'I'm sorry,' she whispered to Antoine, then turned and marched to the end of the garden, to where a gate opened up to take her down a sandy path towards the beach.

Tyler watched her go, seemingly oblivious to Phoebe's exclamation about how she was only trying to help. He shrugged away her touch, then crouched down and started to pick up the broken pieces of china, not saying a word as Antoine looked over at him, then followed his friend's granddaughter to the sea.

'I get it,' Antoine said, walking up behind Emily, who was throwing pebbles into the waves.

'Get what?'

'The car. The accident.'

Emily picked up some more stones, moved them around and around her palm, then sent them all soaring into the sea. 'I don't want to talk about it.'

'No. I don't suppose you do.' He wrapped an arm around her, gave her a kiss, breathed in the scent of lavender shampoo that Emily had been using ever since there was no one else to wear the memory. 'So, did Catriona ever tell you just how rich I am?'

'She didn't tell me anything about you.'

'No?' He looked hurt, and Emily felt bad for being the cause.

'She didn't tell me anything about any of you. Apart from Charlie.'

'God, she was terrifying.'

'Still is. And Gigi, who's dead.'

Antoine sighed, then gave a gentle shake of his head and grinned at Emily. 'Well, the point is I am rich. Filthy rich. Which means I have the ways and means to get you to Rome without the need for an automobile.' He took out his phone, sent a quick message, then showed her a photograph of a private jet.

'Seriously?'

'Seriously. Now, I know what you're going to say. Confined spaces and all that, which is why I'm giving you these, as a parting gift.' He took her hand, dropped into it a small, silver tin on which was hand-painted a rose. 'Take one about ten minutes before take off and it'll be like you're floating through the clouds.'

Emily opened the tin, saw half a dozen little white pills staring back. It made her picture him as some sort of dysfunctional fairy godmother. Loading her onto a private plane and stuffing her full of drugs.

'Now, there is one condition.'

Definitely a fairy godmother.

'You have to promise me that you will come back and

visit one day, very, very soon, or else I will turn up on your doorstep and never leave.'

'I'm not sure Norfolk is exactly your kind of scene,' Emily said with half a smile, her mood somehow lifted by a man who she felt as if she had known all her life.

'I'm old, darling. Boring is probably exactly what I need. Besides, I want to meet Richard, the man with the Dalmatian who made your grandmother believe once more in love.'

'Richard?'

'Ah, seems she still had some secrets left to share.'

'Too many secrets.' The question as to why her grandmother had told Antoine about Richard, but not her, is one that would haunt Emily, at least for a little while. The idea that her grandmother could possibly think she wouldn't want her to be happy in her final days. That perhaps Emily had somehow diminished her happiness by thinking only of herself, of how she would cope on her own.

'And not enough time. Speaking of which, we best get you off to the airport.'

Time, Emily thought, glancing at her watch and feeling a roll of nerves in her stomach as she once again imagined an egg timer, spilling all the remaining hours away. She tried not to think of what would happen if she couldn't finish the puzzle before it was too late. The cottage would belong to someone new. Another family who would dig up the rose beds, paint all the walls and remove any trace of who had lived there before.

It had happened when her parents died, strangers moving into what had once been her home, and Emily had always hated the idea of someone else being happy there, jealous that it couldn't be her.

'I really don't think I can.'

'Nonsense. If you've come all this way, one more little hop over the sea isn't going to be a problem. You are stronger than you think.'

'It's not the plane.' Emily looked back towards the house, to where she could see Tyler hovering by the back gate, pretending to be absorbed in his phone, but every so often his head would lift in their direction.

Antoine followed her gaze. 'She paired you up for a reason.'

He offered Emily his arm, and the two of them walked slowly up the path. Part of her wanted to stay, to hide away in Antoine's gilded palace and do nothing but paint. To learn all of his secrets and discover more about who her grandmother used to be. But she also knew that hiding was no longer the answer. She just didn't know if she had it in her to keep going, with him, with Tyler.

'I suspect he's not as bad as you fear.' Antoine tucked Emily's hair behind her ear, exposing her scar.

'Would you have said the same thing about Noah?'

'Some people are beyond redemption, my darling.'

Thousands of feet above the ground, stuck inside a metal container that was hurtling itself through the atmosphere, Emily sat, and tried to remember how to breathe. Because accepting you have no control is terrifying and the biggest, hardest thing anyone ever has to learn.

'The bar-headed goose has been heard flying across Mount Makalu, which is over 27,000 feet above sea level,' Emily whispered the words to herself as her fingers flicked against the arm of her seat.

'You OK?' Tyler watched the movement of Emily's lips,

leant forward to try and hear what it was she was muttering, but she turned her head away, lifted a tumbler of ice and whisky to her lips, allowed herself another sip.

The pills Antoine had given her were slow to take effect. The rapid beat of her heart, the way she couldn't keep her toes from tapping on the carpeted floor, all of it was making her feel decidedly uneasy.

Not to mention the very close proximity of the two lovebirds over there, so close that she could see the absence of pores, of any imperfection, on Phoebe's face. Neither of them had even asked if she could join the search, Phoebe had simply hopped on the plane, and Emily now wished she had found the courage to stand up to Tyler, to say no.

'One and a half hours,' she told herself, tried to ignore the small jolt of turbulence. Which meant there was just over an hour to go.

'I'm sorry about your parents.'

Emily looked down to see Phoebe's hand on her thigh but didn't quite have the strength to swat it away.

'I had to explain,' Tyler cleared his throat as he spoke. 'You know, about the car.'

Emily narrowed her eyes, bit back the urge to throw something at him.

'There are no rules to grieving.' Phoebe's hand had moved up to give Emily's arm a gentle squeeze and she shied away. 'When my grandmother died, she requested that no one talk for an entire day, so that we could all think of her in our own way.'

Tyler stretched out one long limb, then the other, the toe of one of his boots resting against Emily's foot and she tucked it underneath her, safely out of reach.

'Really?' he said with a yawn. 'My grandad just told us all to go and get pissed at his local.'

Phoebe punched him lightly on the arm, and he offered up a mock – *oh!* – in response. 'My point is, when they're gone, they're gone, so why does it matter if she doesn't go through with it? Catriona would never know.'

'I. Would. Know.' Emily snatched Tyler's beer from his hand, finished it in two gulps, ignoring the way he was looking at her, like she was some pup that needed to be watched with care.

He opened up the small refrigerator in between the seats, took out another beer and popped off the lid. Emily tried not to watch his lips as they parted, tried not to watch the rise and fall of his Adam's apple as he swallowed.

'And it's her home.'

Shut up, Tyler. Emily screamed at him in her head.

'Sounds like she could buy one hundred homes with all the money she's set to inherit.' Phoebe kicked off her sandals, lay her legs across Tyler's lap. 'Catriona Robinson made *The Sunday Times* Rich List the last five years in a row. And death is always good for sales.'

'That's hardly the point, sweetheart,' Tyler said as he rubbed his hand up and down her thigh. 'If she doesn't complete the trial,' he went on, with a look over at Emily, 'she doesn't inherit a penny.'

Of course, it's money that you're concerned with, she thought to herself.

Emily was aware of how her foot continued to bounce up and down, that her fingers were scratching against her palms and the space in her chest continued to shrink, to make her heart feel as if it were about to explode inside of her.

Not here. She absolutely could not have a panic attack thousands of feet above the earth.

'But that's just awful.' Phoebe sat a little straighter. 'What happens to the money if you fail?'

Emily sat forward, helped herself to another drink. 'The bar-headed goose is thought to be the model for the Hamsa of Indian mythology.'

'Sorry, what?' Phoebe replied.

'I don't care,' Emily said and it was true. She didn't care if she wasn't saying the words properly. All she wanted was to drown out the sound, the nearness, of them both. Normally it would be easy, she could simply listen to music, close her eyes and block out the world, but she forgot to put her Discman in her hand luggage because she was just a little bit nervous about getting in a lump of metal that would then fly through the sky with nothing below to catch them when they fell.

'She does this when she's nervous.' Tyler swigged his beer, crossed his legs so that Phoebe had to move her own.

'The Hamsa is a translation of the Sanskrit word for "goose" or "swan", or even "flamingo". Antoine loves flamingos.'

Tyler put his hand on Emily's glass. 'I really don't think you should have any more to drink.'

'Push off,' she slurred, swatting his hand away. 'A Hamsa is a mythical or poetical bird with knowledge. I know lots about birds. I know lots and lots about all sorts of things, but I do not have anyone to talk to them about.'

Her tongue felt like it had doubled in size and she knew she was lisping because Phoebe was looking at her and her scar in that special, annoyingly sympathetic way people always did when she couldn't get the words out straight.

'How many of those pills did she take, Tyler?'

'Hindus believe that the Hamsa is a supreme spirit, but I can't quite remember the rest. Oh, one more thing, in yoga it's the breath of life.'

'A goose is the breath of life?' Tyler said and Phoebe tried to stifle a giggle behind her teeny-tiny hand.

'Oh, what would you know?' Emily threw her arm out in frustration, sluicing some of her drink all over Tyler's lap. 'All you've done for the past six years is make rich people richer. Except you screwed up, Daddy won't bail you out and now you're searching for penance by helping the weird bird girl find whatever it is her dead grandmother left behind. Which, by the way,' she said, gesturing again with her drink and emptying a little more all over his jeans, 'I do not believe to be her whimsical, no magical, no ... Whatever. I don't think it's a book.'

'You don't?' Phoebe looked aghast. As if it was a personal slight to her existence that she wasn't going to get what she wanted out of this little trip.

'I most certainly do not,' Emily said, and poked out her tongue.

'Anyone hungry?' Tyler opened up the picnic basket prepared for them by Antoine's maid.

Emily couldn't look at the basket directly because it made her think of how easily a creature could hide inside. A small monster with fangs and green eyes who had already eaten all of their food and was just waiting for some idiot to put their hand inside so he could bite it off.

'I wish I had a pet,' Emily said as Tyler passed her a prosciutto and brie sandwich. 'A little monster called Samson. I would feed him banana cake.' She grinned across at Tyler. 'He's scared of bananas,'

'No, I'm not.'

'Are too,' she continued, biting down on her baguette and making appreciative noises as the salty meat hit her taste buds. 'I used to chase him around the kitchen, waving them at him. Daffodils too.'

'I don't like you when you're this chatty.'

'And yet for years, all anyone has ever wanted was to get me to talk.'

'How ironic,' Phoebe sniffed at her own sandwich, then handed it back.

'Isn't it, just? All it took was my entire family to die to open the veritable floodgates.'

Silence. An awkward shuffle of limbs as Emily continued to eat, her jaw clicking in response.

'What's the book about?' Tyler picked up Emily's glass, moved it away and replaced it with a bottle of water.

'Which one?' she said as she leant back her head, felt the weight of it sink into the soft leather upholstery. 'You are going to have to be more specific, because I do not believe I am in full control of my faculties. Or facilities. One of the two.'

Tyler stood, opened the overhead locker and reached inside Emily's bag. He lay the book open on the table between them to reveal a picture of a girl who worked for her father, picking olives from the nearby groves and crushing them into oil. A child with dreams as big as the heavens, but who didn't want to disappoint her family by not carrying on their traditions.

'It's about her,' Emily said as she ran her fingers over her grandmother's words. She could see it now; understood that the story was about how Catriona had left behind a whole other life. One that would have meant marriage, children, normality.

Would such a life have crushed her like the small, green fruit in the story, or would she still have found a way to soar?

Head bowed, Emily felt the first tears fall. She watched as they dropped onto a plain, white envelope she hadn't yet had a chance to open, thinning the paper and showing up the suggestion of words within.

'Let me read it to you,' Tyler took the envelope from her, fingers resting on her hand a moment longer.

Why not? Emily thought as she sank into her seat and allowed her eyes to close. Listened to the soft timbre of his voice as he read her grandmother's words aloud. He'd already snooped through everything else, what difference would one thing more actually make?

11 December, 1965

We are all in the gutter, but some of us are looking at the stars.

Oscar Wilde

More Wilde, I know. I keep coming back to him, to his raw honesty, his 'fuck you' attitude to the world. No doubt it's because of Antoine, because of what happened between us. I probably should have stayed, but I was getting fed up of being tossed aside whenever he found someone more interesting to hang out with. Then apologising, always apologising, when he sobered up, said he was sorry, he couldn't do it without me.

I always forgave him. Because he is who he is and I owe him so much. If it weren't for him, I wouldn't have been able to write Imagination. I'm not saying it's some kind of literary masterpiece, but it's a beginning. And I do think it tells a story that many women can relate to, on some level. I mean, we don't all fall in love with someone like Sebastian, and I've never had those kind of feelings about Antoine (although wouldn't it have all been so much easier if we did fancy each other?).

Men are just so different to us. They don't feel in the same way, or even if they do they won't ever admit it.

Although there are always exceptions to the rules and Gigi seems to have found one, slap bang in the middle of Italy. A man who is neither handsome, nor suave, but he is gentle and kind and he absolutely adores her. He also makes her laugh like no one else can and she does seem to be so very, very happy.

Part of me hates her just that little bit more because of

it – jealousy is such an ugly emotion – and I think she knows it, which is why she showed me the library. Over two hundred thousand ancient books and little, old me. It's so peaceful in here, so stuffed full of history, that whenever I come inside, I can feel the beat of my heart slow, just a little.

I have been working on something new. Gigi has read the opening chapters and told me it was good, but I need to try something more gutsy, more honest. I'm not entirely sure what she means, given how much of its main character is based on myself. I have a feeling she means Noah. But I'm not sure if I trust myself to ever put down on paper all the myriad of feelings I have towards him.

He sent me a letter. Via Paris and then to Antoine, who kept it from me. Which is what the argument was about. As in the big argument. The kind you don't know if you can ever come back from argument. I do understand he did it out of love, believed he was saving me from a whole heap more pain, but it wasn't his decision to make. He was being selfish, thinking only of what he wanted me to do. I'm so fed up of other people deciding who I am, where I should go, what kind of writer I should be. What kind of life I should live and with whom.

I'm angry with Gigi because of this (isn't it amazing what comes out of your mind when you simply sit down and write – I hadn't admitted this to myself until I saw the words on the paper in front of me). She's supposed to be my friend. Supposed to support me. And yet she can't bring it upon herself to encourage my writing. There are a million books out there, a million more still to be written. Not all of us are meant to become the next Shakespeare, or Keats, or Hemingway. Not all of us will become famous or rich as a result of our work. Although it would be nice, perhaps for a few weeks, but then

I know I'd want to run and hide away in a cottage by the sea, where no one could find me, unless I wanted them to.

What is it I'm craving? What is it I want but cannot seem to find? Is this normal, to be so distracted by everything the world has to offer and yet have absolutely no idea how you fit into it all?

It must be this time of year. The countdown to Christmas, when families are supposed to be together, put aside their differences and celebrate with too much food and wine. The Queen's speech on the radio and backgammon played by the fire. Carols and mistletoe and skies filled with the promise of snow.

Only this year I will be here. Well, not here, in Rome, but with Giancarlo's family. Gigi has extended her invitation to include me (luckily, Italian families seem to be ever so hospitable and always have an extra seat at the table). All because my father still hasn't forgiven me for deserting him, for bringing shame to the family name by daring to go against his will. Anyone would think it was the nineteenth century, that women didn't have the vote, or the right to bear arms, or actually have a brain inside their thick skulls.

But Mum wrote and told me it might be best to wait a little longer. At least until Harry and Bess have got married. (Didn't take her long to slip into my place, to provide my former fiancé with some love and comfort. Fine friend she turned out to be.)

I know it was my decision to leave. I know I would have suffocated in that place, but part of me is afraid I might never be able to go back. How much longer before Dad forgives me? Because one day there won't be any time left at all.

I'm trying very, very hard not to regret my actions. To look forward, to focus on everything that I have and I am happy, I am excited about where my next adventure will lead. It's just sometimes I can't help but think I might be asking for too much.

Noah wants me to go to him. That's what the letter was about. He's still in Italy, working at some fancy hotel until he can save enough money to buy his own boat. Gigi is adamant that I do nothing of the sort. But what if he's my soulmate? Not all love stories are simple and without disagreement. In fact, aren't they all somehow tainted and actually tested by the hands of fate? Could it be that Noah and I are actually destined to spend the rest of our lives together?

The end of his letter was like a poem. Just a few lines, but I'm sure he knew the effect they would have on me.

My heart is not as it was, before
You showed me what depth of love was possible.
My body knows not how to sleep, how to
Lie, due to the cold space you left behind.

Part of me wanted to burn his words, destroy his profession of love. For all I know, he's given the same declaration to all his women. But I find him, the memory of him in bed, with me, so impossible to ignore. For when he is good, he is so very, very good. And kind and funny and he makes me breathe differently. As if he's changed the way I choose to rise in the morning, drinking in the day. He makes me see the world anew, block out the noise, the modernity of life. Seek out what was there before and what will be long after we are all nothing more than worm food.

Rome is clearly getting to me. Either that or it's all the pasta and gelato (yes, even in December I will eat my body weight in ice cream, because it is just heavenly). Every morning I hear the church bells, calling me out to the streets. I have ambled through flea markets and spent all my money on antique trinkets that I do not need but hang in the window to catch the light in such a way as to push rainbows onto my notebook.

I love everything about this city. The chatter of women as they hang their laundry from balconies, the shouts of children running up and down the streets. The very history etched into every dusty red brick that makes my heart ache for someone to share it all with.

CMR

16

STARLING

Sturnus vulgaris

Back to the wall Emily sat, legs out straight, with feet turned in, like a rag doll. She felt ragged and bedraggled and agitated and all kinds of other things her mind couldn't find the words for.

So sure had she been that this was where the next, potentially final, clue would be. Hidden in the very same place her grandmother sent Ophelia to at the end of the very last book. In the library where she hid the atlas, ready for the next person to discover it.

It was the exact same library Catriona had sat in, day after day, carving out the beginnings of her second novel. A story of two women living the same life, only three generations apart; one Emily now believed was about the choices her grandmother made and the life she turned away from. It made her question whether her grandmother's decision to leave had haunted her ever since, and she suspected this journey was, in part, Catriona's way of showing her how easy it was to accept your existence. Because owning up to your mistakes could be terrifying.

And you can't escape your past, she thought. *The ghosts just never let you be.*

'Are you sure this is the right library?' Tyler was looking back at the building, eyes hidden behind a pair of aviator sunglasses, but Emily had no need to see to understand his doubts, his frustrations. She wanted to be gone from here, from him, just as much as he did her.

'Yes,' she said quietly, but she felt like screaming at him. Because it was the oldest public library in Rome. It was next to a church. Her grandmother's initials were carved on the underside of the table where she told Emily she had always sat. At the very back, close to the wall, half hidden behind a giant, wooden globe.

'The librarian said so too,' Phoebe replied, kicking her toes against the wall.

The librarian had become rather flustered, rather animated, upon discovering who Emily was and why she was there. He had babbled an apology in broken English about not having a book for her, but asked if she would like to see the desk where Catriona Robinson had sat, written all of her books?

Not all of her books, Emily thought as she shuffled a little to the side, away from Phoebe and those dainty feet. *Only one, and I doubt you've even read it.*

Then there were the questions, the inevitable desire to know whether there was any truth to the rumours. Did it mean that the lost manuscript could be here, in Rome? Did Emily know what was in it? Would she be able to mention the library, and the librarian, by name, if he in some way had proven helpful to her search? Did she know what it was about, or could she, please, give him just one little clue?

Emily had crawled under the desk, traced her fingers over the 'C' and 'R' cut into the wood. Allowed them to venture further, over a scattering of tiny 'V's that made her think of a child's way of drawing a bird. She wondered what had made her grandmother decide to leave a piece of herself behind in so random, so obscure, a place. It gave her some comfort to know that the stories she had been told were true, that not everything in the books was pure make-believe. Even if it was proving impossible to use them, to help her figure out what it was her grandmother was trying to show her.

'What about the shop?' Tyler lit a cigarette, smoke twirling into the sky, making Emily think of bonfires, fireworks, blowing through mittens and stamping her feet on frosty ground.

'No.' It felt like she was going around in circles, and nothing in the memories her grandmother had shared was helping.

'Why not?' Tyler took another drag, looked at Emily with slanted eyes. 'Surely it's worth a try?'

'I said no.'

'But the photograph is of them, here, in Rome. You told us it's where they bought the very same locket you're wearing.' Phoebe yawned, stretched her arms high to reveal a line of unblemished stomach.

Emily crossed her arms over her own torso, pictured the thick, silver line that ran around her left hip.

Phoebe looked down at Emily, then over to Tyler, who was stood at the edge of the street, hands on hips and staring at something she could not see. 'So not Rome?'

'Apparently not,' he called over his shoulder.

'Then where?' Phoebe said.

Emily groaned. 'I don't know.'

'You must have some idea, surely?'

'I. Don't. Know.'

Perhaps if she simply stopped talking they would keep arguing amongst themselves, forget she was even there. Perhaps at some point, if she was quiet and still for a long stretch of time, she could meld herself into the fabric of the church wall. Become no more than the memory of someone who once was stupid enough to believe that any of this was a good idea.

So many pictures of imaginary faces and places that swarmed inside her mind. A lake, birds, music connecting it all. She began to hum, nodded her head in time to the music nobody but her could hear. Her fingers automatically reached for a pen, a sketchbook, turning each page over until there was a fresh rectangle of white.

Emily focused on the reassuring scratch of nib on paper as a picture began to take shape on the page. Tried to block out all that surrounded her, concentrating only on the one thing that stopped her from feeling so alone.

Anything. Anything at all to make the demons disappear.

Because she was so far away from what was normal, what it was she had become accustomed to, that she did not trust herself not to fall apart completely if she did anything other than sit on the cold, hard ground and block out everything other than the sound of nib scratching paper.

Emily's vision was blurred, the lines on the page seemed to be so very far away, and she was trying not to think about what would happen if she couldn't find the next clue. Because there were only five more days before everything would end.

'Emily?'

Tyler's hand was on her shoulder, his face so close to hers, but it's as if she neither heard nor saw him. It's as if she had hidden herself inside a bubble, separating her mind from reality.

'Emily, what's wrong?'

'No,' Emily whispered, shook her head over and over as she looked down at the picture she had begun to draw. It was of a woman sat in a chair under the shade of an apple tree, with a child in her lap, whose head was bandaged up with scraps of fabric that wound around and around her body, stretched beyond and into the tree. Imprisoning her in the garden.

Tyler's arms came around her waist, lifted her high, like a child being carried off to bed. She turned her face towards him, blocked out the view of the city, tried to block out the sound of his voice, telling her it would all be OK.

He carried Emily without knowing where he was headed, knowing only that he had to get her away, to do something to snap her out of whatever place she had locked herself inside of.

As they passed the end of a narrow side street, he paused, sniffed the air, then turned. He stopped in front of a glass door on which was drawn a white cartoon of a girl carrying a pizza, whilst simultaneously balancing a book on her head. Emily wriggled free of his arms, sat down at a nearby table and opened up a menu.

Before long, Tyler and Phoebe were debating where in fact they were supposed to be or, indeed, whether they should go back and ask Antoine, or even call Tyler's mother, see if she could help or had another clue. This last suggestion resulted in a swift 'no' from Tyler as he shoved another slice of pizza into his mouth.

Emily twirled her fork, lifted it to her mouth and bit down on the sauce-laden strings of spaghetti. She chewed methodically, went through the rhythm of eating, but couldn't actually taste what it was that fell down her gullet.

It seemed so familiar, yet strange, to witness people discuss the best plan of action. To listen as they went through all the possibilities, all the parameters for change, without once stopping to even ask her opinion. But it had always been this way. Her taking a step away from reality, allowing other people to decide for her.

Another bite. Another swallow, before she realised Phoebe was talking to her.

'I'm sorry,' she said, resting her chin in one hand and staring at Emily as if she were some relic in a museum.

'What for?' Emily moved her fork about the plate, imagined a whirlpool inside of which a mermaid was trapped.

'For not understanding about your scar. The accident.'

'It's fine.' Perhaps the mermaid could grow legs, like in the fairy tale? Walk amongst others, learn how to blend in, to pretend.

'She really was quite a remarkable woman,' Phoebe said as she pushed her half-finished pizza aside. 'I mean, to raise a child alone even now must be tough, but back then?'

Emily was always jealous of all the people who adored her grandmother. Of all the people who thought they were owed a piece of the great Catriona Robinson, and she used to wish the stories could have just been for her.

Before the second book in the series was published, Catriona had asked Emily if she minded, if she was OK to share the stories, and her pictures, all over again. For years she wished she had said yes. But now Emily realised how empty the world would have been without those stories. Without the one about a boy who was afraid of the dark and so climbed to the top of a cliff with Ophelia and her little grey duck, just so he could see the stars. The two of them dove off the very same cliff to swim with the creatures that lived at the bottom of the ocean, down where the sunshine couldn't quite reach.

As Antoine had told her, Catriona was a woman always searching for more. Always looking out for inspiration that could strike at any moment. Emily had come to understand that her grandmother had written because the desire to tell stories, to share her ideas with the world, was in her blood, it's what drove her every day. It was never just about Emily.

'There must be something more, something hidden in the book that you haven't thought of.' Tyler reached over to steal Emily's discarded olives. It was irritating, his familiarity not just with her, but with everyone. The assumption he could do what he wanted, all the time.

'What do you mean, hidden?' Phoebe asked.

'Don't you remember? Every book had a treasure trail at the back. Something more for the reader to find.'

'And you think one of these might point to where we need to go next?'

'We?' Emily said.

'She's trying to help, Em.'

'Why? Why do you care, Tyler?'

She couldn't shake off the idea that he had never been there for anything other than the money. Because he lied to her, made her believe she was someone worth caring about, and that's what hurt most of all.

Phoebe shifted in her seat, crossed her legs towards Tyler as she looked from him to Emily and back again. 'You know, Rome isn't the only city with a Colosseum.'

'What's your point?'

'I'm just saying, maybe you remember it wrong. Maybe they bought the necklace somewhere else. Maybe she made it all up and Gigi never even existed.'

Emily slammed her fist against the table, was aware of her back teeth biting together as she began to stand, then Tyler leant across her for the pepper, pulling her attention away.

'Who came up with the treasures to be found?' Tyler asked as he tapped the pepper pot against the table, made sure Emily was watching.

'She did.'

But then again that wasn't quite true. At least, not for this story. Emily had been the one to draw Ophelia wearing the necklace before any words were written down. She had found it in her grandmother's room, in an open shoebox sat on the window ledge. Wondered who the lady in the picture was, stood next to a young Catriona with her hair tied up in a scarf and enormous golden hoops hanging from her ears.

Her grandmother had looked over her shoulder as Emily sat in her usual seat by the back door, seen the locket she had drawn, hanging from Ophelia's neck. Then she went to her room, came back with the real thing looped over her wrist, before bending down to fasten it behind Emily's neck and whispering that it belonged to her now. Emily had worn it every day since.

'She ate pasta.' Emily stared down at her empty plate, but couldn't remember taking the last bite.

'Who did?' Tyler asked.

'Ophelia,' Emily said as she went through the story in her mind. 'She ate pasta made by the girl's father.'

A man who lived by an olive grove in the mountains and crushed the fruit into oil, mixed it into flour with egg and water, said it gave the pasta an extra-special flavour.

'Giancarlo.' The man Gigi moved to Italy for, who had loved her grandmother's best friend even more than the food he created.

'Who?'

'The "G" on the dedication has to be for Giancarlo, not Gigi.' It was Giancarlo who had taught Catriona Robinson to toss pizza dough like a native. Showed her how to make it thin enough to see the sky through, to make it extra crispy. Pizza dough she used to toss high, up towards the kitchen ceiling, making Emily giggle with delight.

Burnt edges and melted cheese. Scraps left on the back doorstep for all the birds to feast on when their bellies were fit to burst. All the stories she used to tell Emily, about the people she once knew, but which Emily had never been certain were true, up until now.

'Where is he?'

'Verona.' The city of love. Of Romeo and Juliet. She remembered the balcony her grandmother told her about when she first sat down to study Shakespeare. A place where people left letters of hope, of loss, not only of desire.

'You're sure?' Tyler was already busy with his phone. No doubt mapping out the next part of their journey. No doubt figuring out how to get it all over and done with, so he could forge ahead with his life.

'Yes.' But her head shook itself, no. Because she wasn't sure. Not now. Not when she had brought them here by mistake.

'We could always call ahead?' Phoebe suggested. 'Just in case.'

'No.' How could she call up a man she had never met, or had she? Something was there, a man's voice, low and strong. But it was all hidden behind a layer of doubt, of confusion, so she wasn't able to figure out if it was real or just the memory of something she was searching for but couldn't reach, cobbled together from whatever story her grandmother had told. Reality and fiction always puddled together, making it so hard for Emily to try and see the difference between the two.

'Giancarlo Delucci,' Tyler said as he read from the screen of his phone. 'Together with his late wife Virginia, Senor Delucci wrote a bestselling collection of Italian cookbooks and opened a two-star Michelin restaurant in the heart of Verona.'

'Sounds like our guy,' Phoebe said.

Tyler turned the phone around, showed Emily a picture of a man stood by a workbench, rolling out sheets of pasta and smiling back at the camera. Back in Norfolk, there was a black and white photograph on the mantelpiece in the living room of Gigi wearing a lace wedding dress. She was being kissed by a man, tall and thin, with a sunflower as a buttonhole. The man was the same as in the photograph Tyler had gleaned from the internet, only Emily had never seen his whole face before.

All the people her grandmother adored but never took her

219

to see. People who were a part of her world, her life, but became nothing more than memories after her parents died.

Emily wondered why she had spent so little time with her grandmother before. What was it that made her such a fleeting part of her childhood? She had spent her whole life travelling, exploring, living, and then all of a sudden she had stopped. As if she had simply cut herself free from the past in order to protect her family.

'She's dead,' Emily said, realising that her mother wasn't the only person her grandmother had loved and lost. Began to fear that there was something more about meeting Giancarlo than simply retrieving another book, another clue.

'Who's dead?' Phoebe said, rubbing at her leg and ignoring the look on Tyler's face.

'Gigi.' Despite the heat, Emily shivered, felt the hairs along her arms all stand up in a row, because she was beginning to think that this quest, this puzzle, had nothing to do with the books after all.

'You just said the dedication was for Giancarlo.' Tyler began to gather all his belongings together, checked his watch, then his phone.

'It is.' *I think.* She brushed at her arms, waited for the momentary chill to pass.

'Then what's the problem?'

The problem was that Emily had no desire to arrive on the doorstep of an elderly man and ask him about his dead wife. And if she was wrong, if Giancarlo wasn't the next person she was supposed to find, she would have subjected him to painful, horrible memories that he had probably spent most of his life trying to forget.

Emily pushed back her chair and stood up. 'I want to

go,' she said, picking up her suitcase and making sure it was zipped shut.

'Are you sure you don't want me to call first?' Tyler tossed some coins onto the table as a tip.

'No.' Emily started to walk away. 'I want to go home.'

Something was telling her to flee. To get as far away from Rome and Verona and all of her grandmother's memories as fast as she possibly could. There was no sense to it. No rhyme nor reason for the murky sensation in her stomach. But it was there, a slither of fear mixed through with doubt. Something that seemed to be warning her about what was waiting just around the corner, if she didn't run.

'You can't go home.' Tyler grabbed her arm, forced her to stop.

'Why not?' Emily could see Phoebe hovering just behind and she wanted to shout at her, to tell her to stop looking, stop listening, just stop being there, to leave her alone. For them both to leave her alone.

He hesitated. Looked away and down, which told her all she needed to know and more.

'The money.'

'No, not just the money. I mean, yes, your money. Your inheritance. Your home, Emily. It's not there unless you see this thing through.'

She shook herself free of him. 'What if I don't want to?'

'You don't have a choice.'

Emily hated him in that moment, simply because he was right. 'I could go to my aunt.'

Tyler frowned. 'The one in New York?'

'Why not?'

'You're being ridiculous.'

Probably true, given that Emily hadn't seen her since her twenty-first birthday. When her aunt and her husband did nothing but talk about how fantastic their lives were. The sort of people who would point out a crooked painting on the wall, or say that the lawn needed mowing.

Her father's sister. A woman whose face was as starched as her shirt, with a choker of pearls around her scrawny neck, hair like a helmet and two boys dressed identically in blazer and bow tie. Of course she couldn't go and stay with them, it would be even more torturous than travelling through Europe with Tyler and his annoying girlfriend.

'What's one more day?' Tyler called out as Emily walked away. 'Come on, Emily, you've come this far, it would be stupid to walk away now.'

'Go home, Tyler,' she shouted back. 'Or stay here, with her. Either way, I really don't care.'

The weight of summer fell over her skin as she walked. Heat stuck to every surface, the copper light of dusk that graced the surface of the water as she looked down from the stone wall of the Ponte Umberto bridge. She stared at the reflection of mottled clouds and black trees that stretched to the banks of the river and wished upon wish she could wake up to discover it had been nothing but a dream.

Emily thought of all the lessons her grandmother had taught her. Always asking her to look beyond the facts, to push her mind further than rational thought. Her way of teaching had shown Emily how everything in the world was somehow connected. Like water, which travelled all over the globe in a never-ending cycle of life and death, making you realise just how insignificant one life, one person, could actually be.

A soft swish of leaves as a warm breeze stirred the sleepy city. Ahead was the silhouetted dome of the Vatican. Inside those walls was a ceiling painted by Michelangelo, a masterpiece that he never wanted to work on and took him years to complete. It was incredible and ridiculous all at once.

She could go and look upon it with her own eyes, search out all the clues, all the suggestions that there was more to the painting than you saw at first glance. The secrets Michelangelo hid in plain sight, just like she had done in all of her grandmother's books. Because people have a habit of ignoring what's right in front of them, choosing to see only what they want to, not what they should.

Emily started to become aware of something that didn't quite fit, that shouldn't be. A sensation which made her stand a little straighter, hold her breath, because the dome seemed to be moving, vibrating, and with it came the sound of ... Of what? Emily stretched her neck to see, to hear a hum, a crackle, as thousands upon thousands of black dots emerged from the top of the church.

It was like a cloud, a moving and expanding cloud that changed from one second to the next into fantastical shapes. Except it wasn't a cloud at all.

Starlings. A murmuration of starlings that seemed to expand and retract like an accordion, painting pictures in the sky as they swarmed up and over the city.

Emily saw shadowy shapes that broke then fitted back together, deep pockets of black that fragmented into individual birds, all those wings that rustled and swooped in the darkening sky. The sound made her think of breaking waves on the shore back home. A storm approaching. The wind pushing and pulling the air back and forth. It seeped right into her soul, made her ache for the absence of her family, made her afraid to be alone.

Then it was done. The birds moved on and the city seemed too quiet, too still. Emily turned to see Tyler stood at the end of the bridge, waiting for her.

17

HUMMINGBIRD

Trochilidae

It was raining, thin lines of wet running down the train window as they sped through the Italian countryside.

The rain was a completely inconsequential observation, it was always raining somewhere on the planet, but Emily realised the weather was something she used to pay attention to. It used to set the mood, the plan for the day, determined when to go for a walk, or if they would visit a garden centre, plant some seedlings, bring the washing in before the storm arrived. It would make her decide if it should be meatballs or BBQ for dinner, and whether she needed to take a jumper when she cycled into town.

Still dressed in shorts and a T-shirt, Emily felt the chill on her bare limbs as she rummaged through her bag for another layer. As she shrugged on a thin, black cardigan, she thought about how unstructured, how spontaneous, her life had become, which seemed ridiculous, given she was being sent in a very clear direction.

When was the last time I had a bath? she wondered. When had she last lazed underneath warm bubbles and lost herself in a book? She stared out of the window, rain smudging the view, and tried to think of the last moment she had spent at rest, at peace.

Tyler had turned everything upside down. The feeling of being alone, of being separated from the world, had only intensified since Rome. Because she could still remember the sensation of being carried in his arms, feel the vibration of his heart, beating against her own.

Her sketchbook lay open, revealing a few pictures earlier made of the starlings, all the shapes that she had seen. But they wouldn't quite come together in the way that she wanted and all she had so far was just a tangled mess of lines that vaguely resembled a tornado.

Phoebe and Tyler were sat close to one another in the seats opposite. Her legs were tangled up in his lap, stroking his hair whilst they had a half-hearted argument about *Romeo and Juliet*. Emily had tuned them out, tried instead to focus on the pitch and timbre of voices from the other passengers, not caring that she had no idea what was being said.

There was a woman on the phone, having a heated discussion with someone on the other end. Her words were like staccato drums, every so often rising into a shout that seemed to explode, like the blast from a trumpet, and make the elderly man sat next to her jump.

An orchestra of words. Emily swapped seats, peered behind her down the aisle as she mentally put each person in the carriage into a different section of the orchestra. The children would be the strings, all fighting one another for attention, the group of women hunched close together could be flutes, their whispers and laughter skipping over the surface of all the other instruments. Then the man at the far end, trussed up in a three piece suit and frowning at his computer screen, a bass drum, perhaps, or even cymbals that he would clash together theatrically when he found the answer to whatever was causing that line between his eyes.

'You agree, don't you?'

Emily turned as Phoebe leant across to her, tapped her lightly on the back of her hand.

'Sorry, what?'

'It's a romance, not a tragedy.'

'They die,' Tyler said. 'Not very romantic.'

'Yes, but it reunites the two families,' Phoebe argued. 'It's not romance in its purest sense, but because of what it creates. The sense of sacrifice, not only for the lovers, but their friends as well. It's about all kinds of love, not just sex.'

'It's a catalogue of errors, and they both kill themselves because they're too stupid to realise what's actually happening.' This last part was delivered whilst looking straight at Emily, waiting to see how she would respond.

'What is it about men and Shakespeare?' Phoebe punched Tyler playfully, rolled her eyes at Emily.

'What is it about women and their need for a happily ever after?' he said.

'I'm not taking sides.' Emily picked up her pen, began to recreate the idea she had about turning words into music. An idea she had first come across when sat in a store back in Norfolk, listening to the bookseller telling her about the puzzle her grandmother wanted her to solve.

227

Five days gone, Emily thought to herself. Only five more left to go.

Turning down the volume on all the conversations, she began to hum a tune. One that her grandmother always played whenever she felt in need of a pick-me-up. Her magical go-to that never failed to see both of them leaping about the kitchen, then collapsing in a pile of laughter and exhaustion as 'Dancing Queen' came to an end.

Emily smiled as she realised she had been drawing an orchestra of birds. Hummingbirds, which were sort of her own go-to, her favourite. She had first discovered one on holiday in France and mistaken it for a giant bee. They were mesmerising, with their incredible, iridescent colours, the speed with which those tiny wings would beat. It was a fascination that resulted in her disappearing during one trip to the Natural History Museum, when Tyler accused her of running away. All she had wanted was to see a real one, albeit stuffed, motionless, so that she might try and capture some of that brightness on paper.

'So you do remember?' Tyler was smiling at her, at her work, whilst sat forward in his chair.

'Hummingbirds can fly in the rain,' she replied without looking up, then added a bow to one of the birds that was sat at the front, holding a violin.

'Can't all birds fly in the rain?' Phoebe asked, picking at a cuticle on her finger.

'They have no sense of smell and their tongues look like feathers.' But it was their colours she loved most of all. The blur of wing which changed the pigment, the fragmentation of light that turned into all possible hues on the spectrum. Every time she looked at one, she saw something new.

'She's like a walking bird encyclopedia,' Tyler said as he stood. 'Anyone want anything from the buffet car?'

Emily shook her head and tapped her pen against the side of the can of cola she was yet to finish. It was her third and she could feel the caffeine inside her veins, making her jittery and nervous. Or at least that's what she'd been telling herself. Nothing to do with where they were headed, or who they were supposed to find.

The possibility that she had got it wrong, again. Or even the possibility that she hadn't. Because there was a feeling, a lingering feeling she couldn't ignore. Gigi was dead. Her grandmother was dead. So what could be the message she was about to be given, by a man who had known them both, before tragedy split apart their love?

'You two going to be okay whilst I'm gone?' Tyler asked as he looked between the two women.

'You're not my babysitter.' Only it felt as if he was, because she had never been trusted to do anything alone.

Tyler left and Emily did her best to ignore Phoebe, even though she could see her shifting in her seat, trying to look closer at what it was Emily was drawing.

'What made you change your mind about carrying on?'

'The birds.' The starlings, with all their movement, their frantic activity, yet still protecting one another, always flying as one.

'You like birds.'

'You say that like it's a bad thing.'

'No, not bad.' She turned to look out of the window, at the blur of muted greens and yellows. 'Did you always like them?' Phoebe said, breathing on the windowpane, then using her finger to draw a simple flower that slowly faded away.

'I guess so.'

The first picture Emily had ever drawn was of her favourite toy. Then butterflies and flowers and fairies. Hundreds upon hundreds of fairies who she liked to imagine lived at the bottom of the garden. Tiny, magical people who rode on the back of all the rabbits who came to visit and one day would take Emily off on an adventure, somewhere far away. Perhaps to their secret kingdom on top of a mountain, hidden by pink clouds spun like sugar.

Emily turned to a clean page, began to create a series of concentric circles that formed into a path that led to a castle made of stone. It was somewhere she had never been, but her grandmother once showed her the pictures and told Emily it was a clearing, a mystery of a place, near her childhood home. Then she sat with her by the fire and shared what she could remember about the folklore that surrounded the faery glen.

Emily searched her mind for the first time her grandmother had told her the story, knew it was from long before. She could almost taste the chicken soup bubbling away on the stove in a kitchen, at the back of a Victorian terrace in London, where she and her grandmother would sit, dunking butter-laden bread into steaming bowls whilst the cat slept in the corner, in a circle of autumn sunshine. A house that once was her home, then was sold, passed on to a family new.

So long ago. It felt like the memory belonged to someone else's life. To a little girl who would sit on her parents' bed, sketchbook open on her lap, watching her mother sat at her dressing table in a gown made from pale blue silk. A child who was mesmerised by the sight of her mother putting on her make-up, getting herself ready for a night at the opera.

Emily shook her head as she ripped out the sheet from her sketchbook, scrunched it tighter and tighter, then tossed it aside.

Phoebe watched without saying a word. She must have seen what it was Emily had drawn. The lines that seeped from the circles, twisted and turned themselves into a picture Emily had kept locked away. Surely she must wonder why Emily decided to destroy the image of a woman, sat by a mirror, brushing her hair?

'It must be hard,' Phoebe picked up the discarded piece of paper, put it back down again. 'To be the only one left.'

You have no idea, Emily thought as she smoothed out a fresh page.

'Sometimes pain is necessary, to enable you to recognise when you finally feel better.' Phoebe took a long, slow breath, the exhale coming out as a judder. 'I used to hurt myself.'

Emily looked up. Phoebe was staring out of the window, but Emily could see in the reflection that she was trying not to cry.

'We're all told that we should be the best at something, or at least extraordinary in some way.' Phoebe fiddled with the cuffs of her shirt and Emily noticed how her nails were bitten down to the pads of her fingers.

'No one's the best.'

'I read somewhere that you can get addicted to pain. Or, rather, the feeling you get when the pain goes away.'

'I wish I knew what it felt like for the pain to go away.'

Phoebe offered her a faint smile. 'I learnt to forgive myself. To focus on the here and now, instead of always looking to the future.'

Her words made Emily realise that she had only allowed

herself to live in the present because she was afraid of everything else. Too scared to look back, too uncertain as to think about what comes next.

'How's that working out for you?' Emily asked.

Phoebe gave a small smile. 'Not great, to be honest. I have absolutely no idea what it is I want to do.'

'Join the club.'

'What about your drawings, your grandmother's stories?'

'They're her stories, not mine.'

'When you were younger, what did you want to grow up and be?'

'An astronaut,' Emily said without stopping to think.

Phoebe laughed. 'Seriously?'

'Also a ballerina, a showjumper and a magician.'

'A magician?'

'I wanted a pet rabbit.' But her mother had said no, due to the foxes that lived at the bottom of the garden. Told Emily the poor creature would either get eaten or die of a heart attack whilst the foxes prowled around outside its hutch.

'I wanted to be a conservationist.' Phoebe opened a packet of mints, offered one to Emily. 'To find ways to save all the incredible creatures on this planet, before humans destroy it all.'

'So be a conservationist,' Emily said, turning the mint around in her mouth. Surprised herself by saying a word that would normally have made her lips clamp shut.

'Just like that?' Phoebe was looking at Emily with a strange expression, as if she were deciding whether to leap upon the suggestion or swat it away.

'What's stopping you?'

Phoebe paused. Bit down on her bottom lip. 'After

graduating I applied for a job with a wildlife foundation in Rwanda. I would have been working with the local community to help develop tourism that would benefit, rather than threaten, the gorilla population.'

'What happened?'

A small smile, a shrug of shoulder, a look behind to see if anyone was coming back.

'I decided to spend some time in France. It really helps, you know, to be fluent in something other than English.'

She turned it down for him. Emily was suddenly so angry that Phoebe would turn down her future for someone who was about to move to the other side of the world without giving anyone else a second thought.

Her grandmother's face swam into her mind, from when she was young, from the photograph given to her in Paris. A woman who chose to do it all alone, who chose not to marry, not to conform. Someone who had always told Emily that society took far longer to catch up with the views of individuals than was necessary. Told her that she shouldn't care what other people thought, because at the end of it all there's no one to answer to for your decisions, other than yourself.

'Don't change your life for anyone.'

Phoebe made a small noise, nodded, then shook her head as she stared up at the ceiling. She looked like she was either about to punch something or scream. A look Emily recognised all too well, because it was exactly the same way she felt every single time she thought about what could have been. When she dreamt of the life she could have had, felt she deserved, if it hadn't been for one split second on a summer's afternoon.

It was how she had felt during her recovery. When others

were trying to get her to talk, to walk, because what was the point of it all if they were gone? If her parents, and now her grandmother, weren't there with her, loving her, giving her a family, what was the point? What was the point of anything if you had no one to share it with?

'Like Mary.' Phoebe sniffed loudly, began to drum her fingers on the table.

'Who?'

'Mary,' she said again, peeling back the foil on her packet of mints, then putting two more in her mouth. 'From your grandmother's book.'

'You've read *Imagination*?' Emily was always surprised when people talked about her grandmother's earlier work. More often than not, all they ever wanted to do was gush about the brilliance, the genius, of Ophelia.

'I really liked it,' she said, with a nod. 'More than I thought I would.'

'How so?'

'The juxtaposition between what Mary thinks is going on in her and Sebastian's relationship versus the reality that she's in complete denial about. It's like there are two voices in her head, the yin and yang of the universe.'

'Phoebe studied English at Cambridge.' Tyler slid into his seat. 'We met when I went back for a reunion dinner last year.'

'Really?' A moment ago, Emily would have found this news irritating. Simply seen it as yet more evidence that, for some people, life was a series of fortunate events, whereas for others it was all they could do to scramble to keep up. Now Emily looked at Phoebe with different eyes; understood that no one ever really knows what goes on inside a person's mind, or their heart. That each and every one of us have demons to battle with at some point along the way.

'Fat lot of good it did me though,' Phoebe gestured for Tyler to move, to let her out. 'Twenty-three and working as a waitress in a cocktail bar.'

'You still have time,' Emily said, watching as Phoebe made her way towards the toilets in the next carriage, saw her offer up an apology when she tripped over a bag someone had left in the aisle. It made Emily wish she could go back, start again, offer up more than hostility to someone who was clearly just as lost as she was.

Tyler unwrapped a toasted panini, the scent of roasted tomatoes and basil closing the gap between them. He took a large bite and waved the sandwich in Emily's direction. 'You of all people don't get to judge her based on what she looks like.'

'I wasn't.' Only she was.

'You're still beautiful, no matter what you think.'

Hand to her scar, Emily dipped her chin. 'Stop.'

Emily had been beautiful, as a child. She knew it because of the way people always commented on her appearance, or looked at her a certain way. It's also what made her so acutely aware of the difference after the accident because of how everyone stared at her and her scar. At the half of her face which didn't quite fit.

'I mean it,' he said, taking another bite, then handing the rest to her. 'You shouldn't be so focused on things that no one else cares about.'

Emily turned the sandwich over, then around, pulled a string of melted mozzarella from its centre. 'You mean my parents.'

'No, I mean you. Always thinking you're only worth something because of her. She was holding you back,' he said, stabbing his finger onto Emily's sketchbook. 'Stagnating you.'

'Don't say that.'

'You have so much talent. Your drawings are incredible, even you must be able to see that? You don't need her, or her legacy. You can do this without her.'

I wanted to be a writer. The thought popped into her mind without warning. Another thought, another memory, but one that wouldn't quite let her peel back the curtains to see. The same kitchen, this time with snow on the ground and a cake in the oven. The cat was just a kitten and Emily had been teasing it with the end of a ribbon from her mother's sewing basket.

'We're in this together.' Tyler pushed the sketchbook closer to Emily. 'No matter how hard you try to push me away.'

They watched one another as she ate. Bite after bite, neither of them saying a word. When she was done, he took out his headphones and slid them across to her.

'There's more inside your head than whatever idea she told you about.' Then he sat back, folded his arms over his chest and waited.

That's what I'm afraid of.

Emily looked at the crumpled piece of paper containing a memory she hadn't wanted to find, then placed the headphones over her ears, switched on the music and tried to drown out the world.

If she opened the floodgates, anything and everything could come tumbling out.

RAVEN

Corvus corax

Someone was singing. There was a church, from which a wedding party was spilling onto the street, a cloud of confetti covering the bride and groom. Emily bent down to pick some up. Saw they were rose petals, pink and soft but already beginning to wilt. Her hand began to shake as she watched the happy couple kiss, bodies pressed tight together, the wide smiles of all who had gathered to witness their union.

She thought of Tyler and Phoebe, of their offer to come with her. How she had turned them down, said she was fine. Now she wasn't so sure, because she couldn't shake the feeling that had followed her all the way since Rome. It had been there when they arrived at their hotel, late last night. Emily had collapsed into bed, too exhausted to fight sleep, the after-effects of valium, whisky and a belly full of Italian food finally catching up with her. But the feeling was still there when she had woken. It whispered in her ear as she attempted to swallow her morning coffee, tapped her on the shoulder as she asked for a map from the hotel reception, circled the address she needed to get to.

It had persisted, like a whining child, as she walked the streets, breathing in a new city, all the people that blurred into one. A place full of strangers going about their everyday lives, who knew nothing of her, of why she was there. She had been drawn towards the quiet, to the streets where not so many tourists were ambling about. That's when she had seen him. A raven. Perched on black railings imprinted with centuries of other people's fingerprints.

A graveyard in the middle of a city, protected by birds who always made Emily think of the Tower back in London, where six ravens lived, wings clipped so they couldn't leave, for fear of the curse proving to be true. She felt like one of those birds. Feared that because she was here, something dark and dangerous was about to be released.

Turning her back on the raven, Emily followed the sound of song, stopping just inside the church doorway. There was a monument built into the wall, of a coffin and a death mask, the sight of which made her step deeper into the gloom. A woman was singing near the altar, the vibrato in her voice reaching all the way up to the cavernous ceiling. It made Emily think of her mother and the arias she would sing whilst dancing through the house, trailing a mist of Guerlain behind.

Stop, Emily told herself, wanting to leave but transfixed by the beauty of the song. It was sad and hopeful, all at once, even though she couldn't understand the words. She sat down on the nearest pew, dropped her head automatically and began to murmur the Lord's Prayer. As she did so, she thought of how churches carried all the highs and lows of life, the beginning and the end, all under one roof. She also thought about how she hadn't ever said goodbye to her parents.

It had been decided she was too weak, too vulnerable, to attend the funeral, that the ordeal would prove too much for her, and she needed her rest. It had been decided, for her, without ever asking what she wanted to do.

Her parents were buried, side by side, on a hilltop in London. She was taken there, only once, the last time she visited the city, to leave red roses on their graves. Her grandmother had chattered away about the likes of Douglas Adams and Karl Marx also being lain to rest in the same location. Probably thought that her words, her ordinary, light-hearted, words, could distract Emily from the horror of what she was being forced to do.

Emily wiped at her eyes as she remembered, looked up to see a statue of an angel, knelt in prayer. She had run away from her grandmother that day. Just like a child playing hide-and-seek, only she hadn't wanted to be found. Curled up behind an angel at rest, wings neatly folded and eyes closed. Her grandmother had searched the graveyard, calling out Emily's name until finally she stumbled back onto the path, asked if they could please go back to Norfolk.

It had been so much easier to hide, to bury everything deep, to deny all the sorrow, all the regret. To allow her grandmother to wrap her up in cotton wool and fend off all the demons, anything that might threaten to break her, to make her feel.

'Stai bene?' A priest hovered at the end of the pew, hands hidden inside the sleeves of his vestments and a look of patience, of kindness, on his lined face. Emily resisted the urge to throw her arms around him, feeling like an idiot for imagining how he might take her into the confessional, cleanse her of all her sins, then give her a cup of tea and a biscuit before sending her on her way.

'I need to find someone,' Emily handed over the map, saw that she had torn a hole in one corner.

The priest smiled back, said something in Italian and beckoned for Emily to follow him to the door. He pointed along the street, then gave back the crumpled map. As he did so, he clasped Emily's hand between his own, staring deep into her eyes, then at her scar.

For a moment the world stilled and the two strangers stood, not saying a word. Emily felt the air around her stir, let go the breath in her lungs and registered the beat of her heart as it began to slow. The priest murmured to her, low vibrations of sound escaping his lips, landing on her skin, embalming her with their intent.

Then he let her go. One curt nod of his head, before spinning on his leather soles and walking away, the tails of his robe waving goodbye.

What did he see? It disturbed her. The way he had seemed to look deep inside her soul. The idea that he could understand her pain, had no doubt seen it so often on the faces of his parishioners. Was it because he could accept the will of God in a way that most people never would?

Emily walked without realising where she was going, feeling trapped somewhere between then and now, not understanding where she had been or where she was supposed to go. What it was that she was about to find in a restaurant in Verona.

I wish you were here, she thought as she turned the corner, found herself once again by a river.

Leaning over the smooth, stone wall, she felt a mellow breeze on her cheek, turned her head to follow the water in its perpetual flow. To her right there was a row of potted eucalyptus plants, the sweet, minty fragrance making her think of winter nights with Vicks rubbed onto her chest; of soft hands and a calming voice that sung her a lullaby whilst she slept.

Stop, Emily told herself once more as she watched a woman step from behind the plants with a bright red watering can. She watered each plant in turn, then went over to where a pair of oversized urns were stood, flanking the entrance to a restaurant with a brass plaque next to the door.

'*Scusi,*' Emily called out and the woman turned.

'*Si?*' she asked, a slight crease between her brows as she looked Emily up and down, saw the map in her hand, the pink around her eyes.

'I'm here to see Giancarlo,' Emily said. 'My name is Emily.' There was a flash of recognition as Emily spoke her name, followed by a torrent of Italian that Emily understood nothing of, along with a broad smile and hands that beckoned her to follow.

The woman led Emily through the restaurant and up a small flight of stairs. Everywhere there were people, busy polishing glasses and straightening starched linen tablecloths. Emily could smell garlic, rosemary and something else as she turned her head to peer inside an open door, at stainless steel worktops covered with ingredients, heard the scrape of knives being sharpened, felt a slight drop in temperature as she went back outside.

Giancarlo was sat on the balcony at a small, round table in the sunshine, drinking coffee and doing a crossword. He was wearing a checked shirt, jeans and horn-rimmed spectacles that balanced on the end of his nose as he tackled each question in turn. He looked up as they approached, a lazy smile on his face that turned quickly into astonishment.

Emily sat down, allowed him to simply look at her a moment. She didn't press him for any conversation, any answers, because she saw the way his eyes lingered on the locket around her neck, was certain he knew what photograph was inside.

'For a second I thought you were her.' His voice was low and melodic, but not the one she had been expecting. Not the one she was trying to remember from long ago.

'Apart from the hair.' And the scar.

'I think it's the dress. She wore one just like it the first time we met. I took her and Gigi dancing on the hills behind Rome. The two of them had all the men wrapped around their fingers.' He smiled as he spoke and Emily could tell he was thinking of that night, of when two young women thought they had the rest of their lives to be friends. It made Emily sad and happy all at once.

'I never wear dresses.' She looked down at the red dress she had chosen that morning, but didn't remember putting it in her suitcase, couldn't remember the last time she had worn it.

'You should. Beautiful things shouldn't only be kept for special occasions.'

Emily smiled. Thought of how at home her grandmother used bone china, crystal glasses and silver forks for breakfast. A mismatched collection of things that she had bought, and broken, over the years. Along with silk blouses and diamonds. Never caring if something got lost, always saying that life was too short to care about possessions.

Someone came out, placed a pot of coffee on the table, along with a plate of individual millefoglie cakes. Giancarlo picked one up and broke it in two, handed half to Emily, waited for her to bite down, for the hit of salt and caramel to reach her taste buds. She made the necessary noises of appreciation and he chuckled before eating his own.

'They were Gigi's favourites,' he said, pouring a line of dark, steaming coffee into both cups, then holding up cream and sugar in turn. 'She told me they're what made her fall in love with Italy, with me.'

Emily shook her head to both. Looked over to see the crossword Giancarlo had been attempting was from *The Sunday Times*.

Giancarlo saw her looking. 'Gigi introduced me to it and, I understand, she got the tradition from Catriona. A way to help improve her English, but I think just a way to link them together even when they were oceans apart.'

'We always did it too.' Sometimes it took them all week to finish. Her grandmother would burst in from the garden to announce that the answer to 5 down was 'tyranny', or Emily would wake in the night to realise that the alternative word for 'genie' was 'jinn'.

Another tradition. Another secret that united friends across time and even death. An idea passed along from one to another. Just like Tyler. Emily fingered the earrings he had gifted her, trying not to think about the way the very nearness of him always left her feeling more alive, more invested in the day.

'I wish I could talk to her.' Sometimes Emily would get to the end of the day and realise she had nothing to talk about, and no one to talk to.

'You should still talk to her,' Giancarlo dropped two lumps of sugar into his coffee, stirred through the liquid with a teaspoon. 'It helps, weirdly, to tell them about your day. That's why I still do the crossword. It makes me ask her what the answer should be, and I try to imagine what she would say.' He gave a small chuckle, a longer sigh as he thought of his wife. 'Even if she didn't know, she would come up with some crazy idea, make me laugh, make me remember once again how very much I loved her.'

At home, Emily would communicate through email, or say a few passing words to the people she came across during everyday life, but it had only ever been with Catriona that she had formed a real conversation. Or Milton, but that was always decidedly one-sided. The very fact she couldn't ever talk to her grandmother again had fallen, like a stone, inside her soul and was refusing to budge, no matter how many times she reminded herself she had known it was coming. Her death wasn't a surprise, although it was still a shock whenever she went to make a cup of tea and automatically took down two cups.

'It's too hard,' she said, picking up her silver teaspoon and twirling it between her fingers.

'We are all dying, Emily. It's how we choose to live that we can control, nothing else.'

'Don't you miss her?'

Giancarlo sighed as he took hold of her hand, patted it gently. 'Every day. But Gigi lived life to its fullest. She ate everything, drank everything, danced in a thunderstorm and chose not to regret a thing, because it was a complete waste of time to look back.'

'Sounds like something Grandma would say.'

'I didn't have to watch her suffer, like you did. It was the most horrific experience of my life, but she went without pain.'

'I wanted her to fight.'

'Catriona was powerful, she had such strength, even in the darkest of times.' He looked at her then, opened his mouth, closed it, almost as if he weren't sure if he should say what he was about to. 'She read a poem at Gigi's funeral. I hated her for it at the time, but now I understand what it was she was trying to make me, make us all, understand.'

Emily clenched her jaw, ignoring the spasm down one side of her neck and how her hands balled into fists as he began to speak.

'*A total stranger one black day, knocked living the hell out of me.*' Giancarlo spoke slowly, taking care over each syllable.

Stop. Please stop, she thought as she realised that Giancarlo was reciting a poem by E. E. Cummings. The words pushed inside her mind, swirled all around, pulling up all sorts of memories and emotions she wanted to ignore.

'*Who found forgiveness hard because, my (as it happened) self he was.*'

'Giancarlo, please.'

He was crying now, but the words kept coming. '*But now that fiend and I are such immortal friends the other's each.*'

'I can't,' she gasped between breaths, aware of the tears that were falling from her own eyes, because she knew the poem. Her grandmother had made her read it, dissect it, along with countless others about death, about sorrow. So

245

many lessons her grandmother had tried to teach her, things she had steadfastly refused to hear.

'Can't what?'

'Forgive myself for surviving.'

'It wasn't your fault,' he said.

'What would you know?'

He didn't reply, he simply sat quite still, looking at her.

The same waitress came back, carrying a parcel that she lay on the table between them. Giancarlo nodded at Emily, but she didn't want it, nor what was hidden inside. That damn feeling had returned, the one that had been lurking in her subconscious, only dealt with momentarily by the priest, but now it was back and ready to be set free.

'Can you do it, please,' she whispered, watching as he pulled the paper apart to reveal a picture of two girls holding tight to the back of an enormous bird with feathers the colour of fire. They were soaring over the earth, high into the heavens, looking down on a village through the centre of which a river ran.

Emily let go her relief as she reached across for the book, because it was a story about love. About a girl who carried a bird with damaged wings through a thunderstorm, only for it to die. So she buried it under her window and the next morning a phoenix rose from the ground to take her and Ophelia flying through the clouds to visit a rainforest, where a whole host of creatures was nesting in the tallest of trees. Ophelia had asked what happened if they fell, only for the phoenix to reply that they simply had to learn to fly.

Giancarlo sipped his coffee, put the cup gently on the table and Emily noticed that his hand was shaking. She could feel that doubt, that fear, slink back inside her heart as she pulled out a plain, white envelope from between the pages of the book.

'There's something about death that makes you appreciate how fleeting, how precious, life really is,' he said, looking at the envelope as if he might have some idea what it contained. 'After the initial pain and horror fades a little, then you realise how fragile we all are. How easily all of this – this life – can be gone.' He paused to wipe his spectacles with a handkerchief. 'She wanted you to understand that you were her reason for not giving up.'

Emily thought again about the story within the book Giancarlo had given her and when it had been written, shortly after their return from London. They had gone for a book signing at Hatchards, with all those people staring at her, followed by the disastrous visit to the cemetery, when Emily hadn't even been able to look upon her parents' grave. Back in Norfolk, she had locked herself in her room and refused to come down, to engage in anything that remotely resembled conversation.

Catriona had tried everything: pleading, cajoling, not to mention bribery, but not even the sight of Milton at her window had been enough to pull Emily out of her nightmares. For close to a week she had done nothing but cover her thoughts with music turned up to full volume, Jimi Hendrix and his guitar pushing everything else from her mind.

It wasn't until her grandmother had slipped a few sheets of paper under her door, pages filled with the beginnings of a new story, that Emily had found a way to rid herself of the darkness. Only then had she been able to open the window wide, let in the light and begin again.

This is different, Emily thought as she stared down at the book's cover. She understood the message her grandmother was trying to send; knew what it was she was expected to do. But knowing and succeeding were two very different things.

'I don't know how to start again.'

'Then you have to try.' Giancarlo opened the book, pointed to the dedication on the first page.

For Noah – I should have said yes.

'Do you know where he is?'

'There is one more thing.' Giancarlo rose from his chair, reaching around the side to take hold of a wooden cane with a silver parrot on its end. He held out one arm and Emily took it, escorting him back inside the restaurant and to a small windowless room, which served as an office. The walls were filled with black and white photographs, all hung in haphazard fashion, all of people she did not know.

Apart from one.

Emily's eye fell on a photograph of Catriona and Gigi, both in bikinis, with hair soaked through with water from the sea. They were having a tug of war with a towel, Gigi bent double with laughter and Catriona leaning back, as if she were about to fall.

'I was angry for such a long time.' Giancarlo gazed at the photograph as he went around the desk. 'Angry at God, at myself, for wondering whether knowing Gigi for only a moment was better or worse than never knowing her at all.' He opened a drawer and took out another book, slid it across to Emily with a tear in his eye.

It was a copy of *Ulysses*. The same book her grandmother had seen a stranger read on a train headed for London and, years later, asked Emily to hide in the story Giancarlo had just given her.

'She said you would understand.'

'I don't.' She flicked through the pages but found nothing out of the ordinary. The book was a puzzle within a puzzle. A parody, a story set over the course of one day. Where was the link she was being asked to find?

'You will.' Giancarlo put the book back in his desk drawer. 'But don't be alone when you try to figure it out.'

'Why not?' Emily swallowed away the lump that had reappeared in her throat as she remembered the way he had looked at the envelope tucked inside her grandmother's book.

'You have someone with you?' He was staring at her again and she could see a certain sadness behind the lenses of his spectacles. It made her understand that every time he thought of Catriona, he remembered too the wife he had lost.

'I do,' she replied, thinking of Tyler and Phoebe, not certain they were with her in the way Giancarlo, or her grandmother, hoped.

'Just remember,' he said with a kiss on each cheek, then one more for luck. 'If you block out everything, you end up with nothing.'

It felt as if Emily's feet were moving, but she had no idea whether or not she wanted to go where they were taking her. She began to hum the tune to a long-forgotten hymn as she walked away from the river, away from the man who taught her grandmother how to toss a circle of dough into the sky. One more step towards the unknown. Like a lab rat in a maze from which there was no escape.

Don't panic, she told herself as she came into a square alive with noise and smell and people. Everywhere there were people, on all sides, like walls closing her in. She longed for the stretch of shoreline she could find so close to home. Part of her ached for the sight of the ocean that continued over and beyond the horizon and the endless curve of sky that she liked to watch the passage of time play out on. The rising sun, the dance of cloud, the myriad of stars that spoke to her of people from long ago, who had stared up at a light so far away, that guided them as they explored an unknown world.

Where was her constant, her Northern Star, keeping her safe from harm?

Emily sat on the pavement outside a café and checked her watch, spotting a couple as she searched through the chaos. Tyler was taking pictures of people on his phone and scribbling in his notebook. Phoebe was sat next to him, eating an ice cream and reading something Emily could not see.

Not exactly what Giancarlo meant, but they were all she had and, right now, she had no desire to carry on alone. Right now, she needed someone to tell her it was going to be okay.

Tyler looked up as Emily approached, saw the anxiety written all over her face. 'What's the matter?'

'I don't know,' she replied, turning the envelope over in her hand, wishing she could peep inside, just for a second, to decide whether or not the words it contained would do more harm than good.

'Have you read it?' He was staring at her. Everyone was always staring at her.

'No.'

'Do you want to?'

'I don't know.'

There was a sudden cheer and Emily looked across to see a woman throw her arms around a man, who then picked her up and turned full circle. As he did so, something caught the sun, flicked a patch of light onto Emily's face and she turned her head away. She had no desire to look upon their happiness when she could sense something else, waiting. With a deep breath, she slipped her finger under the envelope's seal and pulled out the pages of palest blue.

28 July, 2003

*'All we have to decide is what to do with the time
that is given to us.'*

JRR Tolkien, *The Fellowship of the Ring*

My child died and I wasn't there to say goodbye. To tell her
how much I adored her. How she changed my life the very
moment I first saw her pink, crumpled face. No, before that.
When I decided to keep her, happy accident that she was.

And now she is gone and everything is dark and filled with
shadows of what was, what should have been. Shadows of the
future that I catch glimpses of whenever I hear someone singing.
She had the most beautiful voice and I miss it so.

Adrianna had to identify the body because I was too far
away to get back in time. It haunts me, that image I will never
see. Of two women separated by the split second that turns life
into death, one carrying that moment around with them forever.
Never being able to unsee the cold, brutalised body of her best
friend. It should have been my duty, my burden, but I am also
so selfishly grateful I didn't have to see her that way. That I at
least get to think of her alive and full of joy.

Hospitals are hateful places. Not least the stench of
antiseptic and death, but the strange stillness that seems to cloak
everything. No one talks at a normal volume. It's all hushed
conversations in the corners of rooms. Making up sentences that
contain a multitude of sins — false hope, lies, counter-lies and
bucketloads of positivity thrown in for good measure.

But I have to be here, for her, for Emily. Her body is being held together by so many different materials, I'm not sure I can remember them all. All of her injuries. All of her broken bones and torn muscles and skin that the doctors have stitched back together like she's a patchwork doll. Her beautiful face. Her innocence. Shattered the very moment a stranger took the turn too fast.

She keeps pointing to the window. She likes to watch the birds even though it makes her cry. I'm terrified of what will happen next, because she hasn't said a word in over two weeks and part of me thinks she never will. Not because she can't, but because she has nothing left to say. What are words other than an expression of feeling, and how are you supposed to convey those feelings when they are raging inside of you, shredding your heart and burning your soul?

Too many people. We are surrounded by too many well-wishing people, who want to help, want to touch, want to comfort, but none of them know how. None of them will ever be able to fill the bottomless pit of despair that Emily and I are now trapped within.

I must take her away. Far from all the reminders of home. All the people and places she knows. Give her a chance, a fighting chance, to recover. Give me a chance to figure out what the hell I'm supposed to do now.

I am left behind. Empty and bereft, with no desire to carry on. But I must, and I will. Because she has lost her entire world too and I swear to do all that I can to try and piece it back together somehow. I will love her with all my heart and show her that, despite all the sadness, we can always rely on one another to search out the light, the song, the laughter.

CMR

253

19

ROBIN

Erithacus rubecula

'She was singing to me.' Emily gasped.

'What? Who?'

A web of tangled memories with the merest suggestion of something more. Something that was asking Emily to draw back the shutter she had put over the past and force herself to remember.

'She was singing to me. Then all of a sudden she stopped.'

'Emily?' Tyler was looking at her, waiting for her to say something more.

Time suddenly slowed, revealing gaps and cracks she had never dared to look through before, and then the memories began anew. Swirling through one another, a series of images on a loop she could not escape from.

Images from the day she had no desire to see.

'Make it stop,' she gasped, clutching at her heart, the words coming out between laboured breaths. 'Make the pain stop.'

She fell against the table, sent glasses and cutlery scattering to the ground, sank into a chair and looked out at a world she was unable to see, to focus on.

'She's having a panic attack.' Tyler glanced at Phoebe.

No, this is worse, Emily thought to herself. Like a long, sharp needle pressing against her heart. Bringing new stabs of pain each time she tried to breathe.

'Put your head between your legs.' Phoebe placed a hand at the back of Emily's head, but she pushed her away.

'Get off me,' she cried, and her grandmother's pages tumbled to the floor. Phoebe picked them up, took a few steps away.

'Emily, what's wrong?' Tyler bent down to her height, tried to make her look at him. 'What was in her diary?'

Her body and mind were at a loss for any kind of reaction. It made her feel like she was back in that hospital bed, seeing the world through an unwanted but familiar lens.

All was changed and she could never go back to how it was before. Just like then. Just as when she woke up to a room silent apart from the sound of her grandmother breathing. She was slumped in a wing-backed armchair, over by the window through which Emily could see the sun rising over the rooftops of London.

There were people, words, tastes. A biscuit on a plate that crumbled like ash and she hadn't been able to eat because her jaw was wired shut. But she could remember.

She had never wanted to remember.

The low note of pain that had escaped her chapped lips, woken her grandmother from a restless sleep, who then came over and tried to give comfort when she had no idea how.

'I don't want to remember,' Emily screwed her eyes tight, tried to shut out the past.

'Remember what?' Tyler was there, close enough that she could smell the coffee and tobacco on his breath.

'Make it go away.'

She wanted it all to leave her: all the memories of her parents, the images in her mind of that day. Unwashed dishes in the sink, a pan dirty with eggs and bacon. A window left open when they skipped from the house. A pale green dress trimmed with lace and her mother's hair wild and free, with sunshine on bare arms, reaching high and singing at the top of her voice.

There had been a picnic basket on the seat beside Emily, with walnut cake and fresh pineapple that she was slowly eating, piece by piece. They were in a sleek, black sports car with its roof down, one her father had borrowed from a friend, from Tyler's dad, just for the day. It was supposed to be a surprise trip to the river, where they would take out a rowboat and have a picnic on the water.

Her father leant across to kiss his wife, and then a flash of metal came towards them, too fast to miss, sending a tumble of sky overhead as the car flipped over and over.

A cry, a scream, a hiss, then a sharp pain in her head as all turned quiet.

'My mother told me to look up,' Emily whispered. 'To see a flock of birds flying overhead. Told me to count them all and made me promise not to look back down.'

Two magpies were on the road and came hopping onto the car. They looked at Emily before flying up and away from the sound of sirens that drew close.

Shouts, voices, the feeling of being lifted high. Looking back to see her mother's body, eyes closed and at peace. A red stain on her dress. Her father's face was turned away, which was no doubt a blessing as he took the full force of the truck.

Screaming. A child screaming over and over. Fighting against the people who were trying to save her, to stop the flow of blood from her face. To hold her tight, to keep her safe. Then another sharp pain and Emily's world went black.

Emily had told herself those magpies transported her parents to Heaven. She looked for them every day from her hospital bed. She would sit by the window so she could look at the sky and count all the birds that simply disappeared whenever they wanted, to somewhere new.

'Emily?' Tyler's hands were on her arms, trying to stop her from scratching at the scar on her face.

'Why?' she whispered, rocking slowly back and forth, tears intermingling with droplets of blood on her cheek. 'Why did she want me to remember?'

Tyler glanced across at Phoebe and he saw the look on her face as she finished reading, then passed the pages to him. He scanned Catriona's words, one fist clenching as he realised when they were written.

Emily looked up at Tyler, hoping somehow that he could piece together all the fragments, all the questions in her mind. Except he had betrayed her. He didn't care about her, he was only there for the money.

Struggling to her feet, she swiped at her nose, surprised to see red in amongst snot and tears. Snatching back the pages from her grandmother's diary, she stuffed them into her bag and began to walk away.

'Where are you going?'

'Home.'

'Emily, wait.'

'No,' she spun round to face him. 'It's over, Tyler. Go home, or wherever it is you would rather be.'

'You can't go, not like this.'

'Like what?'

His hand lifted, then fell back to his side, all the confusion on his face not quite translating into words.

'You were only ever here for the money, Tyler, not me. Besides, you still have a family waiting for you back home, only you're too selfish to understand how lucky you are.' Emily pointed over at Phoebe, her voice rising into a higher octave as she shouted out her frustration. 'She gave up a life-changing opportunity for you, and yet it's still not enough.'

'That was because of me?' Tyler turned to face Phoebe.

'There's nothing wrong with living a normal life,' Emily said, realising how much she resented him in that moment for thinking it wasn't enough.

'Who says I want normal?' He was looking again at Emily, seeing the way her body was shaking uncontrollably, but her eyes told him to stay away.

Emily saw Phoebe place a hand on his arm, holding him back, telling him to let Emily go. So she did. Simply turned around and walked away, her battered leather suitcase trundling along behind.

There was nothing wrong with normal. It's all Emily had ever wanted. To be like any other girl, with parents who used to read her bedtime stories, built sandcastles on the beach or sipped hot chocolate by the fire after coming in from the snow.

With no idea where she was headed, Emily walked on, her mind a blur of all the memories she had hidden from. All the moments shared with parents taken from her far too soon.

Verona's railway station was just like any other, only this time Emily was without direction, without purpose. She scanned the black departure board, so many destinations flashing up in yellow, just waiting to be chosen.

Where to? Back to St Tropez? To Antoine and his mansion and all that money tied up with guilt? Because of him, her grandmother never had a chance – a real chance – to be with Noah. Had he not interfered, would Catriona have married Noah, been as happy as Emily's parents? People who had given her something to hope for when she was all grown up. Her very own living and breathing fairy tale, only without the happily ever after.

They had honeymooned in Paris, and there was a photograph, in their bedroom at home, of them kissing under the Eiffel Tower. Emily's mother was dressed in a fifties-style skirt, her hair tied back with a pink ribbon, and she was holding an enormous balloon. It was ridiculous, but it always made her father smile because he said it was the happiest moment of his life, right up until he first held Emily in his arms and felt her tiny fingers wrap around his own.

Emily wondered where that photograph was now. No doubt boxed up in the attic back in Norfolk, along with all the other reminders too painful to look at, too precious to throw away.

Paris. She could go back to Paris. To the city where she felt so free.

And do what? She had no money, no job, nothing apart from a legacy that didn't even belong to her because she couldn't finish her grandmother's stupid test.

There was no more home. There was no one to whom

she could turn. How much pain did she have to bear? How much loss and remorse and suffering of heart?

Tears kept appearing on her cheek, surprise lines of wet that she tried to wipe away, only to find her fingers dotted with specks of red. She glanced around, saw that she was the subject of much interest – eyes that darted away, whispered words into another's ear and fingers that tapped away at smartphones. Mounting speculation and curiosity that she had not noticed up until that point. Which made her do what she always did when there was too much attention. She found somewhere to hide.

The station washroom was stark and white and bright, with two cubicles and a mirror above a plastic sink. Emily turned on the tap and watched water that ran over and through her fingers, the cool bringing momentary relief to her flushed skin as she cupped the water in her hands, brought it to her face, again and again. Looking up, she was startled at the sight of a young woman, staring back at her. She had full lips with a pronounced cupid's bow, hair like strips of sunlight and bright eyes that looked right back. It was as if she was asking Emily to see the memory of the girl she used to be. Screaming at her to be remembered, to be allowed once more to live.

'I look just like her,' Emily said as she turned her head a little, tilted it up, then down. She leant closer to the mirror, then stepped away, laughing at the similarity between her reflection and the portrait hanging in Antoine's house, and the photograph given to her in Paris, too. How much she looked like the woman who she had kissed every morning and before she went to bed. But she never saw what others did, didn't realise part of the reason why they stared. Because she had been paying no attention to the woman she, herself, had become.

A decision to be made. To stay or go. To follow this test, this puzzle, all the way to its bitter conclusion, or go back to England. Figure out another way.

Emily smoothed back her hair, and tried not to look at how those earrings really did show up the flecks of gold in her eyes, which only made her think of where Tyler could be. If he was still in the city, somewhere, or already making his way back to London, with her.

Suitcase in hand, she went back to the station concourse, watched the names on the board flicker as another train departed.

The sound of laughter pulled her attention elsewhere. To a couple, wrapped around one another, him kissing her just below the ear. Her reaching around his neck to pull him closer. A diamond on the third finger of her left hand, making Emily think back to another couple only a heartbeat away from the table where she had sat, drinking in her grandmother's words. Realising and remembering the horror of that day all over again.

A memory of when she found a ring tucked away at the back of a drawer in her grandmother's study. A simple gold band in which a stone of deepest blue was set (the exact colour of Lake Garda, her grandmother had said). It was given to her by a man who once loved her enough to ask for her hand in marriage, but Catriona knew it would never last. Her grandmother had smiled softly as she recalled the exact time and place he dropped down on one knee, placed a kiss on the pulse of her wrist and said he would never leave her, not again.

'James Joyce,' Emily whispered, reaching into her bag and taking out the book Giancarlo had given her, in which one of the clues listed at the back, one of the clues to be found, was a tiny depiction of *Ulysses*, resting on the nightstand of a girl back home. It was a novel Emily had read out of curiosity after hearing the story of how someone had once asked Catriona Robinson to marry him in the exact same place James Joyce seduced his wife.

That very same day, her grandmother began to map out the idea of a new story. She'd asked Emily to draw her a phoenix with feathers the colour of a setting sun. Emily had asked what love had to do with a phoenix and her grandmother had replied that there was always time to start again, to become someone new, if only you were prepared to try.

'*Scusi.*' Emily attempted a smile as she approached a man in a flat cap and uniform. The collar of his shirt was damp against tanned skin, with a shaving cut on his neck that he had tried to cover with a piece of now dried-up tissue. He lifted his head, gave Emily the swift once-over, then adjusted his belt, leant forward as he spoke.

'*Si, belissimo, come posso essere di servizio?*'

'Sirmione? Train?' Emily made a chugging motion with her arms and tried not to notice his amusement.

'*Il suo più rapido per guidare,*' the man responded, miming a steering wheel and pointing towards the exit. '*Il gruppo taxi e fuori.*'

'Perfect,' Emily muttered as she nodded her head in thanks, before looking up at the yellow sign with a black symbol of a car glaring back at her. She headed outside, looked over to where a line of taxis was stood, all neatly in a row, and tried to imagine they were like ducks, simply stood by a pond and waiting to go for a swim. Or school children fidgeting with conkers in their pockets. Ready to soak them in vinegar after school and tie them up with string.

Anything and everything to stop her from thinking about the last time she got into a car. It had been fifteen years since she'd heard the clunk of the metal doors locking her in; since she sat on the red leather seat and looked ahead through an unbroken windscreen. No speck of blood on the glass; no one trapped behind the wheel.

She propped her suitcase against the wall and sat on its edge, felt the ancient leather sag a little under her weight. A glimmer of red in the corner of her eye and she turned to see a robin pecking at the ground by a nearby tree. She gave a low whistle and he cocked his head, regarded her a moment, then came hopping over, stopping just shy of her foot.

'Hello,' she smiled down at the bird, watching him circle around the suitcase, looking for ants or stray crumbs. A second later and he fluttered up to land next to her, on the very edge of her case. He gave a chirrup, the ruby feathers on his breast quivering with the sound.

'No,' Emily crossed her arms. 'I can't. I absolutely cannot get into a taxi driven by a complete stranger.'

The robin gave his tail a little shake, depositing a tiny dropping down the side of the yellow leather before flying away.

'Fat lot of help you were.' Emily watched the bird loop up and over into the branches of the tree. She heard him calling out, either in warning or in search of a mate.

Robins are solitary birds. Emily looked across to the taxi rank. *And they often sing at night, which makes people mistake them for nightingales.*

'Oh,' she said as she stood all of a sudden, stared up at the tree. The bird was gone, but the memory of when she had first learnt about them came rushing back to the very centre of her mind.

A crisp Sunday morning. Her father in the back garden, digging out his beloved vegetable patch. No matter the weather, he would be there every weekend, tidying the greenhouse, planting out seedlings or trimming back the rose bushes. Emily liked to sit and watch him, sometimes handing him a trowel or helping plant out the seeds, press them down gently with fingers that would still bear traces of the earth when she went to bed.

Another morning, heavy with snow. When she and Tyler had been taken to the very top of Primrose Hill, toboggans at the ready and misty cheers as they flung themselves down the slope. The toboggan had tripped over a rock, and she fell, with hands lain flat, only for another sledge to shoot straight across them, pushing her fingers into the ground, making her cry out in alarm.

Her father picked her up, brushing her clean of snow and turned her hands over, slipping off sodden gloves. Then he had declared all was fine, no harm done, but Emily was too afraid to get back on the toboggan, crying and asking to go home.

'*If you don't go back up now, you never will,*' he had said with a smile, then kissed her cheek, straightened her scarf and made her climb once more to the summit. He had waited with a wave at the bottom until she got back on, kicked off from the ground and went soaring through the snow, feeling in that moment as free as any child ever could.

Face your fears. Don't give in to the voices of doubt.

264

Embrace the terror because you never know where it might lead you.

So many lessons taught, but all those memories pushed away.

He always told her to trust her gut, but she had been ignoring it for years. Which meant she ended up as nothing more than a girl, stood outside a train station, too afraid to finish what she started. Too afraid to find out what was waiting for her on a town by a lake.

This one's for you, Dad, Emily thought to herself as she picked up her suitcase and walked towards a waiting taxi.

20

HERON

Ardeidae

On the southern shores of Lake Garda sits the town of Sirmione. At the far end of its peninsula and completely surrounded by water is a medieval castle, a fortification used by the Scaliger family to protect the town from invasion.

It was at the top of this fortress that Emily stood, staring across the gentle waters of the lake. Watching as hundreds of boats criss-crossed the horizon, carrying tourists from port to port. One of them could well belong to the man she was looking for.

Below was an assortment of streets, and buildings with tiled roofs, evenly spaced windows and thick shutters to keep out the heat. The land stretched out into the lake on either side, clusters of Cypress trees breaking up the blue with leaves so dark they almost looked black, and the Italian flag sitting limp atop its pole, with no breeze to make it dance.

The taxi driver had dropped her on a strip of road, no doubt glad to be rid of the strange English girl who insisted on having the windows down and music turned up full for the whole journey. Emily had sat on a bench, head between her knees, waiting for her heart to return to a normal rhythm. In her hand she clutched the scrap of paper given to her by the taxi driver, with the name and location of Bailey's Boats. Noah Bailey, the man who asked Catriona Robinson to love him forever, in sickness and in health. Except she rejected him, and Emily wanted to know why her grandmother had turned her back on the man she loved most of all. Was it something he did, or did not do? Or something entirely more complicated?

Tyler was in her head now too. Had her grandmother an ulterior motive for choosing him as her guardian and ac-complice? Had she hoped they'd find one another after all these years and become something more than just long-lost friends? Would it have made any difference if he had kissed her in the bar in St Tropez, or if Phoebe hadn't turned up?

Because she can see the romance now, hidden in amongst all the tragedy. The reminders of love, of forgiveness, of the fleeting pocket of time that is life, which her grandmother kept chucking at her. But romance was never happily ever after. It was never just the highs, but also all the lows.

Emily stared down at the quayside, with all its tourists, far below, and out across the vast expanse of water. She imagined a time when the castle was filled with soldiers. When ships brought goods from all over the world, and her fingers itched to draw the images forming in her mind: a stowaway hidden in a crate of tea brought all the way from China; a young girl who dreamt of being an explorer.

There was a rumble of engine as a sleek black boat traversed the waves below. A man stood at the helm, steering his vessel beneath one of the bridges that would bring him back to land. He had short, dark hair, smudged with grey at the temples, his sleeves were rolled up to reveal strong, tanned arms and there was a cigarette tucked behind one ear.

Two by two, she ran down the steps, round and round until she reached the bottom, then had to lean her head against the cool stone to wait for the world to stop spinning. Through the crowds, she went, in and out of a group following a woman shouting in German, along with a screaming child trying to escape from its buggy and a mother smiling her apology behind tired eyes.

The man secured his boat to shore with a thick length of rope, before assisting each of his passengers back onto dry land. He turned as he felt someone's eyes on him, raised one hand to his mouth and said something Emily could neither hear nor see.

She watched as he walked towards her, held her breath as he pulled her into a tight embrace. He was crying, talking in a mixture of English and Italian. Hugging her, then holding her at arm's length, staring at her face, then shaking his head and crying all over again.

'Emily,' he said her name like he was afraid of it. Quiet and slow. 'Emily,' he said again, exploring every part of her face, resting a moment on her scar, then back up to her eyes.

'Noah.' She attempted a smile, but there was something about this man that bothered her, because she couldn't shake off the feeling of déjà-vu, that she had met him before. Except she didn't remember his face, so what was it? The fact he had been expecting her, or even the knowledge of what he did to her grandmother? Disappointment? No, because he was just as alluring, just as whimsical, as she had imagined. All crinkly eyes and designer stubble, with navy blue shirt, white jeans and a diver's watch around one wrist.

'Are you hungry?' He was looking at her in a different way now. As if he was seeing her, not her grandmother, noticing the ways in which they were unique, as much as how they were so very similar.

'A little.' In truth, she didn't really know what she was. Food seemed somehow irrelevant, disconnected from this man, this place. She wanted something, but couldn't put her finger on what it was.

'Do you want to see the castle?' He pointed to the stone walls behind them.

'I've been up it already.'

'Did you know that it is built on stilts? Just like in Venice.'

She liked the way his words were curling around one another, as if he was struggling to piece them together. It may have only been because he was more used to speaking Italian than English, but it made her feel more at ease, less aware of her own impediments.

'I tell you what. Let me take you out on the boat. To a place I know a little further up the lake. Somewhere I took your grandmother, a long time ago.'

He was waiting for her to reply. To give her consent. To get on a boat with a man she knew only by proxy but who could, for all she knew, be an axe murderer.

'Do you have time?'

Three more days. Emily calculated. Three more days until

the timer ran out of sand and everything she thought she had would be given away.

'If we go now,' he held out his hand, invited her on board his boat. 'We can be there to watch the sun set, with a glass of Prosecco and some fantastic linguine.'

The boat thrummed to life and Emily sat up front, next to Noah at the helm. She closed her eyes to feel the salty spray on her face as they cleared the small marina, and he opened up the throttle, sending them hurtling across the water.

Did you swim here? she wondered, knowing how much her grandmother loved the sea, even on the coldest of mornings, even when she was tired and frail.

Eyes wide open, she saw houses with terracotta and lemon walls, children playing on pebble beaches and snow-topped mountains looming in the background. It was spectacularly beautiful, like a film set, or something stolen from the depths of her imagination.

A heron was perched on one of the rocky outposts they sped past, all skinny legs and long beak. Motionless, the bird waited, staring into the water for its prey.

The Greeks believed herons to be messengers from the Gods, including Aphrodite. Emily stole a glance at Noah. Was her grandmother trying to send her a message, or was she simply looking for clues, for signs, that this was where she was supposed to be?

Watching the casual way he navigated the lake, with only the slightest movement of his hand on the wheel, Emily imagined what it would have been like to have loved someone as deeply as her grandmother loved this man. For someone to love you that way in return.

It was clear he was at home here, speaking with reverence

and delight as he pointed out various landmarks along the way. He was at peace, and she couldn't help but wonder once again why her grandmother hadn't wanted to be here, with him.

'Over there,' he said, pointing to a huge villa with a thin, wooden jetty that was flanked either side by candy-striped poles, and Emily could make out an ivy-covered entrance to the house at the top of a long flight of stone steps. 'Wait here one moment, I'll see if they can provide us with something to eat.' He dipped his head, took hold of her hand and placed a gentle kiss on her skin, watched her a moment more, then disappeared up the steps and into the house.

Emily followed a neat, gravel path around the side of the house to discover an immaculate garden with a line of palm trees that flanked a swimming pool, the surface of which was perfectly still. There was no one else about and so she decided to slip off her shoes, dangle her legs over the side of the pool and stir her toes through the water, sending ripples over the surface all the way to the other end.

'Why did you ever leave?' she murmured, looking beyond the villa with its stuccoed walls and to the houses that reached all the way up the hillside.

A high whistle and she looked back to see Noah come outside, beckoning her towards where he was waiting on a covered terrace with curtains drawn back to reveal a panoramic view of the lake.

The terrace floor was pink and white chequered marble, the light fittings were the same colour as candyfloss and the chair Noah pulled back for her to sit upon had a satin bow tied around its back. But it was what lay beyond the terrace, back towards the jetty and a little to the right, which stopped her from sitting. Something that Emily thought she had seen before made her go back down and around the pool before running towards a view she had looked upon, over and over, without knowing where it actually was.

'She was here,' Emily whispered, leaning both hands on the back of a wooden deckchair with deep green cushions. A pair of them, either side of a stone table, positioned under a tree with branches that reached down to wave hello.

'I was working here, at the hotel, when your grandmother came back.' Noah was there beside her with a far-off look on his face. Almost as if he knew which photograph she was thinking about. A photograph that lived on her grandmother's bedside table, of Emily's mother as a toddler, peeping out from the top of one of those very chairs, her grandmother stood behind with both arms either side for protection. Both of them smiling at whoever was taking their picture. 'The house used to belong to Mussolini, before it became a hotel.'

He was talking for the sake of having something to say. She was used to people behaving this way around her, filling in the gaps created by her silence, but this was different. It wasn't because she didn't want to speak, to talk to him about her mother, about why she was here and all the thousands of other questions she wanted answers to. But rather she had no idea what to say, or how to convey all of what it was she was feeling.

'Did you know about Margot, about my mother?'

He exhaled with relief. As if he had been holding his breath, afraid of what she was going to say.

'Not at first, and I wish I could tell you she was mine, that you are mine.'

Emily swallowed away her disappointment, gave a small

smile as she realised it didn't hurt half as much as she had expected it to, because on some level she had always known her grandfather wasn't the treasure to be found. And it felt as though she had found something wonderful and unexpected in this man, in Antoine too. They were pieces of her grandmother that were still here for her to discover.

'So why did she come back, if you weren't the father?'

'I think we were always drawn to one another, in some way. But we both also understood that I wasn't right for her, no matter how hard I tried.'

'She loved you.'

'And I loved her. More than anyone before or since.'

'What happened?'

'I asked her to stay, to marry me, again. For us to become a family.'

Emily stared at him. He was seated in the same spot where her mother once played. She could imagine time unwinding, going back to that summer. She could picture the three of them on the shores of this very lake, with her mother, Margot, having her toes dipped into the wet and giggling with delight as those pudgy legs kicked out.

Emily listened to the rush of waves over the shore, heard how the water here was more gentle, less aggressive, than at home. As if each stretch of ocean or lake had its own personal melody. Just like a person has their own unique scent, or tone of voice, or the exact beat of their heart.

'She said no.' Emily sighed. It made her sad to think of her grandmother here, with him. Being asked to love someone and telling them it wasn't possible.

'Three times.'

'Three?'

He laughed, a rich note of sound that filled his lungs before escaping, making Emily smile in return.

'The first was after a drunken argument, about Antoine no less. In Sirmione, when we barely knew one another but couldn't deny the attraction, the pull of both our hearts.'

'He's still mad at you.'

'I know, and I probably deserve it.' Noah lit a cigarette, drew on it in a gesture so reminiscent of Tyler that it hurt her to watch, to see the similarities between the two men who had never met. It pained her to realise how much she cared for them both, in completely different and surprising ways.

'She left him to come here, when she still had faith in me. It lasted for a couple of months, but then ...'

'Then?'

'I was young, and arrogant.' There was no need for him to fill in the gaps.

'You're an idiot.'

'You sound like Antoine, but you're right. I was, and it is something I regret every single time I think about her, about what could have been.'

'And?'

He took another drag of his cigarette, gave himself time to think before replying.

'I came back to find her gone. No note, just a copy of *Villette* left on top of an unmade bed.'

'She was punishing you.' Emily laughed as she considered her grandmother's choice of book. So typical of her to leave nothing but a clue as to what it was she was really thinking. A book about a lonely woman's love for an unattainable man. Not too dissimilar to a cryptic clue that had led Emily all the way back to him now.

'Again, I deserved it. But after a while she started writing to me. Told me she was happy, that she forgave me my sins.'

'Do you still have it?'

'I have all her letters.'

'Can I . . . Can I see them?'

He dropped the cigarette to the floor with a slow shake of his head, ground out the embers with the heel of his shoe.

'I don't know that it would help.'

'Help with what?'

'With saying goodbye.'

She could feel a blockage in her throat. One that swelled and pushed from all sides, fighting to escape. Wet lines appeared on her face as tears fell fast and determined, no matter how many times she tried to wipe them away.

He stepped forward and wrapped his arms around her, enveloping her in a hug as the hurt from deep inside eventually let go, and so he held her tighter still, tucked her safe against his heart.

It wasn't the sight of him, nor the sound of his voice, although the two of them combined had been enough to send her a little off-kilter, ever since she first saw him steering his boat to shore. She couldn't, up until that moment, quite put her finger on what it was that made her a little less certain today was the first time they'd met. It was what was hidden beneath the scent of clean linen with a hint of lime, the undertones of spice and nutmeg in his aftershave, that made her remember, made her pull away.

'You were there.'

'You remember.'

'Yes. I mean, I didn't. But, you were there.' In the clinic, where Emily had been taken to recuperate, to recover, away from all the well-intentioned friends and family back in London. A place where she and her grandmother lived for just shy of two years. Where she learnt to walk, to paint, to live once again.

'You used to read to me.'

'I did. *Wind in the Willows* was your favourite, if I remember correctly.'

A storybook that used to help block out the nightmares. The low rumble of his voice when he imitated Badger, the crazy flap of arms supposed to be Toady that almost, almost, made her laugh.

More often than not, she would turn her head away; close her eyes as she didn't want to see the way he looked at her grandmother. It was the same way her father used to look at her mother – with so much love. Only *their* story was tangled up with a lifetime's worth of pain.

'I'm sorry,' she said.

'What for?'

'Forgetting.'

Noah exhaled slowly. 'It's not something you need to apologise for. You were broken in so many ways. All she ever wanted was for you to get better.'

'What about her?'

'What do you mean?'

'She was broken too.' Emily was crying again. Thinking about how hard it must have been for her grandmother. How for years all Emily could focus on was her own pain, what she had lost. Never stopping to think about the ways in which her grandmother had suffered too.

'Losing a child isn't something anyone can ever even begin to imagine. The tragic unfairness of it all. But she had you.'

'All I did was push her away.'

'You were her reason not to give up.' He took hold of her shoulders, brought his face close to hers. 'Do you have any idea how much she loved you? How much she adored the time you had together?'

'I miss her.' It was no more than the suggestion of a whisper. Words felt but hardly spoken.

'So do I, *mio cara*, so do I.'

'Why didn't you stay, or come back to England with us?'

'She didn't want me to.'

'Because of me.' Everything her grandmother had turned her back on, abandoned, was because of her.

'No,' he said firmly. 'That fault lies entirely with me. I was trying to save her, always trying to save her, and that's never what she wanted.'

'What do you mean?'

'You have to understand, back then, for her to decide to raise Margot by herself, was more than hard. Everyone was telling her not to. Everyone had an opinion on it, but she felt completely alone.'

'She had you.'

'Yes, but I didn't have her. She was fierce and strong and annoyingly stubborn,' he said with a poignant look at Emily. 'But she was also right. We would never have worked because I was trying to make her into something, someone, she was not.'

Emily thought of the heroine from her grandmother's second book, who, at the very end, when she had what others would deem a perfect life, decided to walk out on her fiancé. A woman who took passage on an ocean liner to Australia, hoping to start a life of her own with nothing in her pocket but a handful of hope.

'You are more like her than you think,' Noah said, holding out a brown paper parcel, tied up with string. 'Come,' he said, taking her arm and escorting her back to the terrace. 'You can read whilst we eat.'

Someone had set down two enormous silver domes and placed a bottle of Prosecco in an ice bucket next to the table to chill. Emily lifted her dome high to reveal the scent of sweet chilli, salt and lashings of lemon.

'Eat,' Noah said as he poured her a drink. 'You look like you need fattening up for Christmas.'

Taking a long sip, feeling the crisp explosion of bubbles against her tongue, Emily pulled apart the brown paper and lifted out the next clue.

There he is, she thought with a smile, tracing over the cover with her fingers. She remembered when she first showed the drawing to her grandmother and how shocked she had been when she had started to laugh and cry all at once.

It was Emily's favourite of all her grandmother's book covers – an enormous, violet dragon with eyes of gold and teeth like shards of glass, soaring high over a river filled with lantern-lit boats, all heading out to sea.

It was also the last book in the series, written just before Catriona first fell ill. When Ophelia had learnt to walk again. A medical miracle according to the doctors, but of course she and Terence knew better. The miracle was Ophelia swimming in enchanted waters at the bottom of a waterfall, behind which lived a fearful dragon. A dragon who the local villagers believed to be wicked and cruel, but Ophelia heard him crying whilst she swam and asked him what was wrong.

The dragon was grieving the loss of his brother, who had been shot down by a canon as he flew over the seas. His grief made him angry, made him roar and breathe fire over the villagers, burning their houses to the ground.

'Don't be too quick to judge the monsters,' Emily said as she opened the book to read one more dedication.

For Beth — thank you for saving us both.

'Monsters?' Noah asked as he wiped his mouth with a napkin. It made Emily think again of Tyler, of that first morning back in her Norfolk kitchen, when he helped himself to a snack and told her they had a train to catch.

'Everyone has a secret pain they're trying to hide,' Emily replied, staring down at the name of a woman she knew only too well. Someone she dared to think might possibly be the final piece of this puzzle, and might just be the last step on her journey back home.

'She loved to watch you draw,' Noah said, as Emily slowly turned each page. 'She said it was when you were most at peace.'

'Not any more.'

'What do you mean?'

'I'll show you.' Emily reached into her bag, found an empty space where her sketchbook should have been, then looked across at Noah as she tried to think back to when she last had it. 'Verona.'

'What about it?'

'I must have left it in Verona.' Along with all the other people and places she had been trying to forget.

'What was it you wanted to show me?'

'I can't.' Emily shook her head, no. Squeezing tight her eyes, she tried to block out the memory, all the memories, that she had been shown, that she had been drawing ever since she left England.

'Yes, you can.'

He told me to talk to them. Emily remembered what Giancarlo had said. He told her not to forget them, because then they would never be gone.

'She used to sing to me.' Her words came out all tumbled together, as if they had been trying to escape for a very long time and were afraid she might change her mind, keep them locked away.

'Your mother.'

'Every night before I went to bed.' The same lullaby. A softer, quieter version of *The Magic Flute*. During the day she would dance through the house, pouring out arias from *Tosca* or *La Traviata*, never caring who was listening. But at night, when it was just the two of them, she would sit Emily in a rocking chair by the window, always open so they could see the ever-changing moon, and sing to her about Tamino and his magic flute.

'You can always start again.'

'What?' It was something her grandmother used to say, whenever Emily thought she'd made a mistake. When a picture didn't appear on the page in the same way she saw it in her mind. How much of what she taught Emily had been learnt from Noah, from all the people she used to know?

'That's the beauty of tomorrow,' Noah said as he raised his glass in a toast. 'I think it's time for you to move on. Find something new to paint.'

'I'll try.'

'There's a line in this story, one I keep going back to, again and again.' He reached out for the book, flipped through the pages until he found the words he was looking for. *'Put your hand in the water, and watch all the ripples appear.'*

It was a line from when the dragon asked Ophelia to swim in the waters once more, waters he had warmed with his own fiery breath.

'I think she meant it as a message for you.' His hand was on hers now, his eyes filled with tears. 'That each ripple should be seen as a possibility, and she wanted you to chase them all.'

'But what if I can't?'

'Then at least you tried. That's all any of us can ever do.'

Emily looked out to the lake, to where Noah's boat was gently pitching on the water. Always water. From the very beginning, she had always taken Emily to the water.

'How long will it take to get to Lugano?'

'It's not far. But stay here, just for one night, and tomorrow I will take you back to Beth.'

There was a canary-yellow sofa with tassels all around its base. A pale, grey marble bathroom with roses set by the sink. A bed as soft as a dream and a mahogany writing desk positioned by an open window, from which Emily could hear crickets rubbing their legs together in unison, singing their strange dusk chorus.

'I get it,' she whispered to the moon, to all the birds that flew through the darkening sky. 'I get it,' she whispered again, taking out a plain white envelope and steeling herself for those sheets of palest blue and what they might contain.

She understood how she had been trapped in the memory

of a thirteen-year-old girl. A girl who took flight, like a bird, to try and escape the pain she had witnessed. But now she needed to take a leap of faith, rid herself of the past and set herself free.

25 May, 1968

The sky is hanging down in slithers of purple and blue, with no more than a sprinkling of stars reflected back from an inky pool of water.

It is so very, very peaceful here. Margot is sleeping on the bed next to me, Noah on the sofa next door. If I listen carefully, I can hear them both breathing in their own unique rhythms. One long and laboured, the other all in a rush, a quickstep then pause as she dreams.

He wants me to stay. Asked me again to marry him, this time with a beautiful sapphire ring, and I was so very tempted. But is he asking because of me, or because of Margot? I see the way he looks at her, with a different kind of longing to the way those eyes would land on me. He wants a family, a connection, a reason for getting up in the morning. I want it too, but not like this. We would argue, we always do, and Margot doesn't belong to him. She doesn't belong to anyone and neither do I.

He would make me into a wife, which comes with its own set of unspoken rules and I don't do rules, not any more.

I suppose I could go to Gigi. Raise Margot there as part of a larger, extended family. But it's not my family, it's not where I want to set down roots in this world. I still want to travel, to see what delights are hiding around the next corner, but I also understand how unfair that would be on Margot, at least when she is bigger and needs a life that isn't dictated by her mother.

This is the part I wasn't prepared for. Always thinking about someone else. Always basing your decisions on whether it would work for them, as well as you. But it's my life too, so why can't I just live it? The constant pull of the heart, the constant need to remember that I chose to bring her into this world, she was not of her own making. It is my responsibility to teach her about life, but also let her discover it for herself. How to find the balance? How to ever know if what I'm doing is right?

Or I stay. Give her the traditional family, with two parents, a home and, perhaps, one day, a sibling or two. But it would stagnate me and at some point I would come to resent the decisions I made on her behalf. I do not ever, not for a single second, want to regret anything about her.

But where to? The stigma of being an unmarried mother isn't one that you can easily shake away. All the questions, the knowing looks, the judgement. Do I really want that? Do I actually care? Of course I do. We all care about the opinions of others. No one is completely immune to how we are perceived by the world.

Then there's always the option of going home, but not to Scotland. To London, where Charlie is now working for a publishing house. She's had some interest in my first two books, wants to know if there's a third in the making (easier said than done with a curious toddler to contend with!). But I know she just wants me to go back so she can play at being mother, at keeping house, at having something in her life other than her work. She also told me I could do some freelance work, as an editor, help pay the bills whilst I write. It sounds so very tempting, but also a little bit like the easy way out.

One day I know I will have to put down roots. One day Margot will have to go to school, make friends, follow the same path that everyone else does. I wish it could be different. I wish we could simply see where fate sends us. Travel the globe with nothing more than a notebook and our dreams. But that's just it, it's my dream, not hers. And she still isn't even close to being of an age where she can try to figure out who she wants to be, what she wants to do. I suppose neither have I, but that doesn't mean I can't stop trying.

And men make you stop. Men make you question everything. Make your heart sing then weep in the blink of an eye. Make you forget all rational, sensible thought and think only of the way he makes you feel when he kisses you slowly and whispers again about love.

Noah is my undoing, as I knew from the very first moment we met, in that cramped, dusty, incredible bookstore in Paris. He is my soulmate, but that doesn't mean I should stay. It doesn't mean I should sacrifice my own wants and desires, my own ambitions, just to fit in with his. Because this is his forever. It is beautiful, it would be the perfect place to raise a child, but it does not come from me, from who I am, who I want to try and become.

I haven't yet found my forever place in this world. Haven't yet discovered where it is that I fit. Although there is an image that follows me wherever I go. Of a house in a village by the sea. With apple trees in the back garden and a desk by the window so that I might watch all the comings and goings of nature as I write.

Maybe that's what I've been looking for. Somewhere hidden away from the world, just for Margot and me. We don't need anything more.

CMR

21

NIGHTINGALE

Luscinia megarhynchos

Everything happens for a reason. Everything will be okay in the end. He's not going to kill you, stop panicking.

All of these thoughts and more raced around Emily's mind as she gripped her battered yellow suitcase in her lap. Every bump in the road could be felt through the thin metal casing of the motorbike sidecar in which she was sat, a pair of old-fashioned goggles strapped to her head and obscuring the view.

Had she known this would have been Noah's suggested mode of transportation, she would have gladly taken a taxi back to Verona, knocked on the door to Tyler and Phoebe's room and asked if they could accompany her back to England instead, on the Eurotunnel no less. Or called Antoine and asked him to put her back inside his tiny private plane, all enclosed spaces with no means of escape.

If she had she known this was where she would end up when she first entered the bookshop back in Norfolk, no, when that man and his dog turned up on her doorstep, she would have laughed in the face of all things fateful and seren- dipitous and told the Gods to leave her be.

She could hear the sound of water, could see the church steeple rising from the hillside, taste the scent of pine mixed through with salt. It was all so familiar and yet she wasn't yet able to link together now with then. The reality of what was staring her in the face versus the memory of a place she never thought she would come back to, having been so desperate to escape.

Noah was stood by her side, hands on hips, still wearing his helmet. They were both looking up at the front façade of a house that had been extended in all directions. It had a picture-perfect porch that wrapped around the side, with an oversized swing hanging from the rafters, on which was sleeping a pair of fat, ginger cats.

Beyond the porch was a gate to the vegetable patch, where Emily and her grandmother helped plant out seedlings, pulled away weeds and dug up carrots to be taken to the kitchen for supper. On the first floor, around the back, were two bedrooms, connected by a Jack 'n' Jill bathroom. One of the rooms had lilac walls and a corner seat by the window, overlooking the water. Scratched into the base of that seat was the shape of a duck, along with her initials, E.C.D. Emily Catriona Davenport. The name her parents gave her. The name she felt stopped belonging to her the moment they were gone.

'Are you going up?' Noah nudged her with his foot.

'Aren't you coming in?'

'This is where I say goodbye.'

She stared at him. 'Goodbye?'

'For now.' One hand on the back of her neck, so familiar, so comforting. 'This part is up to you. But you know where to find me and I will always be here for you. Remember that you are not alone, that there are people who care for you, and not just because of her.'

He kissed her cheek gently and she watched him mount his bike, roar up the engine and disappear off and down the road, out of sight.

Come on, then, Emily told herself as she picked up her case, climbed the steps to the maroon front door, rang the bell and waited for her past to open up, invite her in.

The clinic was like an old hotel, designed to make people believe they were anywhere but a medical facility. It was all polished brass doorknobs, oversized chairs and fresh flowers in cut glass vases. But the people in wheelchairs, or with tubes attached to various parts of their anatomy, draped in such a way as ordinary folk accessorise with a necklace, made it apparent this wasn't a holiday retreat.

Emily hadn't been back for well over ten years, during which time subtle changes had been made: a sound system had been installed, there was new carpet on the stairs, and a grand piano by the French doors that opened on to the garden. But the security cameras remained, there to make sure you were safe and sound in the rehabilitation clinic dressed up as a country lodge.

She was asked to wait, to sit in the reception area just like any other guest. Absently flicking through magazines with pictures of strangers smiling back, not taking in any of the articles about the benefits of acupuncture or aromatherapy baths. She couldn't focus because of the smell that was permeating from the kitchen that she knew was down the hall and off to the right. Roasting meat and cinnamon, all mixed in together, along with antiseptic and furniture polish.

It transported her back to a time when she was so very angry with the world, with herself, because she'd survived. A time when she couldn't hold on to any happy memories. When she kept asking to go home, then realised there was no point because her parents were gone. Her room, her things, her life, had all been destroyed by the knowledge that she would never get to enjoy them again. Her school, her friends, everything, gone, changed, ruined, never to be the same again.

No one looked at her the same way, or spoke to her, or paid her the same amount of attention, because she was damaged and bruised and was just someone to pity. Not a person, not a child, just a body in a wheelchair that everyone was trying to fix. But they never understood she didn't want to be fixed, she wanted to be gone.

'Emily?' Emily was pulled back to where a woman was stood before her, a smile on her face and concern in her eyes.

It was the same woman who had treated her, here, when the hospital in England could do no more. When her grandmother decided to take her away from all the people, all the memories, of her life before the accident, deciding to bring her to a clinic where her friend was training as a psychiatrist. A woman whom Catriona first met in Paris but had never told Emily the connection, instead waiting until she herself was gone before revealing the truth about all those people, all those lives that dipped and weaved through one another.

'My goodness, aren't you just the most wonderful surprise?'

Beth pulled Emily into an embrace and she relaxed into the older woman's arms, breathed in the familiar scent of her, felt a sense of peace settle in her heart.

'She gave you the earrings,' Emily stared at Beth, taking in the hair now cropped close to her head, the deeper lines around the eyes, the softening of skin at her throat. 'And it was you, stood next to Antoine in the photograph.'

'What photograph?'

'In Paris. By the bookstore.'

'My goodness, I'd forgotten all about that. Trust Catriona to have it all this time.'

'No, it wasn't her.'

Beth didn't catch the words Emily whispered because she had picked up her case and stashed it behind the front desk. Nor did she see the way Emily was staring at nothing as they walked, side by side, feeling a little off-kilter, a little faint, because she was thinking back to that bookstore in Paris, to the place where they had all met and how very, very envious she was that it couldn't have been her life instead.

Six people, brought together by a twist of fate. Their lives interlinked in so many ways, most recently by another death, but also the possibility of a new beginning. *Her* new beginning, and she saw how they had all played their part in bringing her back here, each of them carrying out her grandmother's wishes, and yet she still didn't understand why.

Beth took her to a familiar room, with a large desk at the far end. On top was a computer, a stack of papers and a silver photo frame that held a photograph of a family Emily had never met. Her eyes flickered to the back of the room, where an old-fashioned music system still sat, nestled in amongst books, photographs and keepsakes.

Emily went over to it, knelt down on the floor in the same spot as she always used to. She felt the room sway a little as she remembered all the time she had spent in here, locked away on her own, listening to music and painting pictures of everything she couldn't say.

'Why didn't you tell me?' Emily thought of her grand-mother's funeral, of all the people paying their respects. Some of them had been complicit in keeping a secret from her.

'She made us promise not to.'

'She wouldn't have known.'

'But we would.'

Emily wished she could put those six friends back together again, take their photograph once more. Have them share a bottle of wine or two over a long meal, swap stories of their lives as they laughed and reminisced and swore not to leave it so long before next they met.

Except that would never happen. Two of the six were dead and Emily wasn't certain she would ever be able to get Antoine and Noah in the same room for more than a few minutes before they started arguing. But then death does strange things to people, makes them act completely out of character.

They were the people who had shaped Catriona, made her the woman she became.

Every single interaction, no matter how small, has an impact on who you turn out to be. Every conversation, every disappointment, every touch, they all combine into one huge mess called life.

Emily heard a drawer being opened, then the sound of something being placed on top of the desk.

I don't want it. Emily dropped her head. *I don't want to know what it is she made me come here for.*

But she *did* want to know, or at least part of her knew it was pointless to try and resist. So she stood up, went over to the desk and opened up the package, because she had come this far and it would be a complete waste of time, of life, to give up now.

Inside a white Manilla envelope were a few familiar sheets of palest blue, folded in half, along with a handful of lined pages, tied through a hole with red string.

Emily took a breath. Could they be the missing pages, the story Catriona Robinson was rumoured to have written?

'I don't understand,' she said as she flicked through the pages, only to see that most of them were empty. A few ideas, places and names. Nothing more substantial than what was in the notebook given to Emily by the bookseller, all the way back in Norfolk.

'Where's the finished book?' Emily looked at Beth.

'I'm sorry, Emily,' she said with hands splayed. 'I don't have anything else.'

Emily flicked through the pages once again, back and forth, as if somehow more words would appear. 'Where's the rest of it?'

'That's all she sent me. That,' Beth pointed at the Manilla envelope, 'along with the real will, and a letter.'

'The real will?'

Emily looked back inside the envelope to find something she had missed, then scanned the words typed neatly on several pages and signed at the end by her grandmother.

'It says here that the house is mine.' Emily sank into a nearby armchair.

'Yes.' Beth perched on the end of her desk, watching Emily closely.

'It says that it's always been mine.' Emily's hands began to shake as she drank in the enormity of what she had just discovered. 'That the estate, the rights, the books. It all belongs to me.'

Emily felt light-headed, but wasn't sure if it was due to shock, relief or something more.

'Who else was she going to give it to?'

'It makes no sense.' Emily's hands dropped to her lap. 'Why bring me here, back to the beginning, like in one of her stupid books, only for it not to be finished?'

'Maybe that's the point.'

'Why make me go through all of this,' she said, waving her arms out theatrically. 'If the house belonged to me all along?'

'Would you have left if she'd given you a choice?'

Emily opened her mouth, then shut it again. In that moment she realised how, only a short while ago, she never would have believed it possible that she could be sat here, having a conversation, an argument, with the woman who had inadvertently taught her how to hide behind her paintings. The woman who, though she helped put her back together, also made her shy away.

Only a short while ago, Emily wouldn't have been having a conversation with anyone, other than the birds who she fed the crumbs of her life to.

Looking again at the Last Will and Testament of Catriona Robinson, she bit back the urge to rip it to pieces; swallowed down the distinct sense of anticlimax.

'Come with me,' Beth held out her hand to Emily. 'I want to show you something extraordinary.'

Arm in arm they walked through the clinic, past the day room, past the library with floor-to-ceiling bookcases and a squishy sofa by the window. A small group of children were sat in a semicircle on the floor, listening to one of the nurses read aloud a story about a little girl and her duck.

'The two of you really did create something rather magical.' Beth smiled as she continued to the end of the corridor, opened a door that never used to be there. 'Those books have helped people in more ways than you could possibly know.'

Together they stepped inside an enormous greenhouse, filled with exotic plants and the sound of running water. Emily felt damp on her skin, looked down to be surprised by the sight of a butterfly, opening and closing its wings on a nearby leaf. There was a mosaic path running through the centre and out to the gardens, and Emily could see a couple of patients tending to a rhododendron bush in the far corner.

'There's also a new swimming pool, a Pilates studio and we even have a couple of ponies, as well as all the chickens you used to chase.'

'What's this got to do with me?'

Beth pointed to a sign above the door through which they had just come.

Built with the kind support of The Emily Davenport Foundation.

'It's because of you. Because of the money Catriona donated from the sale of all those wonderful books. And not just us,' she continued, looping her arm through Emily's and escorting her out to the gardens. 'Charities the world over have benefitted from her generosity. You have helped so many people put their lives back together, Emily. It really is quite remarkable what that little girl and her duck have achieved.'

'She never told me,' Emily said in disbelief.

'She never wanted you to feel obligated. She knew how much you loved to draw and didn't want to take that joy away.'

'She did it because of me.'

'You gave her a sense of purpose. Something she never quite found with your mother, they were simply too different. You are so very much like Catriona. Your spirit, your determination, your creativity.'

They walked on and Emily breathed in, slow and deep, feeling a sense of calm begin to seep into her mind. Thought of all the things she now knew about Catriona Robinson. About the person, not just the grandmother. About who she was trying to get Emily to be.

'I still don't understand why she did it,' she said with a frown. 'Why she gave it all up, her life, her friends, her freedom.'

'Where are we?' Beth asked as they reached a simple wooden bench close to the shore of the lake.

'Is that a rhetorical question?' Her tongue slipped through the words, almost stumbling, but Emily didn't flinch, didn't waver, because she no longer felt ashamed.

'How did you get here?'

'On a motorbike.'

'Who brought you?'

'Noah.'

'And how did you find him?'

How did she find him? How did she manage to find any of it? How did she manage to leave behind her familiar, stagnating life to set out on an adventure dreamt up by the mind of a dead woman?

'Just sit here a moment,' Beth eased Emily onto the bench. 'Sit here and think of her, of where she's brought you. Where you've come from. Sit here and think of all the ways in which you are mad at her, all the ways you wish she was here, just so you could scream at her for dying. But allow yourself to remember, too, what it was she was trying to show you.'

'So this is the end?'

'Or the beginning, depending on how you look at it.' Beth handed her the envelope containing her grandmother's final clue. 'As a little girl I would rise early in the morning, listen for the *gokotta*. I liked to think they were singing just for me.'

'The what?' Emily stared at what she held in her hands, not wanting to think about what she was supposed to do now.

'Cuckoo. They used to live in the woods behind my home, back in Sweden. Do you remember?'

'I remember.' A memory popped into her head, of making angels in the snow, then back to the house for a hot drink and to toast her toes by the open fire. A visit one winter, before relocating to Norfolk. Walks in the forest, listening to the call of birds, staring into the face of a deer that didn't care how broken or disfigured she was. Water like ice that her grandmother dared to swim through. Her skin pink and bright, her smile wide and pure as she wrapped herself in layer after layer of blankets and shook droplets of cold onto Emily's face.

'You should go back,' Beth said. 'Make some new memories.' A gentle pat on Emily's shoulder and then Beth was gone, back towards the house, towards her patients. Because Emily didn't belong here, not any more. This place held nothing more than memories for her, which is why she couldn't figure out what it was she was meant to have found by coming back.

No more clues. No more signs or stops along the way. This was it, right here and now.

The soft call of a nightingale singing in the trees, a rustle of leaves as an accompaniment. It seemed that birds would follow her wherever she went, or did she seek them out? Find comfort in their presence, their meanings? Did she always have such a fascination about them, or did that only come after the accident, when she looked for hidden meanings in anything and everything all at once?

So much had happened. So many people and places forced upon her, but for what? Why make her come back to this place, with all its reminders of the long, slow recovery she had to endure? Why force her to go through it all if there was no manuscript to discover, if, in fact, there was never any need for her to leave home at all?

Sheets of palest blue fluttered in the breeze, pages from her grandmother's diary that were waiting to be read. Emily had been shown a piece of her grandmother's life, several pieces that all slotted together but didn't quite make the whole story. One summer that changed it all. One moment, one decision, one resounding 'yes' to an idea, an adventure, presented to her via a book.

Would Catriona have become a writer if it weren't for what happened in Paris? Meeting Antoine and Gigi. And Noah. All of them. They all touched her, impacted her life, in some profound way. Charlie published her books. Beth put back together a broken, wounded child. Stories linked them all.

Somewhere in each of her grandmother's books there was a message, a lesson, a hidden truth. Something she had learnt along the way and wanted to impress upon her granddaughter, on all the children who read her stories. Each character, each place, took inspiration from her own life, her own highs and lows. Because it's not possible to appreciate the good without the bad. The light without the dark. The joy without the sorrow.

'But most of all,' Emily whispered. 'Most of all, we have to try.'

Shoes off, Emily curled her toes into the grass; imagined them digging deeper, exploring the earth and all the creatures hidden below. She shuffled off the bench to lie on her back, felt the soft blades like a cushion beneath her, spread her arms wide and stared up at the great curve of blue. She breathed in the crispness of the air and watched the clouds that passed overhead, reaching out to one another, something joining to make something new.

'Come on, Poppet.'

A fragment of a memory from this exact spot. On a day so similar to today, when a girl and a woman sat by this lake, waiting for something to change.

'Tell me what you see.'

The girl turned her head away, closed her eyes as a solitary tear splashed to the ground. She began to pull at the blades of grass, ripping them from the soil and tossing them away. The woman sighed, a heavy slant of shoulder suggesting just how tired she was. For a while they sat like this, together but so very far apart. Then a duck appeared from the rushes by the lake, followed close behind by a line of ducklings. One by one they toppled into the water to swim after their mother, a dozen or so little, webbed feet, working frantically under the surface in order to keep up, not wanting to be left behind.

'Once upon a time...' The woman sat a little straighter,

watched the ducks as they swam away. *'Once upon a time, there was a little girl called Ophelia who had a pet duck named Terence.'*

The girl's hand stilled. She gave a small sniff, then turned her face back towards her grandmother, a question forming in those hazel eyes.

'What do you think she looked like?' Catriona Robinson asked her granddaughter, a picture already forming in the child's mind.

Emily sighed as she remembered thinking of how the girl would be short, but not too short. With hair tied up in pigtails and a green woolly hat. Terence wore wellington boots, and a scarf when it was chilly, and they both loved hot chocolate with pink and white marshmallows floating on top. Drunk in front of the fire whilst they sat, side by side, warming their feet.

It all begins and ends here, she thought, picking up the last of the blue sheets of paper, the very last piece of the puzzle, the very last thing left behind for her to discover.

12 August, 2018

I feel free in a way I haven't for years. Taken back the control which cancer stole from me. The months of treatment, the sickness, the absolute exhaustion of it all. I was also so very aware of what it did to Emily. How it made her even more reclusive, even more reluctant to engage with the world.

She is angry with me, at me, for giving up the fight. But this way I can simply be. Swim in the sea. Eat ice cream, drink champagne and actually live again.

One day I hope she will understand, forgive me for dying in a way she never could forgive her parents. I know I never could forgive and forget the torturous hand of fate, but I have learnt, somehow, to accept it. To believe in a better tomorrow.

I met a man this morning. His name is Richard and he has kind eyes and a great, big dog who licked my toes with glee. I'm wondering if he is to be my leaving present. The last person for me to love before I go. I want that for my darling Emily. For her to know the exquisite pain of loving someone and wishing only that they will love you in return.

Often I lie awake at night, thinking of him, of Noah, and all that could have been. He was my first love. After him, no one ever came close. But perhaps I was partly to blame, because I was afraid of ever hurting that way again.

I know now of all the different ways one person can love. I wonder what ever happened to Margot's father? What would have happened if we had never met? Never shared the briefest moment that went on to create another life, another future. Oh, my beautiful girl, my baby, my beloved. I loved you so and have missed you every single day. I loved them all so very, very much and only wish that there was more time.

I wish I could go back and do it all over again, to know that I didn't need to compete with Margot over Emily. To know that I was allowed to simply be her grandmother, to show her a different side of life. To make her see that she had choices, could be whoever she wanted to be. To embrace the weird, the odd, the absolutely crazy side of her personality – the one that went to the park in a swimming costume, wellington boots and superhero cape! To be the girl who wasn't afraid to climb trees, swim in the ocean, challenge people and question it all.

I loved Emily for her passion, her madness, her desire to always push for more, but I was so afraid of influencing her, of getting in between her and her mother. Which, of course, I now see was ridiculous. How could I be afraid of not being loved or not being wanted?

I never really understood Margot, her decision to become completely reliant on a man. I thought it was weak, it was needy and made her too vulnerable. After everything I had battled with, alone. After all the lessons I tried to teach her, and she gave up her education, her career, her independence for him. I didn't understand that she was making her decision based entirely on what was inside her own heart. I didn't understand that she looked at the world with different eyes, with different dreams, than I did.

I wish I hadn't convinced myself that Margot didn't need me, once she found Peter. Once she fell in love and gave up everything to be a wife and a mother. Because I understand now it's what she wanted. She was not me, just as Emily is not me.

The first time I saw them all together – Margot, Peter and Emily, just after she was born – it made me miss Noah, like a physical pain that would not leave me be. It made me miss what could have been and, of course, I couldn't help but think about whether I should have said yes. He was the one person who knew me, the real me, and never tried to change it. He understood why I said no (three times, the poor man!), but he didn't give up. He must have thought that one day I would give in to his relentless offerings of love, to finally realise that it was the right thing to do, that he would make me happy.

I have made so many mistakes in my life. Agonised over too many decisions, and quite possibly this has done me more harm than good. Regret is nothing but a mess of emotion that we can do nothing about. Fear is altogether different. The fear I have always carried with me, of being left alone. After Gigi died it made me cling tighter to Margot. Made me rush back to Noah, only for me to leave him once again. It was unfair of me, but I didn't know at the time how much more pain was still to come.

After the accident, he came back into my life, for a while. We reconnected over my grief and I allowed him to take care of me, which is all I think he ever wanted to do. But it was a malevolent sense of déjà-vu, seeing him interact with Emily, the same way he did with Margot. Perhaps I should have given him more of a chance, given us more of a chance, but once again I was so very acutely aware that any decision I made would affect a little girl, not just me.

Did I suffocate Emily with love? Did I wrap her up so tight in that damn cotton wool that I forgot to teach her how to be independent? Probably shook it all out of her, tidied it away like all those memories in boxes, instead of reminding her who she used to be.

I seem to be questioning everything now I know my time is coming to an end. The idea that there is nothing I can do to change what has happened is terrifying, but part of me is ready to go, to accept that this crazy mess called life is confused and muddled but also exhilarating and glorious, if only we are brave enough to grab hold of it and wring out every last drop of happiness whilst we still have the chance.

I remember when she first began to draw again. How she needed it, we both needed it, as a way of communicating with one another. The stories I would tell made her disconnect from her pain, made her focus on what she could do, rather than what she couldn't. I could see the pictures behind her eyes as she drew, couldn't wait to see if what she produced made sense, matched, with what I imagined in my own mind.

She is better than me. More talented, more creative, and I know that I encouraged her for selfish reasons as well as good. The books were just words on a page, it was her illustrations that really brought them to life, that fired up the imaginations of children the world over. That made Charlie see the potential of that very first story, written by the side of a lake in Italy, surrounded by the sound of nightingales. All I ever wanted was for Emily to be happy, to get better. I had no idea what would become of our creation, our distraction from reality. I had no idea how far that little girl and her duck would take us. How much it would act as a way to keep Emily hidden from the world, all over again.

It was never my intention to use her talent for personal gain. It was circumstantial, but I do understand that it might have stopped her from being so much more. That by keeping her so close, I never let her learn how to fly. It is partly my fault, this cocoon, this life, she has stumbled into. At first it was necessary, the only way we could both bumble through our grief. But by allowing her to remain silent, even when the words began to

303

take shape inside her mouth, did I only make it worse? By squirrelling her away in the clinic, then in Norfolk, by allowing her to escape into made-up worlds, did I prevent her from being able to live in the real one?

Stories are my life force, my way of coping with all the shit this world throws at you. But did I ever let her choose for herself?

She needs to start again, but I am afraid of how she is going to be able to cope without me. If I have done enough to make her see just how capable, how brilliant, she is. I want to be able to show her, make her understand the risks you have to take if you are ever going to be happy.

There is one possibility. But I don't know if it's too much. Or if I have the energy to make it happen. I must, I owe her that much.

Come what may, this is the life I have lived. This is what I am choosing to leave behind, for Emily. This has been me, Catriona Mairi Robinson, 67, a woman who has had time to count all the blessings I have been so very lucky to have.

CMR

22

PHOENIX

Phoenix

Emily was back where it all ended, where it all began. Next to a lake, with nothing but the birds for company, she sat, thinking about all the people she had met, and all the places she had travelled, the fears, the demons faced along the way.

She folded up her grandmother's words, placed them safely inside her pocket and allowed herself to cry. To really cry. For each of those tears to represent a piece of her heart that had been broken, been existing in a state of fear, for far too long. To mourn the death of her parents, her grandmother, the life she was too afraid to embrace.

She cried for the little girl who once was. Whose life became fractured in a split second. By a cruel twist of fate that changed everything, because time wasn't something you could grasp onto, it could only ever be understood when there wasn't any of it left.

Her spine curled over, waves of sorrow flowing up and down her back as she sobbed until there was nothing left inside to come out.

'Emily?'

Her head snapped up. She watched him approach and allowed him to sit next to her, curl his arm around and draw her close. The nearness of him made her cry all over again.

'It's OK,' Tyler whispered against her hair. 'It's OK.'

'No, it's not OK,' she shook her head, saw streaks of wet on his shirt. 'I've wasted so much time. I've spent years stuck in the past, and for what?'

'You nearly died, Em. You were a girl who had her body broken in two, not to mention the psychological impact the accident must have had on you.'

'All I did was hide.'

'All you did was survive.'

'What was the point of it all, if I can only ever draw what she wrote?'

'I think you did a lot more than that.'

Emily felt him shift beside her, sat back to see him holding out her sketchbook. The one she left behind in Verona.

'You brought that all this way.'

'I did. For my sins.'

'Why?'

'Because you need to see, to really see, what you're capable of.'

He opened it to the first picture drawn on their journey. A drawing of a couple of seagulls, stood opposite one another, beaks open as if having a conversation. One of them was sat on top of a unicycle, the other held a newspaper under its wing. A newspaper with a headline printed in bold, reporting the death of Britain's favourite children's author.

The next was of Tyler, walking through a field of silver and blue grass. All those notes twisting up to become a flock of migrating birds, heading off to unknown lands. What she hadn't realised at the time was that she had drawn herself into that very same picture. Walking along beside him, with a battered yellow suitcase in tow.

More pictures. More surprises, but each of them linked somehow to the journey she was being forced to take. A sketch of her grandmother and a man, sat on a bench in a town by a lake, heads dipped close together and a baby asleep in a pram, close by.

A group of hummingbirds, sat on a branch, watching as a couple danced under the Eiffel Tower, illuminated only by the moon. The woman was wearing a fifties-style dress, the man was holding tight to a small velvet box, inside of which Emily knew was a diamond ring.

So many pictures she did not remember creating. So many tiny details she had hidden in them all.

Then the last. All those starlings she saw in Rome, minute specks of brown that she drew over and over to form the face of a woman. Her face. Her torment and fear all gathered up in what she mistook for a tornado.

'You've always done it,' Tyler said, going back to the picture of Ophelia on her bike, pointing to the shepherd with his flock. Only then did Emily realise whose face she had really painted. Only then did she understand what it was Tyler had come to show her.

'I didn't know,' she gasped, turning each page in reverse.

All the way back to a pearlescent cockatoo, with wings stretched wide, ready to soar towards the setting sun as it dipped below the horizon. Back to the very first one in the book, showing her grandmother propped up in bed. Emily had drawn it as she slept, unaware of how she had replaced Catriona's face with that of her mother, imagined her old and worn through with time. How she wished she could have been allowed to survive, for them all to have been a family.

By putting them down on paper, she had kept them trapped, kept her grief trapped and unable to be set free. But she had never learnt to deal with any of it. Never learnt to grieve, to mourn, to accept that death is an inevitable, horrific, part of life.

Emily closed the sketchbook, wiping at her face with the back of her sleeve.

'How did you find me?'

He was looking at her again, in that way of his. It made her wonder if she seemed different. If the tears had changed the contours of her face, revealed a part of her that wasn't there before?

'I called my mother.'

'That must have been fun.'

'I sent her a copy of this,' he said, showing her a snapshot of the photograph taken outside the bookstore in Paris. 'Asked who the last woman was.'

Emily allowed her eye to travel over them each in turn, then go back to rest on Catriona. She drank in the freedom, the joy, in her grandmother's smile. And even though she was dead, Gigi too, they were not gone, because there was still someone left behind, to remember.

'Where's Phoebe?'

'She decided to go home. Said she needed to find her own way. Something about saving the gorillas …'

Emily let out a small laugh before folding her face into a frown. 'I'm sorry.'

'It never would have lasted, not with me going to Nashville. Besides,' he bumped against Emily, let his shoulder rest against her own. 'She was way too normal for my liking.'

'When do you go?'

'Now. Tonight.' He took a breath. 'My flight leaves in a couple of hours.'

'Why are you here, Tyler?'

He replied by bending his head to kiss her, just once. A gentle touch of lips, and she wanted to lean into it, to lose herself in the moment, but something made her move away.

So much had changed in such a short space of time. So much for her heart and mind to contend with, but she had not yet had a moment to try and make sense of any of it, least of all him. So much time that she didn't know what to do with. Days and nights and stolen moments in between that were all now hers to do with what she wanted.

'Come with me,' he whispered, resting his forehead against her own.

Emily stared at him, wanting to be able to simply say yes, to be swept off to Nashville, to immerse herself in the romance of her very own story.

The only problem was, she remembered what her grandmother had written in her diary. About Noah asking her to marry him, about why she said no. Because he would change her, make her into someone she didn't want to be.

Going to Nashville, falling in love, would be the easy option and in a way would allow her to hide again. To hide from herself, from the choices she knew she had yet to make. She had so much time to explore and decide, to make peace with being alone.

'I have this image in my mind and cannot recall if it's a memory or a dream,' Emily said, watching Tyler closely for some kind of reaction. Trying not to think about how easily the words now spilt from her mouth, how she didn't care if her tongue got caught around one of the syllables, or if she stumbled and lisped, because it was him. Because he knew her, he saw her, not the idea of someone who used to be.

'Go on,' he smiled at her and for a moment she thought he was going to kiss her again.

'I'm looking down to see the shadow of a plane, skimming over the ground. I'm thinking that the shadow was in fact another, hidden, plane, which only existed when the sun shone, revealing it to the world. I have lived so much of my life like that plane. Hiding, waiting for the light to shine on me.'

'I take it that's a no.'

So much time spent pushing people away, but she had never really been alone. There had always been someone to check up on her, even when her grandmother was away on a book tour, or had meetings in town. Charlie, the vicar, even that man and his dog, and now Tyler.

'Nashville is your dream, and if I came with you I'd only end up regretting it.' An idea for a story began to form in her mind. A map made out of the memories of thousands of people. Each of them unique yet somehow linked by the paths they tread. Ophelia grown up, exploring secrets, like an excavator of the truth. Reuniting people with objects, memories they thought were lost forever.

'Sounds pretty final.'

'I'm sorry.'

'Don't be.' He blew out a long breath of acceptance. 'I was unfair to you and Phoebe. Even before that, with the whole enormous mess of it all.'

'Neither of us asked for this to happen.'

'I'm glad that it did. I'm glad I got to see you again, to remember who I used to be, when we were young.' He stood, then pulled her to her feet and kissed her, once, on the cheek.

She watched him walk away, bent down to pick up her bag and sketchbook, noticed something tucked into the inside cover. A postcard, on the front of which was a picture of a bright red bird, wings open as it soared towards a setting sun. Turning it over, she saw where he had scribbled a few lines, the letters almost jumping around on the paper as she tried to read through her tears.

> *To me, you are a phoenix.*
> *Brilliantly coloured with a fire that burns deep inside.*
> *But when the rhythms of your heart can only cry,*
> *Know that I think of you.*
> *Because you are my reason,*
> *You make me want to try.*

He's my Noah, Emily gasped as she looked up, saw Tyler at the very edge of the lawn, one hand reaching out to open the gate, poised and ready to leave.

'Wait,' the word was no more than a whisper as she felt it catch against her heart. 'Wait,' she said again, then began to run as he turned his head to smile.

Arms around his neck, she kissed him deep. In that moment, she forgot it all. Forgot the pull of scar tissue across her cheek, the ache along her spine, the years spent hiding away, believing she wasn't deserving of love. In that moment, she became once more the girl she used to be. A girl kissed on a summer's night, with all the hopes and possibilities of tomorrow flickering inside her heart.

Just like that, she felt herself give way, to slip inside his soul, and allowed her heart to open to the possibility of what could be.

'You changed your mind?' He pulled away, a little breathless, a little surprised.

'Yes. No. I mean, I can't come with you.'

His face fell as he let go of her. 'Oh.'

'Because it's your dream.' There was no space between them and yet he felt so far away.

'You said that already.'

Emily ran her finger around the collar of his shirt, felt him stiffen then relax against her touch. 'If I came with you, it would be for the wrong reasons.'

'You said that too.'

'But that doesn't mean you couldn't come back.' She stepped closer, placed both hands on his chest, felt the rise and fall of his breath. 'Or I meet you halfway?'

He chuckled, the sound vibrating through her fingertips.

'Halfway is the middle of the ocean, Em.' Two arms came around her waist and she leant into him, breathed in his nearness.

'My point is, I need to figure out what it is I want to do.' She tilted her face to look up at him. 'And I can't do that if I'm following you.'

He was smiling down at her, a new look on his face. One she hadn't seen before.

'What?'

'You look very beautiful when you're all fired up about something.' He kissed her forehead, her scar, her mouth, and she waited for the moment when she would choose to step away, surprised herself when it didn't come.

'Where will you go?' he whispered against her lips.

Emily smiled. 'Home.'

23

MAGPIE

Pica pica

The garden was still. The leaves were beginning to turn, signalling a new season was on its way. There was a freshness to the air, which carried the sound of the church clock, chiming out another hour. Emily stopped a moment, let the sight of her home fill her heart anew.

Could it really have been only nine days since she'd left? So much packed into such a short space of time. So much more she now wanted to do, to discover, to begin to live the way her grandmother would have wanted her to.

A magpie swooped down as she opened the front door, hopped in after her and called out his greeting.

'Hello, Milton,' she said, bending down to give him a stroke, but he jumped out of the way and onto the answerphone, which was blinking all of its messages, none of which she had any inclination to listen to. There was a pile of post stacked neatly on the hall table, a thick, padded envelope on the top, with a foreign stamp, a postmark telling her it had been sent from Italy.

Noah. Perhaps he had decided to send her the letters from Catriona. But it could wait, and maybe she didn't need to read anything more, not just yet.

The house was as it was before, but something had changed. Was it the space around her, or the way she now stood in the space that was different?

On the wall hung a mirror she had avoided for as long as she could remember. Her reflection showed the same face as when she left, yet it was altogether different, because she was changed from the person who had woken one morning and assumed it was a day like any other. A day when she received a letter that would turn her entire world inside out.

She was no longer the person who had been existing but not living. Nor could she pretend that she hadn't been affected by Tyler, and how he had made her heart dare to give in, to finally say 'maybe'.

What now? How to start again, how to figure out the future?

'Tea,' Emily told herself as she went into the kitchen, paused at the fridge to rest her fingers on her grandmother's favourite Leonard Cohen quote still taped to the door.

She had been dying, slowly, from the inside out. Her grandmother was the only one who could see it and chose to save Emily, to make her notice all the little cracks in the world and not always see them as a bad thing.

Emily filled the kettle from the sink and set it on the stove. Then she opened the back door wide, let in the familiar scent of apple and honeysuckle as she looked up to the sky, at the great, comforting stretch of blue, and sighed her relief to be home.

It was only when she turned around, ready to reach into the dresser for her favourite mug, with turtle doves around the rim, that she saw it.

A box. A simple, cardboard box, sat on the kitchen table by the window, waiting for her to pay attention. Underneath was tucked a note, written by an unfamiliar hand.

Emily pushed the box aside, read the words sent to her along with the unexpected gift.

For Emily. She asked me to tell you that the rest is up to you. Yours, Richard Thomas. P.S. Max says hello and invites you to walk with us both along the beach one day, whenever you're ready.

The man with the dog. Apparently tasked with leaving Emily one last surprise from her grandmother.

'I don't want to look,' Emily said as Milton jumped onto the back of one of the chairs, tilted his head towards the box. 'I don't want to look,' she said again, but found her fingers reaching out to open her gift. Those curious, pesky fingers that always wanted to see, to touch.

Inside was a stuffed toy, a photograph and a small, red notebook.

'Oh.' Emily took a step back, then peered inside once more.

The toy was a duck with patchwork feet and bright green eyes. Emily remembered he used to have a spotty bow tie, but that it got lost long ago. She picked him up, brought him to her nose and inhaled the scent of her childhood. She could picture her old room, the wooden doll's house by the window, a thin layer of dust on its roof betraying how little she played with it. A canopy bed with fairy lights strung all around, a cupboard stuffed full of books, and a chair by the window, in which she would sit with her mother, reading stories each night before going to sleep.

With a shaking hand, she picked up the photograph. Saw it was of her as a baby, cradled in her mother's arms, and her father bending down to place a kiss on top of her head. Baby Emily was holding tight to the very same duck now sat on the table, looking back at her with pebbly eyes.

Emily went next door to the living room, put the frame front and centre on the mantelpiece, next to the one of Gigi and Giancarlo on their wedding day. She looked across to where other memories were caught within a frame. Now she knew that the pain, the sorrow, she felt at the absence of all she once had was shared by her grandmother. She could finally accept, understand, that it was felt the world over by anyone and everyone who had ever lost someone they loved.

Next door, her grandmother's study waited, still and quiet, with the desk by the window on which her ancient type-writer sat, its keys shining in the afternoon light. A shelf full of red notebooks, just like the one in her hand, filled with all the imaginings of that incredible mind.

But this notebook was different somehow, with one of the corners worn away and the pages felt stiff and crackly as she eased apart the spine. In the centre of the first page was a title, written by a child's hand.

The Adventures of Ophelia and Terence
By Emily Catriona Davenport (age 9)

'Oh,' she whispered, turning the page to see a drawing of a little girl with pigtails, holding tight to the hand of a pale grey duck.

'Oh,' she said, louder this time, as she leant against the desk and a memory began to unfold. A memory of herself, as a girl, sat at the kitchen table, asking her grandmother how best to write a story.

'There's no magic formula,' Catriona had replied, cutting into a freshly baked lemon cake and handing Emily a slice. 'But make sure you write about something you know.'

Then she had gone into the hallway of the house that Emily used to call home, came back with a brand new red leather notebook, still wrapped in plastic. She had told Emily that it was the very same type of notebook she used to write down all her own ideas.

'It was my story,' Emily said as she flicked through the pages, written by a child whose mind was filled with dreams and wild imaginings. A child whose existence had not been tarnished by pain and suffering. Someone Emily was beginning to believe in once again.

'It will always be our story,' she said as she went back into the kitchen, looking for someone to tell. For Milton, only he was suddenly nowhere to be seen. She was alone, but not lonely. Fearful, but not afraid. Ready to start again, to find out how she fit into this so-called life. To discover what it was she wanted to do with however much time she had left. To decide what happened next in the story.

Emily looked around the kitchen, sat down in the chair by the back door, opened up the notebook and began to read.

Epilogue

DUCK

Anas platyrhynchos

Once upon a time, there was a little girl named Ophelia, who lived by the seaside with her parents, and her pet duck named Terence. Ophelia longed to do all the things any normal boy or girl would do. Like climb trees, jump through the tide, or simply ride a bike. But Ophelia's legs didn't work properly, and so she had to use a wheelchair instead of being able to walk.

This often made her sad, but Terence was ever such a happy little duck, and every night before she went to sleep, he would tell Ophelia that one day the angels would grant her a single wish. One that would change her life, forever.

On Ophelia's tenth birthday, she woke to the sound of someone singing. Her father carried her downstairs, with Terence trotting close behind, to where her mother was in the kitchen, scrambling some eggs and bacon.

Her mother announced that today was an extra-special day, not only because it was Ophelia's birthday, but because they were taking her to the oldest bookstore in the world. It was a place filled with magic and adventure, and Ophelia was allowed to choose any book she wished ...

Birds and Their Meanings

Emily always struck me as someone who looked for the hidden meanings in life. It made me want to give her a fascination, an obsession, that she would use to distract her from the pain and grief she had to endure.

In turn, it led me to research the superstitions and symbolism behind birds, with a view to include some of them in the book as an extra insight into Emily and her journey. There were countless to choose from, and what I have listed below is just a fraction of what exists for each bird, but they are the ones that resonated with me, and with Emily's story, the most.

1. Cockatoo – show your best colours, but also a symbol of change, of embarking on an important learning process which requires strength, determination and courage.

2. Robin – beginning of a new idea, symbolising renewal and new birth. Can also be the symbol of wisdom and patience, of learning something that could take time to come to terms with.

3. Magpie – listen to what is being communicated by the world around you and be more vocal about your own thoughts and emotions. Can also symbolise unpredictable behaviour or situations.

4. Peacock – in Hinduism, the peacock is associated with Lakshmi, who represents patience, kindness and luck. The feathers are seen as talismans to protect from accidents and misfortune, whilst also serving as a reminder to show one's true colours.

5. Pelican – overcoming loss by looking into ourselves for understanding. Also symbolises a need to let go of judgement and speak one's mind with confidence.

6. Sparrow – companionship, specifically teamwork, but also self-worth and the understanding that even the smallest of things can make us happy.

7. Pigeon – resilience and physical strength, but also a devotion to a goal involving loved ones.

8. Canary – freedom from old wounds of the past, a feeling of inspiration, hope and a new cycle that is about to begin.

9. Seagull – messengers of changing times, but also encouraging you to step outside your comfort zone, to be fearless in your search for freedom.

10. Parakeet – trust and loyalty, but also the use of improved communication in order to accomplish a specific goal.

11. Owl – in Greek mythology, the owl was a symbol for Athena, the goddess of wisdom and strategy. They are also considered to be symbols of mystery, magic and the ability to see beyond perceived deceit.

12. Bluebird – in Russian fairy tales, the blue bird is a symbol of hope. They are also seen as symbols of a spiritual awakening, of a need to give yourself up to the world around you in order to achieve happiness.

13. Cockerel – Celtic and Norse lore believe the cockerel to be a messenger of the Underworld, calling out warnings of danger. They also symbolise an awakening of ideas, of illumination, and the need to accept the truth.

14. Flamingo – strong, hidden emotions and a reminder not to jump to conclusions. Also represents loyalty and a need to belong to a tribe.

15. Goose – desire to escape one's problems, but also a fierce protectiveness of those you love. Can represent a need to remember the people who got you to where you are today.

16. Starling – a message that blessings are on their way, but also a reminder that communication is vital for any kind of relationship to blossom and thrive.

17. Hummingbird – optimism, a need to move away from negative thoughts, but also the idea of being present in the moment, of seeking independence and embracing the resilience needed in order to travel along life's path.

18. Raven – in Greek mythology, ravens are associated with Apollo, the god of prophecy. Often seen as a symbol of impending bad luck, they can also symbolise a warning to listen carefully to the messages you are about to receive.

19. Heron – in many Chinese legends, a heron's job was to take departed souls to heaven. They also symbolise self-reliance, independence and fidelity.

20. Nightingale – eating a nightingale's heart was once thought to inspire creativity and Shakespeare compared his love poetry to the bird's song. They also represent healing and love.

21. Phoenix – in Greek mythology, a phoenix obtains new life by rising from the ashes of its predecessor. Most commonly seen to represent spiritual rebirth and transformation.

22. Duck – aggressive when confronted by an unknown force, but if left alone is sensitive and peaceful. Also symbolise curiosity for the world around you and freedom to explore.

Acknowledgements

For me, writing a book is a bit like a leap of faith, trusting that the snippet of an idea which randomly pops into my head will at some point become a story. But the words would never come if I didn't believe that I was good enough to write them, and belief takes both time and a whole host of people to help along the way.

Thank you to my agent extraordinaire, Hayley Steed, who saw the potential in my writing and who has been on my side ever since.

To Ben Willis and his ferocious editing eye, thank you for believing in the story and helping me understand how to get to the heart of it. Thank you also to Charlotte Abrams-Simpson for the beautiful cover and Helen Ewing for the incredible bird chapter headings, as well as Lucy Frederick and all the team at Orion for helping create an actual, physical, bona fide book.

For the encouragement, the pep talks and all the words of wisdom when I feel like throwing all my toys out of the cot, I have to thank my gang of amazing writing friends: Debs, Kate, Hannah, Rachel, Tom, Noel, Hynam, Chloe, Sophie and Natasha, you are incredible and I am very lucky to know you all.

Of course, there is my family, without whom none of this would be possible. The love and support, along with giving me the time and space to write are the reason why this book exists. Oh, and thank you to Cookie (the dog), because my children seem to think you had a role in this too ...